THE WAR INSIDE HIS MIND

A Soldier's Struggle with the Emotional Damage of Combat

Y.M. Masson

Middle River Press
1498 NE 30th Ct
Oakland Park, FL 33334
www.middleriverpress.com

ISBN: 978-1-946886-11-8

Library of Congress Control Number: 2020906216

First Edition

THE WAR
INSIDE HIS MIND

A Soldier's Struggle with the Emotional Damage of Combat

Y.M. Masson

MIDDLE
RIVER
PRESS

To all the soldiers who have experienced combat

regardless of the flag they fought for.

They are all brothers and sisters.

Chapter 1

Southern Alps, Wednesday, August 15, 1962

It was a long ascent over a steep remote trail to reach the summit; tired, I sat on a rock at the top of the ridge and let my legs dangle over the two-thousand-foot drop. Although intrigued by the faraway horizon where the darkening sky blended with the slowly graying blue of the Mediterranean Sea, my eyes were drawn to the abyss below me.

Alone again in the mountain wilderness, depressed, and full of guilt and anger, I stared at the dark chasm below my feet and my thoughts went to the soldiers I saw lose their lives: the ones who were mine, as well as the rebels we fought. More pain came when I saw the images of the innocent children and civilians who were maimed or murdered.

My journey through the French-Algerian conflict started three years ago and ended thirty months later. But there was no end in sight to my inner struggle, to my own war. My heart heavy, I stared at the deep black chasm wondering if my agony would ever end.

Suddenly, looking down at the black hole, I had the answer.

This summit is the perfect gate to exit this savage and unforgiving world. I can end it all, right here, tonight, just one step from the edge and an endless flight down to eternity.

Chapter 2

Algiers, August 1959

It all started when I stepped off the ship in the port of Algiers late one morning in August of 1959. Unaccustomed to the bright sun, I blinked and looked at the rusty corrugated metal building a hundred or so yards from the pier. There I would find out where I would fight the war for which I had been drafted. I checked my uniform one last time to make sure it was in order, lifted my regulation canvas bag over my left shoulder, and walked toward a Senior Sergeant who stood at the door, a piece of paper in his left hand. We exchanged salutes, and I gave him my name. The Sergeant looked at his sheet.

"Ah. Number one on the list," he said. "Right this way, Lieutenant." And he directed me to the office of the man in charge.

I dropped my bundle and entered the sweltering room which reeked of stale cigarette smoke. Major Roberts, the man who would decide where I would spend the next three years of my life, sat behind a desk with only his name plate and my personnel file on it. He looked at me and took the papers in his hands. With excitement and a knot in my stomach, I saluted him and stated my name.

"At ease, Lieutenant." He opened the folder, scanned the first page, and did a double take.

"Lieutenant Alain? Infantry? Most top graduates from Officers' School shy away from that branch of the army."

"Sir. My uncle led an infantry platoon during World War II. He was decorated for bravery but died prematurely two years ago. I want to serve my country honorably like he did."

"Decorated?" The major asked.

"Yes, Sir. One of the few French troops to enter Germany in 1940, then taken prisoner in the Saar region, he escaped several

The War Inside His Mind

times from German POW camps, only to be recaptured, and eventually sent to Colditz, the bad-boys camp, reserved for the enemies of the Reich."

Major Roberts nodded his approval. "Any idea where you want to go?"

"Sir, I wondered if I could be assigned to the western sector."

"Lieutenant, you're the first to choose. You can pick wherever you want to go. Most officers prefer the northern cities; there are quite a few nice-looking women in these places. I have openings in Algiers and Oran."

"Sir, on the ship from France an officer returning from leave told me that in Algiers, the soldiers do more police work than infantry duty because of the bombings and the lawlessness."

"There's some truth to that, but the Atlas Mountains and the Sahara are hot, arid, and inhospitable. Also the fighting is tough."

"That's what I have worked hard for, Sir, to be an infantry lieutenant."

The major continued to read my file. He suddenly raised his eyebrows.

"Your instructors stated you have exceptional leadership qualities." He stopped and sized my five-foot-ten body as if he saw it for the first time, and looked me in the eye.

"A company stationed in Mascara lost one of its lieutenants, shot and killed, two days ago. The commander, Captain Dufour, a friend of mine, asked me to find him a tough leader; the troops need a firm hand."

He turned to the easel behind him and pointed at a little dot on the map of Algeria. "It's about fifty miles east of Sidi Bel Abbes."

"I'll go, Sir. I have no combat experience, but I'm well trained, and I always give one-hundred-and-ten percent in everything I do. I'm sure I can help."

"Okay, the job is yours, Lieutenant." He wrote a few words on my file, sealed it in an envelope which he gave to me. "Give this paperwork to Dufour when you get there." He looked at me. "He'll be glad to get you."

"Thank you, Sir."

"Wait in the outer room; we'll get you transportation. You'll have to spend the night in Algiers and travel tomorrow. Good luck, Lieutenant."

"Thank you, Sir." I saluted and left the fateful room.

The fighting is tough, the captain said. The guy I'm replacing was shot. What did I get myself into? I guessed I would soon find out.

A sergeant outside the major's office gave me a pass for the Algiers officers' quarters. The corporal who drove me there in a jeep through wide tree-lined avenues with dazzling three-story stark white buildings pointed out the beautiful main post office with its Moresque façade and asked me, "Your first time in Algiers, Sir?"

"Yes, I got off the ship this morning."

"Sir, you should go to Place De Gaulle. It's only a couple of blocks from where you're staying. That's where everybody goes, lots of places to eat and drink. A bomb exploded there yesterday, so you should be safe today."

A bomb? Just like the captain said to me on the ship.

I had not heard the sound of explosions since the liberation of Paris in 1944. A little apprehensive, I strolled toward the plaza that afternoon. The streets were crowded and the traffic heavy. Place De Gaulle, loaded with palm trees, was indeed full of cafés. I chose the one with yellow and red umbrellas. I had never been that far south of Paris and never experienced sun that hot. The sky was almost as white as the buildings, and the light blinding.

My driver mentioned yesterday's blast, but I had no sense of a war going on. Some people walked around leisurely, others hurriedly. Well-dressed Europeans went about their business and spoke French with an unfamiliar singing accent; Arab men in their djellabas, the loose hooded cloaks they all wore, seemed to talk with their arms, but the most intriguing were the local women. Each wore a long white robe down to their ankles and a white piece of cloth wrapped around their head, which they held with their teeth, so that every part of their bodies but their eyes were covered. They showed modesty the Islamic way. It was a world away from Paris. I felt a bit out of place in these bright white surroundings.

I had not been sitting down for more than five minutes, enjoying my cool Pilsner and listening to the latest Edith Piaf song *Non je ne regrette rien* – I don't regret anything—how appropriate, when a little Arab boy with hair as dark as mine offered to shine my shoes.

They were perfectly polished. They always were since that day in training camp when the sergeant who checked uniforms on morning inspection had me shine my boots seventeen times before he was satisfied. By then, the leather, the sole and every hobnail shined like jewels. I had learned my lesson.

"*La, la, la.* No shoeshine," I said. *La* means no in Arabic, one of the most useful words to know in this part of the world, a crusty old sergeant instructor told me.

Pointing at my feet, I told the little boy, "See; they're clean."

He looked at them, wandered away for a minute, and came back with dirt in his hand that he dumped on my shoes. He looked at me, and said, "Shoeshine, General?"

I had to laugh. "Okay, Soldier. Go ahead."

He put the last touch on his polishing job and saluted me. I returned his salute and asked him, "What's your name?"

"Ahmed."

I shook his hand. "How old are you, Ahmed?"

"Seven."

I gave him a good tip. His face lit up. He was resourceful and an independent spirit like I used to be during World War II in Paris at his age. I used to cut the line to make sure I got bread, and I befriended Mimi, a young prostitute who shared with me fruit she got from her German customers.

I had just ordered another beer when a deafening explosion followed by rifle shots shattered the delusive peacefulness of the afternoon. The commotion erupted not far from where I sat. People screamed and ran for cover. French gendarmes on patrol shouted, "Down, everybody down." I hid behind a huge flower pot. A few Arab men fled the area, soon pursued by soldiers. I ran to the site of the explosion to see if I could help. The smell of cordite invaded my nostrils; bodies littered the pavement and to my horror, I saw Ahmed lying in a pool of his own blood, clutching his tip in his right hand. I ran to him, but I could not do anything for him. He was gone.

An innocent little boy lost his life in a senseless attack. It could have been me in Paris, fifteen years ago. I went back to my room shaking my head in disbelief. Now I had no doubt there was a war on, and as usual, a child became a victim.

The next day, in the white-walled, tiled-roof train station, I boarded the train for Oran. The familiar smell of the locomotive smoke and the rhythmic rumble of the car on the rails lulled my mind into thinking of my first day on active military duty, three days ago, after three months of final military training following my graduation from the best engineering school in France. I spent that day filling out forms, suffering inoculations, and receiving summer uniforms before shipping to Algeria. Some of the officers, drafted like me, fretted at the thought of possibly never seeing their loved ones again. I had no such worry. I was estranged from my parents, and raised by my beloved uncle, who died of cancer two years ago. Other lieutenants were buoyed by the French Government urging the army to fight to keep Algeria French. I just wanted to serve my country and do my job like my uncle had.

Some job! In the mid-fifties, Arab extremists, who wanted Algeria to end its status as a colony, had started their war of independence from France by killing French farmers in the mountains of Kabylie. They did it because they felt that the French had stolen their land in the colonial war of the previous century. Retaliation had been severe; some say overly so. But when General De Gaulle became the French President in 1958, he escalated the uncoordinated skirmishes and random violence into a national conflict: the French-Algerian war. All young French men of military service age were drafted and most thrown into the fight.

So here I was, on the train, going to war, not knowing what to expect, and unsurprisingly apprehensive. Choosing to be an infantry lieutenant and serving my country with honor had a nice ring, but now I had to confront the reality of my ideals. A high-spirited peaceful young man, fun loving and popular with his many friends, I looked at an unknown future which would include seeing my soldiers shot at and having me kill insurgents, mostly young men. Yesterday I witnessed Ahmed's death, which reminded me of the people I saw killed by German planes at the beginning of World War II. I learned at that young age that violent death is usually swift and final, but I always wondered if one felt excruciating pain for the brief instant when the bullets or the shrapnel entered one's body. Did Ahmed suffer?

I expected to be in danger, but hoped to make it back home. Would I be hit? I shivered.

In Oran I changed to the local train south to Sidi Bel Abbes, and after a short ride got off onto the platform. A Senior Sergeant came toward me. About my height, five-foot-eleven, obviously fit, a face tanned and wrinkled by the constant exposure to the sun, he wore a summer uniform: sand color shirt, pants, and a beret. An impressive array of multicolored ribbons brightened his chest. He looked at me and saluted.

"Sergeant Clavery, Lieutenant. I'm here to bring you to Mascara."

I guessed he had no trouble picking me out of the crowd; I had no suntan. I saluted him back. "Thank you, Sergeant."

"Sir, you'll be my commanding officer."

I tensed up. Wow! Such a decorated warrior.

Curious about how the lieutenant I came to replace was killed, I asked the sergeant, "You lost your lieutenant last week. Are casualties heavy in the area?"

"Not really, Sir. Mistakes were made. It shouldn't have happened."

We walked off the platform into the stone station building where it was surprisingly cool, and then out on an unbearably hot large plaza. In the middle of it was a little garden with a small pond and a few palm trees. Smelling like hot steam, the air muted every sound. Starkly white buildings bordered the square. Several military vehicles were parked a few yards away.

"Is Mascara a big town, Sergeant?"

"No, Sir. There's not much going on there. Actually, our base is just outside of town. There are four platoons in the company."

"The major who sent me here told me that Captain Dufour is a great leader."

"Yes, Sir. He's been around. He's fair and knows his business."

I assumed he had many decorations too.

The sergeant stopped by a jeep. Two men stood next to it. "This is your driver, Private Lebon; he's also your radioman." He turned and put his muscular hand on the other soldier's shoulder. "This is Private Vidal." He pointed at the back of the jeep. "He mans the machine-gun."

Both soldiers looked smart in their clean, well-pressed uniforms, and saluted me. I returned their salute and gave my bag to Private Vidal, who dumped it in the back seat.

Five fit-looking, suntanned, clean-shaven young men in combat fatigues, all with ultra-short military haircuts and holding MAT49 submachine guns, stood by a small truck parked next to the jeep.

The sergeant pointed at the soldiers. "Your escort, Sir."

We exchanged salutes.

"I'll follow your jeep in this truck, Sir. The trip will take about two hours." The sergeant added, "The road is safe enough during the day. We should have no problem."

This did not promise to be a casual ride in the countryside. Would we drive through dangerous areas? The past military summer camps and days of what I thought then was hard training looked today like Boy Scout outings.

I got in the front seat, and the driver started the jeep. We roared east.

An hour into the trip, automatic fire directed at our little convoy erupted from the top of a hill on the side of the deserted road ahead of us. It startled me. I did not know what to do, but Private Vidal immediately returned fire while the driver accelerated. The soldiers in the truck fired their weapons also. We had been shot at, but unharmed. My escort took the attack in stride.

"Not to worry, Sir," Private Lebon chuckled. "Those Fellaghas, that's what we call the insurgents, aren't too accurate with their weapons; there's no way they can hit a speeding jeep."

Mascara, August 1959

In Mascara, the driver brought me to the Captain's office, which had a dirt floor, no door, and no windows. It was hot and smelled of warm sand. Sergeant Clavery did not mention the incident on the road and went in with me. "Sir, our new platoon leader."

Captain Dufour sat behind his desk. He sported a well-trimmed blond mustache and was almost bald. He sized me up and gave me a friendly smile. "Welcome, Lieutenant. I've been expecting you. You'll command the second platoon, a good bunch. They can get the job done, but they need a strong hand to lead them."

I saluted him and said, "Sir, Major Roberts told me to give you this." I gave him the envelope.

The Captain chuckled. "The old rascal got himself a cushy job in Algiers. I'm glad he remembered me. He called and said you were the right man. I'm looking forward to working with you."

"Thank you, Sir. I'll do the best I can for you."

"You'll be all right. You have the right attitude. Go settle into your quarters and get your equipment. I'll see you at dinner. You'll meet the other officers in the company."

I left his office, impressed by the seasoned soldier. I liked him.

Private Lebon took me to my simple room: White walls, grey concrete floor, a metal cabinet, a bed, a desk, a lamp and a chair were all I needed. I went to get my gear: shirts, socks and such, combat fatigues, and a helmet I tried on for size. The boots had rubber-like soles and a coarse fabric top instead of the heavy, old-fashioned hobnailed leathered ones I wore in training camp.

I went to collect my weapons from the armory. Sergeant Clavery, who had come with me, recommended I get an M1 carbine.

"It's light and accurate to three hundred yards. More, if you are a good shot. You should test it at the range. It should fire true."

I also received a revolver with a rough wooden handle and a nasty-looking sharp knife with an eight-inch-blade. It came with a strap to attach it to my leg or my arm. I hoped I would not have to use it in a fight. I had no training with that kind of weapon.

The sergeant helped me stow my equipment in my room. We stepped out to the courtyard.

"Sir, I'll assemble your soldiers so you can meet them."

"Good idea. Thanks, Sergeant. How many men in the platoon?"

"Forty-five, Sir. Three squads of riflemen, each with a junior sergeant, two corporals and ten men. The fourth squad, with a sergeant and four men, handles the two B.A.R.s, the Browning Automatic Rifles. And I'm your Senior Sergeant, your right hand."

"Thank you, Sergeant."

He called the platoon to attention in the courtyard. I saluted them, scanned the ranks, and looked every soldier straight in the eye. I could not help but wonder how many of these young men would not make it to the end of their tour.

"At ease. I'm Lieutenant Alain. I'm proud to be your leader. I'll be with you all the time and I'll never ask you to do anything I won't do myself. We'll work to keep casualties to a minimum. Tomorrow we'll start to learn how to function together. The Captain told me you always get the job done; I know you'll continue to do so and I'll help you succeed. You have displayed courage and I know you'll live up to your reputation. It is an honor to serve with you."

My right-hand Sergeant dismissed the platoon. They broke

ranks, and I met with the sergeants and corporals. They introduced themselves and shook my hand. They made me feel welcome. One of them said to me, "Sergeant Lupin, Sir. You got to be from Paris; we have the same accent."

I went to shake his hand. "I can hear that. I'm from Montmartre, Sergeant, and you?"

"Menilmuch." He used the Parisian slang for Menilmontant, a rough district in the north-east of the city. "Welcome to the platoon, Sir."

Sergeant Clavery came to me and said, "That was the right tone, Lieutenant. The first step is always important. Tomorrow, we'll go to the firing range. Arms inspection will be at seven. Good night, Sir."

Three lieutenants stood around in the mess room. We introduced ourselves. The one with a red complexion and a large grin, a first Lieutenant, ran the support platoon. A short and skinny second lieutenant led the first platoon. The third officer, a lanky man, spoke with the accent of the north of France; he was the only draftee officer, like me. The Captain walked in; he was sitting down when I met him, so I had not realized he was a tall man.

Captain Dufour said, "Gentlemen, please, welcome Lieutenant Alain. He'll run the second platoon."

During the simple dinner of chicken, potatoes and a lot of the local red and heavy Mascara wine, almost offensive to my taste buds, the banter was about news from France. I had left Paris two days before, so I was up on the soccer rankings and the rugby championship. The two second lieutenants were Lille supporters and were distraught when I told them they were next to last in their league. The first lieutenant, a big strong man from the south of France, cheered when I told him that the Toulouse rugby team ranked way ahead of the others. The French newspapers did not reach Mascara. No news came in from France or from anywhere in the world unless someone brought them.

At the end of the meal, the Captain said to me, "Lieutenant, I've read your paperwork. We don't usually get the top people from the officers' schools." The Captain continued, "You have a reinforced platoon. Are you familiar with B.A.R.s?"

"Yes, Sir. I trained with them."

"Your platoon has two of them; that's why it's reinforced. I know you have not experienced combat, but your men are good soldiers."

"I'll learn fast, Sir."

"Sergeant Clavery is from Morocco. He has been through it all: Italy and Germany campaigns in World War II, Indochina, and then here. He'll help you gain experience fast. I understand you are good with a rifle. Your people will appreciate that. Welcome and good luck, Lieutenant."

"Thank you, Sir."

Outside the mess room, the first platoon lieutenant said to me after dinner, "It's obvious that Captain Dufour likes you."

"He's a neat guy."

"He started in the army before World War II and went up through the ranks." He shook his head, "He won't ever be a general, but he's a soldiers' captain. He gets the job done and he takes care of his men. He does not send them on crazy missions."

"Good, I want to be a soldiers' lieutenant. I don't want to lose any of my men."

He looked at me and tilted his head. "It would be nice, but you might be here over two years. It's too long a time to go through combat without casualties."

"I'm afraid you're right. Can I ask you a question?"

"Sure, what's on your mind?"

"No one mentioned the lieutenant I'm replacing. How did he get killed? What was he like?"

"A nice guy, but loose on discipline, and disorganized. He was shot in the head by a sniper on a routine patrol. He made many mistakes. The day he bought it, he did not have his platoon in sweep position; he had no point-men, and got himself killed. Not a leader. Your soldiers will watch you in the early days. You have to earn their respect, but be firm, and restore discipline."

"Thank you for being open about this."

He shook my hand. "It is sad to say, but he won't be missed. Welcome and good luck, Lieutenant."

I went to sleep knowing that my life had changed the minute I stepped off the train, and *thinking I am now in charge of the lives of forty-five men, and I won't let them down.*

Chapter 3

The next day, at seven, I inspected the men's rifles and subma-chine guns. The soldiers were combat troops and knew to keep them clean. I complimented everyone, but I remember one of the instructors telling us, "You have to keep checking the rifles. They must be always oiled and clean, not only for inspection."

The platoon boarded the trucks to go to the firing range, about ten miles to the west, in the middle of a barren area with no trees in sight. One could see parched, sandy ground forever.

There were tall dirt and sand dunes behind the targets to stop the bullets. The men who manned the B.A.R.s had their own area at the edge of the range.

The second and third squads took turns firing their rifles at their targets, a hundred-and-fifty yards from the firing stations. First they fired from the ground, then on one knee, and finally standing. It is easy to secure a rifle when elbows rest on the dirt or on one's thigh, but much more difficult standing up. I noticed a young sol-dier from the second squad who missed the center of the target on every shot when standing up. I saw that the strap of his rifle was not tight on his arm.

"What's your name, soldier?"

"Private Boule, Sir."

"How long have you been with the platoon?"

"Five of us came six weeks ago; it's my second time at the range, Sir."

"Do you know why you just missed the target?"

"No, Sir. I do okay if I kneel or lie on the ground, but I can't do it when I stand up."

"That's because your rifle moves when you pull the trigger. Let me show you how to hold it so it's steady in your hands." I took his

The War Inside His Mind

weapon. The men were watching. I had to hit the target. I made sure the strap was tight against my left elbow. I fired three rounds, pulling the trigger softly. They all hit the mark.

I showed the private how I braced the rifle with the strap. "You see, you have to hold your Garand tightly but be gentle with your finger on the trigger. Fire another five rounds."

"Yes, Sir."

The soldier got the strap taut and was pretty close to the center of the target.

"See, you're doing better already."

The big smile on his face showed he was proud of his new skill. "Thank you, Sir."

I wanted to maximize every soldier's skill because it meant better safety for all.

I remembered my first time at a firing range, when my military training started three years ago. I had never held a rifle before that day. The only time I had been near such a weapon was when, as a little boy, German soldiers held me and fifty other people at gunpoint. I had stared at the little round black holes at the end of the guns, wondering for an hour if death would come out of them. Hostages were shot in Paris that same day, but fortunately for me, my group was let go.

First the instructor told me to fire three cartridges at the target a hundred yards away. My trial shots ended up grouped close together, low and left of the center of the target. Interested, the sergeant said, "Aim high and right to compensate. The next five shots will count in your rating." I did as he instructed me. When he looked at my target, he smiled and told me, "You are a natural. Your five shots are right in the bull's eye. You have a sharp eye and a soft finger."

When all the soldiers had completed the drill, I was anxious to test my new carbine. I knelt in one of the firing stations and fired several clips. The carbine was light and reliable; none of my rounds deviated from the center of the target. The soldiers had stopped to watch me. They found out I was good with a rifle. I thought it was an important first step in earning their respect.

The afternoon was the first squad's time to practice with their submachine guns. These weapons, MAT49s, were less precise than rifles but deadly at short distances. The targets were changed from the concentric circles to larger ovals and moved closer.

The drill was more risky than the rifle one because the submachine guns were short and could inadvertently point at other soldiers with a quick turn of the torso. One private kept his finger on the trigger too long and as a result fired too many rounds with each burst. Because he did, the ejection of the empty cartridges from the weapon pushed the muzzle of the gun up and left, which was where the bullets went instead of hitting the target. It would be ineffective in combat and was dangerous on the range.

I hurried to his spot. "Soldier, it's best to fire only two or three rounds with one squeeze of the trigger. It makes your weapon more effective."

A soldier next to him said to me, "That's hard to do, Sir."

"Not really, let me show you." I took the submachine gun, secured it to my shoulder, aimed, and lightly touched the trigger as I had learned. I shot the twenty-one rounds in six bursts. They all hit the target. I reloaded and fired from the hip in short bursts too, with the same results. I showed the two soldiers how I dealt with the trigger.

"Try it; it works." The soldier did and was able to shoot bursts of six rounds, an improvement.

His eyes opened wide when he realized what he was able to do. "Thank you, Sir."

Sergeant Clavery watched the exchange and said to me, "Somehow, many soldiers use their submachine guns to spray their fire without really aiming at a target. They make a lot of noise and sometimes are lucky enough to hit something, but you're right, Sir, with short bursts, it's easier to aim and more damaging to the enemy. It's good of you to have them focus on that."

"How often does the platoon have firing range exercises?"

"About once every six or eight weeks and when we get new recruits."

"The soldiers need to be reminded of the basics of weapon handling," I replied. "We have to come to the range more often if we can. Firing discipline is most important and skills must be kept up. Sloppy firing in combat is not acceptable."

"I could not agree more," the sergeant added.

The sergeant had sent the trucks back to the base, so the platoon could hike back. The relatively safe ten-mile walk added endurance training.

As Sergeant Clavery had suggested, I walked in front of the platoon, I ordered Private Boule and another soldier to be my two point men fifty feet on either side of me. The first squad followed behind me, the second and the third on the right and left. The men were spread out at thirty-foot intervals. That was a sound patrol formation.

The hard dirt, mostly flat terrain, had little vegetation, only a few shriveled bushes and trees with sparse, pale green leaves. Gripping my carbine, my throat dry, I started briskly toward our base.

I had been taught that because combat is confusing and messy, it is more effective to use hand signals as much as possible. "There's too much noise and chaos in combat for yelling orders to soldiers other than the ones next to you. Practice what works with your people," the instructor said.

After a few miles, I talked to Sergeant Clavery about practicing hand signals.

"That's what I learned in school. Do you think we should do it?"

"You know, Lieutenant, if our previous leader had not been so used to yelling orders that no one could hear he might still be here today. I'm glad you brought it up."

I used my fingers, hands, and arms so soldiers could see my signals even from the back of the platoon. We practiced stopping, going fast, slow, right, left and forward for a mile or so. We did it one or several squads at a time. I wanted the soldiers to get used to looking at my silhouette and recognizing it. To make sure every soldier knew what to do, the sergeants repeated my orders to their own squads. At the same time, I thought that, if we were attacked, I would have to give the correct signals. I recalled the instructor telling me, "You have to keep your head together."

That was training. Now, I really had to know what to do.

After we finished the exercise, about a hundred and fifty yards ahead to the right, three men in their loose *djellabas* ran to hide behind low bushes. I pointed them out to Sergeant Lupin, the leader of the first squad, who had come close to me. "Let's go find out what that's all about."

He summoned two soldiers. Our weapons pointed at the bush, the four of us walked cautiously toward the hiding place. Sergeant Clavery joined us. When we were a hundred feet from where they were hiding, the sergeant shouted in Arabic, "Stand up and come out with your arms away from your body."

They walked toward us, their hands on their skull caps. They were young, short, and wore black mustaches. Their dark eyes and thick eyebrows gave their tanned faces a menacing look.

"Why did you hide behind those bushes?" I asked them, pointing my carbine at the shrubs they came out of.

They understood my French, because they answered, but in Arabic.

"They say they're afraid of the soldiers," the sergeant said, "Sir, we need to search them. They might have weapons under their loose coats. They can hide anything under these clothes."

As Sergeant Lupin and his men started to frisk them, one of the Arabs jumped to his right, apparently ready to run. I fired a shot on the ground next to his feet. He stopped in his tracks and fell on the ground. Did I hit him?

"Get up and put your hands on your head," Sergeant Lupin shouted at him. The man mumbled something I could not understand, but stood up. Nothing was found on any of the three men. I wondered why this guy tried to run away if they had no weapons.

Sergeant Lupin put his hand on the Arab who tried to run and said, "You sure scared him with your shot, Sir. He's still shaking."

"He's afraid of something. Go check the bush. They may have left guns there."

The sergeant nodded. "Yes, Sir." He took the two privates with him and went to investigate. He came back with three weapons: an old rifle and two AK47s.

He told the three Arabs to lie on the ground. Soldiers tied their hands behind their backs.

I looked at them; they were the first Fellaghas I had ever seen. I put my rifle over my shoulder and went to look at their weapons. "That's what an AK47 looks like," I said. I knew about the Russian Automatic Kanasnikova, but I had never seen one.

"Yes, Sir. It's their basic assault rifle. The Russians supply them to anyone fighting a western army."

The three prisoners got up and walked toward the base with

a squad covering them from behind. We got back to our quarters without further incident.

It was a good first day for me. I thought I earned some respect from the troops, but I was a little shaken up. I didn't even try to hit the Arab, but firing at something besides a piece of cardboard proved to be disconcerting.

"Well done, Sir," Sergeant Clavery said smiling, "You earned your pay today."

The Captain was happy for me too. "Lieutenant Alain, you have done well. I'm sure your platoon is relieved to have gotten a good leader."

"Thank you, Sir. But I was a bit confused. The dissidents were dressed like regular Arabs. They didn't look like fighters."

"That's one of our problems, Lieutenant. It's hard to know who is against us. You smoked them out this time."

"Who are the rebels?"

"They're extremist Arab Moslems who want to free Algeria from France. Most of the Algerians are neutral. Those in the farms and isolated areas are our friends because we protect their properties."

"Do the insurgents prey on them too?"

"Yes, Lieutenant. They attack them to steal their food and their cattle."

"Do you think the Fellaghas have a legitimate quest?"

"That is not a question you and I should worry about. Our job is to fight the rebels to protect the French and the Algerian people."

Chapter 4

The next day, Captain Dufour got the officers together. "Tomorrow, the company will clear the road from Mascara to Saida. It has been unsafe for some time. Fellaghas have attacked trucks. Our job is to eliminate them or force them out of the area."

Before dawn, the company rode a few miles south to Oued Taria, a hamlet on the road to Saida. Each platoon jumped out of the vehicles and took their assigned position. This was my first combat assignment.

The first platoon's job was to walk on the road and sweep fifty yards on either side of it, the second's to sweep on the right of the first platoon, slightly back.

The terrain was open, but for a few bushes and trees in the low areas. Every soldier had to search behind every tree, bush, rock, and inside buildings, to find rebels who might be hiding behind them. This morning, the Captain warned me, "The insurgents are masters at camouflage. They can hide in the alfalfa around trees, or in the foot-high grass. They dig into the ground and put dirt over themselves. Keep your eyes open."

It was rugged scenery. I scanned the ground in front of me. I hoped I would not walk into a camouflaged rebel; I kept thinking that if I missed one, he would probably shoot me in the back; that added to the uneasiness of my first patrol.

The road, which had been going straight south for miles, suddenly turned east to the hamlet of Sidi Bouhekem. The company came to a halt. Captain Dufour called for me. "Lieutenant Alain, the first platoon will go in the village and search all the houses. Stay on the west side and stop anyone trying to leave. Shoot anybody who runs away. Also, don't let us be surprised from the west."

"Yes, Sir."

I motioned to Sergeant Clavery to come over. "I'll take squads one and two and seal the hamlet from this side. Take the rest of the platoon and stop anyone coming down from the hills."

When everyone was in place, the first platoon went into the village and searched every single structure. With the two squads, I waited and stared at the alleys between the houses. No one tried to run out. The first platoon found no suspect. We had reached the middle of the day and the sun had become close to unbearable. My fatigues were soaked with sweat. The company secured its perimeter and took shelter in the shade of the few meager trees and that of the walls and buildings.

Captain Dufour came to talk to me. "Lieutenant, we're going to come to a few abandoned buildings in a few miles. A couple of those will be in your area. They need to be searched. You need to be careful approaching them; the doors may be booby-trapped."

"Would there be dissidents hiding inside the huts, Sir?"

"I'd be surprised if the Fellaghas didn't leave a couple of guys to slow us down while others run further south or east toward the hills. Hopefully, we can capture one of them and find out how many men are in their group, and where they went."

The platoons proceeded further south. After a few miles, in front of us I saw one of the buildings the Captain had told me about. I stopped the platoon a couple of hundred yards from the old farm. The Senior Sergeant explained to me how to proceed to check out the structure. I placed the squads so they could stop anybody from running away from it.

Next to me, Sergeant Clavery surveyed the shack, a one-story old shed with probably only one room. A captain told me in officers' school that the only way to lead was by example. I told the sergeant, "I'll take a couple of men and go in."

"Sir, you've only been here a few days; you don't have to do it yourself. Have one of the sergeants check the structure."

"I have to get my feet wet. Get me two seasoned soldiers."

Private Martin and Corporal Gaston introduced themselves as they reported.

"Ready, Sir."

"Follow me." I started toward the barn.

More nervous than I wanted to admit to myself, I ran toward

the old shack, stopped midway, and dropped a knee to the ground, looking for signs of life.

When nothing moved, I jumped up, the men following behind me. I reached the wall of the farm. The door was not booby-trapped. There was no door. The corporal threw a rock inside. No one inside reacted to the bait.

I said to Private Martin, "Come with me. I'm going in."

The corporal went to a hole in the wall to provide fire cover, if we needed help.

I didn't know what to expect. My teeth clenched, I went in. I found the room to be empty. I relaxed, lowered my rifle, and took a deep breath. Private Martin touched my shoulder and put his finger on his lip. He pointed at a big square of corrugated metal, a piece of the roof now on the ground in the middle of the room. The private and I put the toes of our boots on the edge close to us and lifted it toward us so that we would be protected if there was a hole with somebody in it. The instant we started to raise the roof segment, gunfire erupted from the hole. I froze. Private Martin, who had a grenade in his hand, motioned me to run out. He did not waste a single second and dropped it in the dugout, let go of the piece of metal, and jumped out too. Even from behind the wall, the explosion was deafening. A gust of hot, acrid air came out of the building.

We both went back in. The piece of the roof did not cover the dugout any longer. Two Fellaghas were in the hole. A mass of blood, bones, and human flesh was all that remained of one body; the other man moaned. Partially shielded from the shrapnel by the dead man, the other rebel had severe injuries.

Sergeant Clavery, who had come into the shack, looked at him and immediately called for a medic.

"This guy is going to need morphine," he said to me.

I called the Captain. "Sir. There were two rebels. One is dead, the other is wounded. I'm not sure he can talk."

"Thanks, Lieutenant. I'll send help to take care of the two Arabs. Secure your area. We'll stay here tonight."

My hands would not stop shaking. If it were not for Private Martin, I would be dead. I almost got sick. I had gone into the structure, but I had done nothing. I had been a spectator. Everything had gone too fast.

I stood outside the old farm with Private Martin. "Thanks, soldier. I could have been shot."

"Sir, the Fells—that's what we call them—dig holes like that all over. They like to hide in them, let us go by, and shoot us in the back. In the open, it's easy to deal with them. Inside a structure, it's too risky to try to ferret them out. It's better to eliminate them right away."

"I'm glad you knew what to do."

"Sir, in this bloody war, you gotta be aggressive and be the first to fire. Instant reaction is the secret to staying alive."

I tapped him on the shoulder. "I'll remember that. Thanks again."

"Glad to help," the private said.

Corporal Gaston said, "May I say something, Sir?"

"Of course, Corporal."

"Sir, the other day, returning from the firing range, you captured three rebels. Today, you went first into the farmhouse. You have never done any such thing before; it's only your first week in this godforsaken country. You have guts, Sir."

"Thank you for saying that, Corporal. But Private Martin did what had to be done. I'm trying to learn the job as fast as I can before I get soldiers in trouble."

Soldiers from the support platoon took the Arabs away. Another smaller building, actually another shed, stood a little further up. Sergeant Lupin told me, "I'll take care of it, Sir. I'm sure there is no one in there."

"Okay, go ahead, Sergeant."

He went in with a couple of soldiers but did not find anybody hiding.

I asked Sergeant Clavery to organize the platoon up for the night. He selected spots for the sentries, and set the first watch.

I went to see the Captain who sat in his jeep, his radio center.

"Sir, I'm afraid that the wounded guy won't be able to tell much," I said.

"On the contrary, Lieutenant, he told me he belongs to a katiba. It's their basic fighting unit, like our platoons. They're usually twenty to thirty men. He said they did their job on the road. They're on their way to join another katiba. He swore they had fled toward the west."

"Why west?"

"Frankly, Lieutenant, I don't believe it's the way they went. I think he lied to me. The closest hills are toward the southeast. They are part of the Ouarsenis Range. You'll get to know these mountains more than you ever wanted to."

"Are we going to go after them tomorrow?"

"No, Lieutenant. That's not our mission. We're a sector company. We're assigned an area to protect. We don't go on pursuits, unless we have special orders. Tomorrow, we'll continue to sweep the road toward Saida. There will be some other old ranches on the way. Your platoon will lead the company. You'll open the road, Lieutenant."

"Yes, Sir."

"Lieutenant Alain, you did well again today."

"Sir, my troops did the job."

"That's not what I'm told."

"I must confess I was scared."

He got out of his jeep. With his great height, he towered over me, put his huge hand on my shoulder, and said, "Lieutenant. We're all scared. We control our fear because we need to be able to do what the situation requires. But fear is inside every soldier and officer in combat. In a way, it sharpens our senses so we can give the right orders and do what we think is best. You'll learn to manage it too. Actually, you already have."

"I have?"

"Weren't you scared before you went through the door?"

"Yes, Sir, but..."

"But you went in all the same. I'm glad you joined the Company, Lieutenant."

Trucks from the support platoon brought hot food. I took a tour of the sentries with Sergeant Clavery. They were to be relieved every two hours. We settled for the night. Although tired, it was not a time to let my guard down. I went to lie against a wall. The bright moon reflected on the light sandy ground. There was no wind, and it seemed peaceful, but I knew better. It was my first night outside in an active rebel area. I was too nervous to sleep.

I went over the events of the day. My soldiers thought I had done a great job. I thought I made a fool of myself, actually almost a dead fool. No training can make anyone ready for the shock of close

The War Inside His Mind

explosions. The Fellaghas were on my mind; I saw the terrible damage on the wounded man's body and the wreckage of the dead one. Yet, I felt no guilt. The dissidents were flesh and blood, but I did not look at them as human beings. That disturbed me who I thought to be a nice guy, but we had killed these men. I guess I have to get used to it. I shook my head.

I got up to check on the sentries.

"How are you doing, Private Vidal?"

"I'm fine, Sir. Nothing to report. Thank you for remembering my name."

"You were in my jeep when we drove to Mascara, just a few days ago. It seems like a year has gone by since then."

"I know, Sir. It's a different world here."

In the morning, the second platoon assumed its new position and I headed south in front of the company. A few miles down the road, shots rang out, and bullets hit the dirt not too far from me. I dove to the ground.

Sergeant Clavery crawled next to me. He pointed to a large one-story white farm building which had holes in the walls and a doorway, but no visible door from where we were. There must be a flat roof from which the sniper or snipers shot at us.

"Sir, it looks like it's a lone sniper." The sergeant said to me. "Either this guy has a long range rifle and is a bad shot, or he got nervous and gave himself away too early."

"Whichever it is, we have to take him out," I said. "I'll take the first squad and get within range. Keep everyone down and send a runner to tell the Captain what I'm doing."

"Yes, Sir. Don't forget to zigzag."

I signaled Sergeant Lupin and his squad to get behind me. My body bent forward, I got up and ran, the men following me. More shots were fired, all from that one rifle. No one took a hit.

I threw myself on the ground and called for the sergeant. "We're not yet close enough to hit him, but I want to make sure there are no other snipers out there. Get a couple of your men to open fire." Then I realized the first squad had submachine guns, ineffective at long range. Damn it, I had made a mistake not to take a rifle squad with me. "They can't hit him; I just want to know how many rifles respond."

I looked at the roof where the shots came from. But somehow I, the sharp shooter, could not hold my carbine steadily. I may have been rattled by my error, but my hands shook, my eyes blurred, and I could not aim. I just could not do it! I hoped nobody saw me. I concentrated and fired in the general direction of the roof, but I could not focus on the target. How sobering. I had never aimed my rifle at a human target before, but I had to do it now, and better get used to this.

There was no response from the sniper, or snipers. I signaled to cease fire, took a deep breath and, followed by the troops, moved forward. When I got in range, I hit the dirt again.

I remembered telling my first rifle instructor, "I may be a sharp shooter, but I hope I'll never have to fire at people."

"It won't be your decision," he replied with a shrug, "But if somebody is trying to kill you, it's a good skill to have." Well, now was the time.

I had regained control of my nerves and told Sergeant Lupin, "I'll be able to see him if he shows himself. I hope he didn't slip away. Hold your fire."

This time, my hands were steady. I waited. After a little while, the sniper slowly lifted his head above the roof. I fired three rapid shots. He disappeared.

"Either you got him, or he's hiding, Sir," the sergeant said, peering in the distance.

I stood up and resumed the same irregular pattern. No shots were fired. The squad got close to the farm. My throat was dry, but we had to go in. The sergeant and I entered the building. There was no hole in the ground, this time. A ladder led to the flat roof where the sniper lay on his stomach, motionless; one of my bullets had gone through his forehead. An M1 Garand rifle, an accurate weapon, was next to him; indeed, he was a bad shot. I looked at him, but again I did not feel anything. He had tried to kill me.

The sergeant and I went back outside. "Sergeant Lupin, signal the rest of the platoon to join us."

My radio man came; I called the Captain and told him what happened.

"Stay there and wait for me, Lieutenant."

I leaned on the wall. The Captain came and asked, "Were you the one who got him, Lieutenant?"

The War Inside His Mind

"Yes, Sir."

"You are good with a rifle; too bad for this guy. You were too far when he first fired, and he paid for it with his life, but he did slow us down."

"Either the rest of the Katiba waits for us somewhere," I pointed my rifle down the road, "or they already fled to the hills."

"They're probably gone from the area, Lieutenant. There are a few more structures a bit further up, then nothing until Saida. Someone might be hiding in one of them, but it's not likely. They wouldn't risk too many men to hold us."

The company started again, in the same formation. More structures came into view; I stopped and looked for any movement. Sergeant Clavery stood next to me. "What do you think?" I asked him, "Anybody in these old farms?"

He grabbed his Garand with one of his powerful hands, and easily lifted it to his shoulder. He shot at a couple of the old buildings. There was no answer, only an echo from the nearby djebels, as the Algerian hills were called.

"No, Sir, there's no one there."

I sent Sergeant Lupin to check the old structures. He verified they were empty. The dissidents had gone to the mountains.

Close to midday, a little further down the road, I met elements of the company stationed in Saida. That sector belonged to them. Its job done, our company boarded the trucks and returned to Mascara.

That night, after some of the strong Mascara wine and dinner, I went to my room and pondered the events of the last few days. Sir Winston Churchill said the most exhilarating thing in life was to be shot at and not be hit. Well, I must have missed the big thrill. I had to disagree with the man I revered. Fear, not exhilaration, was my experience with bullets aimed at me.

Everyone thought I was doing great, but I had many questions and doubts. Deep inside, I dreaded the next few weeks. Would I stop being scared? Would I be able to keep my head in a critical situation? Would I make another mistake like picking the wrong squad for the job? Would my hand shaking happen again? Would I ever get comfortable firing at people? The choice seemed easy if I wanted to survive, but knowingly killing young men would still be hard to accept.

I thought of writing to Ms. Rooth to share my dilemma. She always gave me good advice.

A few years back my uncle gave me money to go to England to perfect my English. I stayed with the Rooth family in South Devonshire for the summer and fell in love with my hosts. Indeed Ms. Rooth became my surrogate mother. She was my guiding light, everything my mom had failed to be. My mother had been distant ever since my brother was born during the German occupation of Paris. Although never nasty to me like my father, she rarely showed interest in me or in what I did. She tolerated me; Ms. Rooth loved me.

For many years, her husband had served as a colonel in the British army in India, so she knew a lot about soldiers in combat. I wrote to her about my working at getting used to being an infantry leader, and to fighting the enemy, but found it challenging.

Mailing the letter proved difficult. Military mail to and from France did not require any stamps. That did not work for England. So I wrote to Nicole, the sister of my best friend, Thierry, and included the note to Ms. Rooth. I asked her to forward it. She agreed to help, and promised to continue to do it. She would forward Ms. Rooth's replies to me.

The War Inside His Mind

Chapter 5

The day after the sweep, Captain Dufour sent for me.

"Lieutenant, let's talk about your job. Each platoon in the company is responsible for an area. Yours goes east from Sidi Boussaid a village southeast of here to the northern side of the Ouarsenis range for about forty miles. Let me show you." The Captain pulled a map out of his desk drawer, opened it on his desk and went around the blue line with his finger. "Here's your sector, inside the blue perimeter. Your sergeant is familiar with it. He'll help you plan the patrols."

"Sir, are there any people living in the area?"

"In the lower elevations, there are a few French settlers' ranches, and Arabs' farms because that's where they can get water. Most of the French have vineyards, orange groves, and other crops. The Arab farms have mostly date palm trees and grow vegetables and grain. Because of their religion, the Arabs don't make or drink wine. You have to meet the ranchers and the farmers."

"Any villages?"

"There are a few hamlets. Your job is to patrol the area to look for and eliminate rebels. They avoid staying in villages for too long."

"Do they hide there?"

"No. They tend to hide in the higher elevations, and use the djebels to rest or to move around. They sometimes bother the farmers or the ranchers. Your main concern is not to let the dissidents set up a fortified hideout in any of the hills."

"I'll make sure of that, Sir."

"Initially, plan day patrols. When you're used to the routine, you'll take your men on patrols that last a few days. You'll get resupplied by trucks. It's more efficient."

"Don't the rebels move at night?"

"Yes, they do, but you have to learn the terrain first. It's easier during the day."

"Understood, Sir. I'll make sure I can patrol at night very soon, "

I had to start acting the full part of being an infantry lieutenant. I had a steep learning curve ahead of me. Luckily I had Sergeant Clavery's experience to lean on. He was unflappable. Although I had been shot at, and had killed a rebel, the couple of skirmishes I went through did not qualify as combat. I had not yet fought against an organized unit. *That'll be my next big test.*

The next morning, in my room, my sergeant pointed at the map on my wall. "Let's plan the first patrol on Djebel Dahja for today," the sergeant told me, "There are few trees, it's not steep and it'll be an easy first step."

Once off the trucks, the platoon started to hike up the mild slope of the front hill. On top of it were a bunch of boulders and a few bushes. Sergeant Clavery came to my side.

"There's no one hiding up there; it's too close to the road. But let me explain how you'd go about it if there were rebels on top."

He showed me how to approach a rocky promontory to minimize the likelihood of having several soldiers downed by the first shots. It was pretty simple. I practiced the maneuver with the platoon so my communications with the squads were as clear as possible.

There were no encounters with Fellaghas in the first patrols. The djebels were quiet. It gave me the opportunity to learn how to be frugal with water, yet drink enough to be able to function. Water is heavy, but so is the ammo. Staying hydrated could wait until being back to base or resupplied at the end of the day; running out of ammo may mean not seeing the end of the day. I also got used to hiking for hours under the hot sun. I actually learned to love the mountains, the big sky, the quietness, and the arid landscape. We walked on hard dirt with embedded rocks; we breathed dry hot air which burnt our nostrils and our throat. We could see forever; the shrubs were scrawny, the scenery pretty drab, but it helped distract me from the constant fear of being shot at unexpectedly by a rebel hiding in ambush.

At the end of the week, the sergeant suggested the lower areas east of Boussaid for the next patrol.

The trucks dropped the platoon five miles past the little village. The day started with an easy walk toward the east. The terrain was almost flat with gentle rolling hills, dotted with small oaks. Late morning, I came up a small knoll with big rocks and a few trees on top. Close to the crest, on our side of the hill, an Arab woman crouched behind a big boulder; a little girl sat next to her. As I approached the two of them, she took her daughter in her arms to protect her from me.

I said, "Don't be scared, I'm your friend." She replied in Arabic and shook her head and hugged the little girl tighter. Sergeant Clavery came up to me. I asked him to tell her I would not harm her or her child.

The sergeant talked to her softly. She seemed to relax and talked to him for a long time.

"What's the story?" I asked him as I pointed at the woman.

"Sir, she was tending to her goats in a barn away from the main building early this morning, when she saw armed men walk toward the farm. She and her daughter hid behind the animals and watched. The rebels entered her house. They are still inside. She closed the gate of the barn to keep the goats inside and ran away to hide behind this rock."

"How many fighters were there?"

The answer was many. The sergeant guessed ten, give or take a couple.

"Where's the farmer?"

The sergeant spoke to her again. "Her man and his two sons went to the village to sell dates," the Sergeant told me.

"The platoon will get the rebels out of her house. Tell her to stay where she is until one of us comes to get her," I told the sergeant. "She should also watch for her husband. I don't want him to walk into the middle of the battle."

The woman lowered her eyes and nodded. I crouched in front of the little girl and held my hand out. She recoiled, but her mom took her daughter's hand, put it in mine, and took both our hands in hers. She said something to me. I picked out the word *Shukran* which I knew meant thank you.

"Aisha," she said putting her hand on her little girl's shoulder.

The fearful eyes and timid smile of the little one touched my heart. "Hello, Aisha."

She clung to her mom.

I crawled up to look at the farm from the top of the hill. The hamlet stood a couple of hundred yards behind it. Several buildings made up the farm; the main one had two stories, three large windows, with no glass, and a wide door in the side facing us, no openings on the side. On the right of it were grain crops, and further away from the house the date palm trees. There were no dissidents I could see on the grounds outside the farm.

Sergeant Clavery sized up the situation next to me. "Some of the rebels are poorly trained and have little discipline. It's our luck that this bunch is sloppy. They did not post any look-outs."

"Great. Here's my plan. The second squad will take position to the left in the bushes about seventy-five yards from the building." I pointed to a bunch of trees and greenery. "I'll take the first squad with me and approach the house from the right. You stay here with the rest of the platoon and open fire at the farm before I jump into the house. That should keep the rebels away from the door and windows."

"It makes sense, Sir. That's what I'd do. What about me leading the attack? I've done it many times."

""For sure, but I'll do it. There's got to be a first time."

"Yes, Sir."

I went back down from the crest, gave the orders to the platoon. Hidden by the top of the hill, followed by Sergeant Lupin and the first squad, I went to my right around the palm trees and then straight for the wall without being detected. Once next to it, my mind worked fast. I positioned half the squad with the sergeant toward the rear of the house to prevent any rebel from escaping through the back of the farm and flee, or come around to attack me from behind. Corporal Gaston and his six men would come with me and rush the farm.

All of a sudden, AK47 fire erupted. The second squad must have been detected. More rebels opened fire from all the openings in the front of the farm. Sergeant Clavery was right. They were firing from all windows in all directions. I had no idea what they were shooting at, and believed they did not either.

I signaled to Sergeant Clavery and his men to open fire. The intense BAR and rifle fire sent the rebels inside the house, away from the openings. It was the perfect time to attack. I held my carbine tightly on my left hand and took a grenade in my right hand. Corporal Gaston

The War Inside His Mind

and his six men were behind me, poised to strike. I was ready to go ... Ready? Was I? People in their right mind did not do what I was about to. Running into bullets?

But I had no choice. I signaled the sergeant to cease fire, nodded to the corporal and jumped around the corner. A soldier threw a grenade through the first window. The corporal and I ran to the door and threw our grenades into the house. All exploded inside. Thick reddish smoke almost blinded us. Screams and yells came out of the farm. As soon as I could see enough, I rushed through the door, the corporal next to me, both our weapons firing. There were rebel bodies on the floor. Two of my soldiers jumped in through the windows. Three rebels fled toward the back of the farm. I pointed them out to the corporal who went after them with one of his men. On my right, a wounded dissident moved his hand toward his weapon. A private shot him dead.

Two rebels retreated, firing their AK47s. One hit Private Boudier who stood next to me. He fell and dropped his gun. The dissidents disappeared into the next room. Furious, I grabbed the private's submachine gun, fired through the wall, and burst into the room. The two dissidents were on the floor, riddled with bullets.

Shots were fired in the back of the farm. Pursued by the corporal, the three rebels jumped out the back of the house only to be shot by Sergeant Lupin's men, but not before one of the insurgents hit one of the sergeant's troops.

Suddenly, all guns went silent. The rebels on the ground, wounded, or dead, the smell of powder, the smashed furniture, and the blood on the dirt floor were the tell-tales of the craze of the last few minutes.

A ringing in my ears, my whole body tense, sweat poured down my face, and my hands shook. Etched in my mind forever was the memory of the intense fight, my first combat test. Having two of my soldiers wounded distressed me. They were my first casualties, and I came out of it unhurt.

Corporal Gaston helped Private Boudier walk out of the farm. He had a nasty blood stain on his right side.

"How do you feel, buddy?" the corporal asked him.

"It hurts like hell. My flesh is burning, but I was lucky. The bullets didn't get into my lungs."

The corporal stabbed him with a dose of morphine from his first-aid combat kit.

"How's the man who was hit outside, Corporal?" I asked.

"Sir, Sergeant Lupin is with him. He lost his left ear and part of his cheek. He's bleeding a lot, but his eye seems okay."

I went to thank him for his sacrifice, but the sight of the soldier shocked me. The soldier's face was half gone. What an ugly wound! I trembled momentarily. It was the first time I saw how gruesome war wounds can be. I could not imagine how the soldier could bear the pain as well as the realization of the damage inflicted to his body.

Sergeant Clavery came down with his men and got all the rebels, dead and alive, out of the house.

I radioed the Captain and reported on the outcome of the patrol, and added, "Sir, I have two wounded soldiers. I need an ambulance."

"Good work, Lieutenant. I'll send an ambulance and a squad of the support platoon right away. The trucks won't be far behind to pick your platoon up."

"Thank you, Sir."

I sent a corporal to tell the Arab woman she could come down with her daughter. She did; her husband and her two sons were with them. The man spoke good French.

"Thank you, Lieutenant, my name is Amin. You saved my wife and my daughter Aisha, and you killed the bastards who went into my home."

"I'm sorry, Amin, but the inside is a bit of a mess."

"Not to worry, we'll clean it up."

The woman went to the shack where the goats were. The poor animals must have been traumatized by the racket of firearms and explosions. Aisha came to hold my hand.

A couple of the soldiers went into the house with the farmer to help him sort out the mess. Amin came out. "Lieutenant, the rebels didn't go up the ladder to the upper level. That's where I store my grain and stuff. So I still have food for the family."

I took Aisha in my arms. "You're safe now." She could not understand what I said, but my tone of voice told her I was her friend. I put her down and let go of her hand. I knew how she felt,

The War Inside His Mind

so young, and in the middle of a war she did not comprehend. She was pretty and had a birth mark next to her left eye. She stared at the dead and the wounded people on the ground. I was five when I saw people strafed to death; I knew she would never forget this. I hoped she would make it through the war and not end up like the little shoeshine boy. It's hard to witness innocent children become the victims of war.

"Bye, Aisha."

So shy, she looked at the ground. She looked so vulnerable.

I went to comfort my wounded men who were about to be taken to the hospital.

I felt guilty. I wondered if they blamed me; I had sent them where they were hit. "Thank you for your bravery. You'll be well taken care of in Mascara." I patted them on the hand; they were hoisted onto the ambulance.

"I'll be back soon, Sir," said Private Boudier.

While we waited for the trucks, I asked Sergeant Clavery, "Sergeant, when Private Boudier was hit, I picked up his submachine gun, fired a few bursts through the wall and got two rebels. Would it not be better for me to carry that kind of weapon instead of my carbine?"

"Sir. You probably would have accomplished the same with the M1. In most cases, on patrol, because you're such a good shot, you can get rebels at two hundred yards. It'd be a shame for you not to have your carbine then. You could never hit anybody that far with the MAT49. If it were me, I'd stay with the carbine."

"Thanks, Sergeant."

Going to sleep that night, I reflected on my first combat test. I had kept my head in the chaos of the fight, and I thought I did the right thing. I might have a chance to survive after all ... or I might have just been lucky.

Chapter 6

A few days later, I received the letter from Ms. Rooth I had been eager to read. *Dear Alain* – it felt nice to be called by my name without the "Lieutenant" in front of it — *I knew it would be difficult for you to get into the routine of war because of your love of peace and your compassion for people. But you will soon look at the rebels as your enemy because of the casualties they will inflict to your platoon, and it will become easier for you to fight them. Trust me; it will happen; it is a matter of time. I think of you every day. Please keep yourself safe. Write soon. I love you.* Now that my uncle had passed away, Ms. Rooth was my only surrogate parent left. Because of her years of experience observing British soldiers in India, she knew the inescapable transformations my mind would go through in the next few months.

I ran monotonous patrols, constantly in a search of dissidents. The crack of a bullet might snap at any time. It could maim or kill a soldier, or me. I had to be vigilant. The hikes ranged from short one-day missions to several-day outings. I worked endlessly at keeping my men focused. Most of the days saw us do routine hikes when nothing happened, no combat, just a tense march in the mountains. We walked endlessly. The scenery was parched but beautiful to my eyes. There was little water. The *wadis* were rivers in the rainy season, but they were dry beds of loose rocks most of the time. Some of the mountainous terrain was difficult, steep, and rocky; at times areas of thorny bushes made it almost impassable; the constant heat during the day made our routine tedious and wearisome.

"Spread out. Keep your distance," I had to signal several times. I can't say I had no fear; I did, but I had to manage it and keep going. From what the Captain told me after my first encounter with armed rebels, all the soldiers felt the same way. I rotated the lead squad

The War Inside His Mind

several times during the missions. The point men were changed every hour. Everyone had to keep sharp.

One day, the platoon intercepted a small group of rebels. Not fully focused, a couple of the squads fired their weapons without concentrating. The rebels escaped; a missed opportunity. Fortunately no one in the platoon got hurt, but it was sloppy weapon handling. I was quite upset about that, and let the soldiers know.

We got back to our base, and the next day at five in the morning, the platoon hiked the ten miles to the firing range to spend the day. I wanted to get their sloppiness out of their fight discipline.

"This morning, we'll do the regular rifle and submachine gun exercises." At the end of the drill, I called the sergeants. "Now we'll practice grenade throws; although not many were thrown yesterday, quite a few miss their targets."

I could almost hear the imperceptible groans that greeted my announcement. Everybody, including the sergeants, dreaded that drill.

The grenade area was about two hundred yards from the range. There were three throwing spots, protected from the target direction by four-foot sandbag walls. The targets, also delineated by a low sandbag parapet, were roughly one hundred to two hundred fifty feet away from the throwing stations.

A soldier would stand next to a sergeant in each throwing well. The first drill involved throwing dummies to the target, and then soldiers threw five live grenades to the target.

One of the last soldiers to go through the exercise, Private Boudier, who had recovered from his wound, had gone through the practice only once before. I could see he was quite nervous. When he had to switch from blank to live grenade, he froze. "I'm not sure I can do it, Sarge."

The sergeant put the little iron pineapple on top of the wall and told him, "Take it, pull the pin, and throw it to the nearest target." The private did not move. His corporal approached the sergeant, "Let me help him." The sergeant nodded.

I had to let him do it, but I held my breath. The corporal took the grenade, placed it in the soldier's hand, pulled the pin, his hand around the private's fingers so the little bomb did not arm. He pulled the private's arm back and helped him throw the grenade. It fell and exploded short of the target, but the thrower and the sergeant had ducked behind the bags. No one got hurt.

The corporal told the private, "Your turn, do the exact same thing by yourself." He put another grenade on the wall. Again I held my breath. The private took it, pulled the pin and threw it way beyond the two targets. "Well done, soldier. From now on, you'll be the one I choose to throw to the furthest enemies," the sergeant said, laughing.

The tension in the platoon broke; the drill ended shortly after a few more minutes.

Sergeant Clavery assembled the platoon. I told them, "You worked hard today, and you all did well. Don't ever forget that careless handling of firearms means trouble, and trouble means casualties."

The platoon assumed patrol formation to hike back to the base.

Being on alert all the time took a toll. Lives were at stake. Anyone in the platoon could get injured or die from unexpected light infantry fire at any time. Most of the dissidents in the Atlas range wore some sort of combat clothing and were trained, but on occasion local village workers or merchants chose, or were coerced, to help the rebels' cause for a day or for a week. They were harder to identify as enemies.

With a record of many Fellaghas captured or killed, the second platoon built a good reputation for getting the job done. I was getting more comfortable in my role. I knew what to do in most situations, and I had earned the trust from my platoon. My men were sharp and effective, but I also knew I did not have the killing instinct yet. When I faced dissidents, if I had a chance, I tried to persuade them to surrender. Most of the time, they refused, and I felt justified to attack them. Days went by, but the end of the conflict was nowhere in sight. There was a price to pay for that; nerves were raw.

A young sergeant and ten new recruits joined my platoon to replace those who had completed over two years of military service. I had to train them, blend them into the strong fighting unit the platoon had become, and slowly get them used to combat.

One afternoon, the platoon went on a search, near *Djebel El Mebres*. Like the Captain had done for me before my first sweep, I briefed the new sergeant and soldiers about the dissidents' mastery of camouflage.

On the flat terrain, there were many trees, irrigation ditches, dry at that time, and a few bushes. Hiding would be easy for the dissidents. I instructed the sergeants to be vigilant and to spread their soldiers in two rows so the squads could cover a wide area. The young sergeant walked in the second row of his squad, with no one behind him.

The walk went on, slow and monotonous; soldiers checked trees and bushes, careful not to miss a rebel hiding under some pile of dirt. After two hours, a burst from an AK47 shattered the silence of the afternoon. I turned around to look at what happened. A soldier lay on the ground, and an Arab ran away as fast as he could. A corporal from the third squad aimed his rifle and shot him. I ran to my fallen soldier. It was the new sergeant.

Face down in the dirt, unconscious, several bullets in the back, he bled profusely. The wound looked deep. I could see his lung.

Sergeant Clavery called for an emergency medical evacuation. A medic who had accompanied the patrol rushed to the wounded man. There was not much he could do. He tried to slow down the bleeding, but could not do it. The sergeant wheezed and made gargling noises. Within a few minutes, the medical Alouette helicopter came. Two army nurses jumped out. They ran to the sergeant and took over from the medic. They worked fast, secured the wound with huge gauze bandages, strapped him on a stretcher, put him on the chopper, and took off.

I asked the corporal who shot down the rebel, "What happened, Corporal?"

"Sir, the rebel hid in a hole, covered with dirt. The sergeant walked about five feet from him and didn't see him. He had gone thirty feet, when the Fell stood up and fired his assault rifle. He hit the sergeant, and narrowly missed one of my men, who only got his sleeve torn away by a bullet. Then he ran away; I got him before he got too far."

"Thank you Corporal."

"Sir, I feel terrible, that was one of his first patrols; such a nice guy."

"Yes, for sure."

I seethed, but I had to complete the sweep. Anxious to get back, I called for the trucks to meet us at the end of the sweep area. I hoped the hospital would be able to save the sergeant's life.

Back at our compound, I went into the Captain's office.

"Lieutenant, your sergeant didn't make it. He died before he got to the hospital."

That hit me like a punch in the stomach. I could not speak. I could hardly breathe. I kicked a chair.

"Damn it. Why did he have to die? It was my fault."

Sergeant Clavery, who had come in too, said, "Lieutenant, there's nothing you could have done to prevent this. It's the problem with the raw recruits. They don't know how to protect themselves. He didn't see the dissident. There's no way you could have taught him how to avoid this. He didn't look. He should have."

"I know, Sergeant. But he died. This is my first fatal casualty since I took command of the unit."

Captain Dufour tried to be helpful.

"Lieutenant. You have nothing to feel guilty about. What happened is what war is about: unexpected and senseless death."

I sat on a chair and looked down at my boots. I had trained my platoon. Everyone was fit, alert, and executed orders well. The first ninety days were the most dangerous for any soldier because they had not acquired the right instincts. But it made me mad all the same. I hated the war, and I started to hate the rebels, like Ms. Rooth said I would.

This was all so new to me. I thought of my uncle. He never talked about his combat experiences; I wondered how he felt when he lost any of his men. I thought he would have been proud of how I handled myself in my early military months, so I decided to write about my war to Madame De Sèvres, the countess who had been in love with him. Because of her nobility, she had social obligations, and my uncle, a common man, could not be accepted by her family. I had met the countess three years ago when he was near death; I had to tell her about his terminal lung cancer and hoped the butler would let me in.

"Yes?" The butler inquired when he opened the door.

"Do you remember me? I came with my uncle on New Year's Day to bring chocolates to Madame de Sèvres. I need to talk to her. I have news that concerns him."

"I see. And whom should I say is calling?"

"Tell her it's Alain."

"Will she know the name?"

"Yes, she will." I looked him in the eye. "It's really important that I be able to talk to her. It won't take long."

"I'll see what I can do. Please wait here."

He came back shortly and said, "Please, follow me."

He guided me through a brightly-lit hall and up a beautiful staircase and opened a French door to a tastefully decorated parlor. "Madame La Comtesse. This is Alain."

Beautiful, middle-aged, elegant, confident and welcoming, she extended her arms out and smiled at me.

I stared at her. "You are so beautiful, no wonder he adores you," I said.

She came close to me and gave me a long warm hug. "Alain, I've heard so much about you, I finally get to meet you. Should I assume these are not happy circumstances?"

"I'm sorry to be the bearer of bad news, Madame. He is dying. He doesn't have much time left. I thought you should know."

Her face turned white. She closed her eyes. "I'm not totally surprised. I've not heard from him in a while."

"Madame, I wondered if you wanted to say good-bye to him."

"Alain, I can't. You're undoubtedly aware of our story."

"I'm sad that you have to live your life like that, Madame."

"I have a name and a title, Alain. I cannot do as I choose. Thank you for coming; I needed to know. I'm so glad to have met you." She gave me a parting hug.

Later she responded to my note telling her of his passing. *Inasmuch as I would like to hold you as if you were my son, you know I cannot. But if you ever need help, you must call on me. I loved Raymond and although I don't really know you, I love you too. Please come by when you can.*

A warm friendship developed between the two of us. Before I left for Algeria, she told me, "Like Raymond, you'll lead an infantry platoon. Like him you'll be brave and make your country proud. Take care of yourself and come back. I'll be waiting for you."

"May I write to you, Madame?"

"Please do. I'll write back. Letters from home will help you keep your head together."

During the next few weeks, I became the officer the army had hoped I would be. I had learned how to do my job well, executed all my missions, ran many patrols, maintained strict discipline in the field, and kept my troops safe as much as practicable. My platoon was credited with more rebels killed or taken prisoner than the other two rifle platoons of the company combined. In addition to sweeps, and the search-and-destroy patrols, I met regularly with the ranchers and farmers who lived in my sector.

George and his family lived on one of the most beautiful farms, with vineyards, an orange grove, and fig trees. I met him on one of my first patrols.

"Hi there, I'm Lieutenant Alain. I'm stationed in Mascara. One of my platoon's missions is to protect your ranch. I thought I'd stop by and meet you."

"Thank you for coming, Lieutenant. My name is George and this is my wife Thérèse."

"Nice to meet you both," I replied, "I see kids over there."

"The oldest one is Michael. He's five. The two-year old is René. If you look at Thérèse, it's obvious that number three is on the way."

"George, do you have weapons to defend yourselves if you have to?"

"Yes, Lieutenant. I have a rifle and a submachine gun. We practice with them. Thérèse knows how to handle them. It's too early for Michael to handle a firearm."

"Do you have a radio?"

"No, I don't. But our family has owned this ranch for fifty years. We know the people in the nearby village. They like us. We don't feel threatened."

"That's great," I said, "But you can get through to me from the village if you need to. The store has a phone. Call if anything changes."

"I will, Lieutenant. Stop by anytime you want."

My life was not all about executing dangerous missions. Between patrols, on some evenings, I became the duty officer for the town of Mascara. In the European side of town, there were bars where young barmaids poured drinks for soldiers who thought they were in love with them. There were many branches of the military stationed in or near Mascara, in addition to the line troops, like we were: maintenance personnel, medical specialists, supply handlers, support companies, and others. Fist fights over the assumed love

The War Inside His Mind

of a barmaid erupted from time to time. The problem arose usually between men of different outfits. The duty officer had to intervene, calm everybody down and send those involved back to their units.

Although this did not further my combat ability and know-how, it provided some relief from the intensity of life in the infantry.

Near the Arab section of the town stood the brothel. Part of my duty demanded that I go inside to talk to the woman in charge. Madame wanted no trouble and relied on the duty officer to make sure no harm came to anyone inside her establishment.

The ground-floor room was quite a sight: lit by several floor lamps with colorful shades, the pink walls and the ghastly red carpeting, the whole room smelled of cheap violet perfume. To complete the warm but seedy atmosphere, there were several sofas and armchairs where women in scanty attire offered themselves to the men who came in. There was no music. Madame wanted to hear everything that went on.

Soldiers would enter the brothel, go to the bar, and have a beer while they surveyed the available women who would tempt them by displaying as much flesh as they thought they needed to and by promising special favors. The prostitutes were a sight to behold. There were mostly pitiful middle-aged Arab women who obviously did not wear any veil, and a few European escapees from Poland, Romania, and other countries from behind the Iron Curtain. They all looked bored. What a life!

Each woman had a sign with her name clearly visible. If interested, the soldier would go and talk to the one they had their eye on. No touching was involved. Once the couple agreed on the encounter, and were ready to proceed, the man went to pay the cashier for the time he could afford. Then they went into a room. A servant kept time and knocked on the door at the end of the session.

The rare times I had to intervene were if two soldiers wanted the same woman and started a fight, or one would refuse to come out of the room when time was up. Once, I bought a beer for a soldier so he could wait for the other guy to finish his business. Madame was very grateful and took a liking to me. She insisted I spent time with any of her woman for free.

"They're all very skilled, Lieutenant. You'll enjoy it."

"No thank you, Madame, I'll pass."

"Okay, next time you're here."

I ended up dreading going into the brothel because I had to keep finding excuses not to indulge in her favors.

To patrol the sidewalks outside the bars and check the brothel resembled the job of a policeman more than that of a soldier. I did not like doing it, but it served a purpose, and all officers in Mascara had to do it.

There were a few nice cafés where local French people went to have a bite and talk. That's where, on my off-duty nights, I learned about mergez, the delicious spicy little lamb sausages one ate with one's fingers. The Pieds Noirs–black feet, as the French settlers were called–were friendly to me. Infantry officers were their protection from the rebels. They looked up to me and often bought me drinks and tapas. There were few young European women in Mascara. Most attended colleges in Algiers, Oran, or in France; the ones who stayed in town were spoken for, married or engaged.

I received a response from the countess. *Alain, I am so proud of you, and your uncle would be too. It is going to be a long war, so be patient. Keep alert and stay safe. It is important for me that you come back. You may think that having lost your uncle, and being estranged from your parents, you have no one to go back to. Well you have me, and you have Ms. Rooth. I love you, and I long for the end of the nightmare, so I can hug you. Keep writing.*

Her letter touched me. Of course I had someone to go back to, and it was comforting to know I had reasons to keep myself safe.

Chapter 7

A small number of armed rebels had been roaming recently around the *djebels* not too far from the town of Mascara. The company had received complaints from some of the farmers. The dissidents entered hamlets and farms, scared children, stole food, and sometimes molested women. They also abducted men and forced them to join them for a few days. They were thought to operate in the zone I was assigned to protect, so it was my job to find them. I had no intelligence reports on their whereabouts, and I did not run into this particular group in any of my patrols. There were few of them, therefore they were hard to find, and probably hiding from me.

One evening, I got a break. A pilot from a light aviation unit spotted a small group of rebels walking toward a little hamlet east of Boussaid, one I knew well because that's where Aisha lived.

In the early hours of the morning, the platoon boarded the trucks to get close to where the dissidents were spotted. Within a mile of the hamlet, the soldiers continued on foot. The sun was barely above the horizon.

"How many Fells are in the group, Lieutenant?" Sergeant Lupin asked me.

"I don't know for sure. From the pilot's report, there must be less than a handful, but there might be more. We'll have to search every structure to make sure we find all of them."

I sent the third and fourth squads around the hamlet to stop anyone from leaving the small village. I wanted the villagers and the rebels, if they were hiding in there, to know that anyone leaving the village would be stopped and checked. Escape was not possible. When the squads were in place, I decided to first search the farm house at the west end of the hamlet, which happened to be Amin's farm.

I asked Sergeant Clavery to take the second squad and surround the farm so no one could run away from it. Once they were ready, I led the first squad toward the main house. It was early but light out, and it surprised me not to see anyone outside. Amin and his family were hard-working folks who hated the rebels. They should have been tilling the soil, tending to the animals, or taking care of the crops. I stopped for a while and listened, but heard nothing. A little concerned, I went close to the building. Two soldiers went to the windows, which had no glass, and peered inside. I called Amin, but received no answer. I went in with two soldiers.

The sergeant and the rest of the troops went to search the court-yard and the sheds.

The inside of the building was quiet. There was not a soul around. Still-warm, half-empty cups of tea and a kettle were on the table.

"The rebels must have been the ones drinking the tea and probably left when they spotted us. Let's look for the family. You search the ground floor," I said to the two men, "I'll go up."

I climbed the ladder that led to the loft where I knew Amin kept his food. Before I poked my head in the open, I shouted, "If anyone is hiding up there, show yourself with your hands up."

I heard soft moans that did not sound threatening. I raised myself so I could peek at the floor. The two sons of Amin were cowering in a corner. I got up into the room and secured my rifle.

I smiled at the two little boys.

"You're safe now. The bad guys are gone. Where are your mom and dad?"

The kids relaxed a bit, but they were still scared. They did not answer me because they did not understand French. Then Aisha showed her head from behind a bale of hay where she was hiding. When we saw each other, I crouched; she ran to me, and put her arms around my neck. Her brothers asked her something; she replied and put her head on my shoulder. The boys knew then they should not be afraid of me. Unfortunately, I could not communicate with any of the children.

I shouted down, "Get Sergeant Clavery here."

I carried Aisha down; the boys followed me. The soldiers had not found anybody downstairs.

The sergeant came and spoke to the children, who told him

their story. The dissidents had sent the children upstairs last night and told them they would kill them if they made any noise. They did not know where their parents were.

"Sergeant, ask them how many men they saw." The answer was three.

The soldiers who went into the shack in the back of the courtyard found the farmer and his wife. They untied them and removed the gags the dissidents had put over their mouths. They brought them to me. Amin had been beaten up. His face was swollen. His wife had apparently not been harmed.

They were happy to see the children were safe. Aisha let go of my hand and ran to her mom.

"Lieutenant, I have to thank you again," Amin said, "It's the second time you saved my family."

"What happened, Amin?" I asked the farmer.

"Four men came last evening. They asked where I kept my grain. They stole bags of it. They said they'd get more food in the village, and come back to take me with them to go to raid the next hamlet. That's why they tied us up."

"Well, they won't take you away now," I told him, "They must have left the farm this morning when they saw the soldiers and gone to hide in the village. They can't escape; the place is surrounded. I'll find them and get your food back. You'll never see them again."

The village had one street, a little dirt road. In the center was a small plaza with a few trees and a couple of benches. There were alleys and a few shacks between the houses which all bordered the main street. There were fewer than twenty buildings to be searched, all two-story, with white walls and a flat roof.

I got my sergeants together. "We'll search from the west to the east, two houses at a time, one on each side of the road. The second squad will stay outside while the first squad searches the houses."

"What about the folks who live there?" One of them asked.

"The people have to get out of their homes. Once the houses are cleared, I don't want the people to go back inside. The buildings are too close together. It'd be easy for anyone to hide if there's confusion. I need to know where everyone is."

"Sir, I'll take half of the second squad and keep the civilians at the end of the road," Sergeant Clavery said.

"That'll do it."

"Sir, the Captain," my radio man said as he handed me the receiver.

"Yes, Sir."

"What's the situation there, Lieutenant?"

"Sir, last night four rebels tied up Amin and his wife, the farmer at the western end of the hamlet. I know that at least four rebels spent the night in the farm and escaped this morning when they saw my platoon coming. But they're in the village. I have it sealed up. They can't go anywhere. I'll find them."

"Okay, Lieutenant. Good luck, and call me when you're through. The regiment's reputation is at stake. The Colonel is anxious for you to clear that situation."

"Yes, Sir."

I had to start the search. The sergeant told the Arab men who were chatting outside to go back to their houses. I did not want people roaming around. Sergeant Lupin cordoned off the first two houses. I told Sergeant Clavery to tell the occupants to come out.

"Sir, they may have weapons inside. What should they do with them?"

"You're right. I don't want anyone to be carrying arms outside. Tell them to leave whatever guns and knives they have leaning on the wall by the door. They'll find them where they left them when they get back to their home. If I find any weapon in the house, it'll be confiscated. Any person who stays inside the house will be taken prisoner."

The sergeant said out loud, "Everyone, man, woman, and child out of the house." He told them what to do with their weapons.

With much groaning from everyone, all came out and assembled on the street. We frisked the men. It would have been inappropriate to search the women. We had no grounds to violate their religious code.

I looked at the men who had segregated themselves from the women and children, and said to them, "You know who we're looking for. If you know where they are, tell me now. It'll save a lot of trouble."

Not surprisingly, nobody volunteered any information. They were scared of what the dissidents would do to the village if they knew someone had revealed their hideout.

The War Inside His Mind

I motioned to one of the old men to come to me. "Which one is your house?" I asked him. He pointed at the one on his left.

"Anyone hiding in there?"

"No, Sir."

"Come with me." We walked toward the door.

"You go in and show me every room," I said to him. I had three men from the first squad with me. The four of us went in with the old man. He did not seem apprehensive, so I was confident there was no one in there. The rest of the squad inspected all the shacks and storage areas that went with the house. After the search, the civilians were ushered toward the soldiers of the second squad who were waiting for them at the end of the village. We repeated the search in the next sets of dwellings. In one of them, I found a trap under a big sheet of metal. We lifted it carefully and found containers of water, but no rebels. Then we got to the plaza.

There were four houses close to one another at the west end of the square. Sergeant Clavery got all the folks from the four houses to come out. Quite a crowd gathered outside. The scene became unsettling. The women complained; some cried. Some of the kids ran around, playing. They thought it was a game. The men went after the kids. No one seemed to want to stay in one place.

I positioned my men so they would cover them all. I shouted, "Stop. Stay where you are." They quieted down. I shouted again, "Nobody moves. Put your hands over your heads."

The sergeant repeated the order, and added, "Stay still, and look at me." The group faced him. Sergeant Lupin covered them with his weapons. The group finally settled down.

I told the soldiers "Take your time. Make sure you go through all the rooms, however long it takes."

It took quite a while to search the four houses and the adjoining barns and sheds, but we did not find anybody hiding.

As I came out of the last house, Sergeant Lupin came toward me. He pulled my arm. I looked at him wondering what he wanted. He pointed at the backs of three women standing with their arms up."Look at their feet, Sir."

I did and almost burst out laughing. All the women wore the traditional long white robes down to the ground and veils to cover their faces, except for their eyes. Because they had their hands over their heads, the robes got pulled up a tad; I could see their bare feet colored with the traditional reddish henna. But the three, so-called women, the sergeant had pointed out to me did not reveal any flesh. On the contrary, I could get a glimpse of the soles of boots. They had no idea I could see that. They were most assuredly three of the rebels we were looking for.

The fourth man or more must be hiding in some other place, and there might be others I did not know about. These were dangerous men who might be armed. I had to secure them and keep the villagers and my men safe. There should be no shooting if I could avoid it. I asked the sergeant to stay where he was with his men and to keep an eye on the rebels, and shoot them if they started to run. I went to the second squad. I asked Private Bernard and two corporals who were physically strong to come with me. I explained the situation to them.

"We'll go around and walk close to the back of the crowd. Once we get behind the disguised men, each of you will grab one of them around the chest and wrestle them to the ground. Sergeant Lupin's soldiers will help."

"Sir, should we frisk them? They may have grenades hidden on themselves," a corporal suggested.

"Sergeant Lupin will do that. Just make sure the rebels can't move."

The soldiers got behind the rebels, as planned, and immobilized them. I tore their robes with my knife and the dissidents were exposed for who they were. No weapons were found on them. They must have left them by the door of the house they were in, as instructed. They were face-down on the ground, and the soldiers tied their hands behind their backs, bound their feet too.

I said, "Sergeant, keep the civilians away." I turned back to look at the prisoners. Most of the Algerians attended schools run by French teachers, and spoke some of the language. I stood over them, staring at the back of their heads, wondering how to get them to tell me where the others were.

One of them yelled, "The Fellaghas will kill you if you touch us. We're mighty Algerian fighters."

I poked him with my carbine. "Fighters? What kind of warriors are you? You scare children, you threaten unarmed men and women, and you steal food. You hide among women and wear their dresses." I laughed. "You're no soldiers. You're a bunch of cowards."

They did not say a word. "How do you like wearing the dresses? How does the veil feel on your face? Would you enjoy cooking and feeding the children?"

I grew impatient. "Do you understand me?"

I turned the talker over with my boot, so he could look at me. He stared at the muzzle of my weapon. I had no doubt he understood what I said. He showed a flash of anger in his eyes.

"Which of you will tell me where the other insurgents are hiding?" The one with his face turned upward spat at me, but the three of them remained silent.

"Okay, someone will."

I turned around and asked Sergeant Clavery to tell the villagers it was now safe to tell us where the other rebels were. Immediately, the dissident who seemed to be the leader of the group, yelled out to the civilians, "I'll kill the family of anyone who speaks." He said it in his language. The sergeant translated it to me.

I towered over him. "Okay, big mouth. Tell me where they are."

He spat again in my direction. I pointed my carbine to his forehead. He blinked and recoiled.

"Don't shoot me. I don't know. They escaped, and they'll kill you."

I stared at him. "You like saying that, don't you? Don't worry, when I find them, I'll do the killing. But I'm not going to shoot you, not right away. I'll have one of my soldiers shoot one of your buddies in the left foot; he'll scream. When he's done screaming, the soldier will shoot him in the right foot. He'll scream again. Then, I'll ask you where your friends are. You'll tell me. If you don't, it'll be my turn to do the shooting. Your left foot will be first and you'll know what to expect, and both of you will never walk again."

As I said these words, I glanced at the other prisoners. One shook his head. He did not want any part of that.

"Lieutenant," he said wriggling his body on the ground, "I'll tell you where he is."

"No you won't, Rashad. I forbid you. If you do, I'll kill you," the first prisoner said as if he were spitting poison.

The man ignored the threat. "Lieutenant, he's in the last house of the village, the one with the three palm trees in front. He's in an underground hole in the back room, with the food and the weapons."

The first prisoner went into a long tirade.

"Put a gag on him to shut him up," I told one of the soldiers.

Now I knew where the fourth guy hid. I sent a couple of soldiers to watch the last house to make sure no one came out of it. I had to continue the methodic search until the last house in case there was a fifth rebel.

I assigned Corporal Gaston and Private Bernard to guard the prisoners. The last houses on the plaza were searched and we found no rebel.

There were two buildings left. Again, the sergeant told the civilians to get out. They had to know where the rebel was, but I did not want to tip them off that I knew about him too. They might yell some warning.

Sergeant Lupin, two of his soldiers and I went into the one where we knew the fourth guy was. The rest of the squad went to search the other house across the road. I had learned the hard way about caches inside houses. I knew where to find the rebel.

We searched all the rooms before entering the one with the hiding place. We saw a rug on the floor. The trap had to be underneath.

"Anybody in here?" the sergeant shouted. We moved a couple of containers and cushions to mask the noise of removing the carpet. The soldiers stood with their backs to the wall, their weapons aimed at the wooden trapdoor. Bullets could go through it.

I crouched so that if the dissident fired in the direction of my voice, he would hopefully shoot over my head. I shouted, "Come out with your hands up. I know you're in there. If you don't, I'll fire through the trapdoor." I shot a couple of rounds in the dirt to make sure he knew I meant what I said.

The rebel lifted the trap slowly. "Don't shoot." The man got out of the hole, his hands behind his neck. Inside the cache, we found several AK47s, grenades, and the bags of grain they had stolen from Amin. Sergeant Lupin frisked him. Everyone came out of the house.

"They got me," the prisoner shouted, obviously trying to warn somebody. Sergeant Lupin put his rifle right on the man's neck. "Shut up or I'll shoot you," he warned him.

"Has the house across the street been checked yet?" I asked one of the soldiers.

"Corporal Raynaud is inside now, Sir."

As he said that, a man jumped off the roof of that house, landed on his feet and started to fire his gun.

"Run, Mahdi, I'll cover you," he yelled at our prisoner.

Sergeant Lupin pressed the end of his gun on Mahdi. "You move and you are dead."

The troops returned fire and hit the fifth rebel. But he had shot a couple of civilians, a man and his wife. He also hit one of my soldiers.

The bullet had gone through his lower leg. It looked like it had been shattered. The blood gushed from it, and a bone stuck out. The private screamed with pain. I went to look at the rebel. He had been shot in the head and was dead.

A corporal gave the wounded soldier a shot of morphine and stopped the bleeding. Sergeant Clavery called for an ambulance. The civilians had minor wounds; a soldier took care of them

I asked the corporal who had searched the house. "How did that happen, Corporal?"

"Sir, he hid behind a pile of boxes, on the roof. The instant we got to the top, the other rebel yelled. He bolted and jumped off to the ground."

I was angry at myself. I should have searched that house before the one where I knew the fourth dissident was. Because of my mistake, three people were hurt.

But we did the job. We had captured four insurgents and killed one.

"Sergeant," I called Sergeant Clavery, "Release the villagers. They can go back to their homes now."

"Yes, Sir."

I looked at my soldier, I asked the corporal, "Is he going to be okay?"

"Yes, Sir. It looks messy, but I think it's only the fibula that's broken. The strong bone, the tibia, is intact. He'll walk normally in a week."

"Did you hear that, soldier? You'll be one hundred percent in no time."

"Thank you, Sir. I guess it'll end up okay, but I probably won't get to go home."

I called the Captain. "Sir, we're done here. The group is annihilated."

"Well done, Lieutenant. Any casualty?"

"One of my guys was hurt; minor wound."

"The Colonel will be pleased."

"Sir. I'm not sure these guys were Fellaghas. They looked like thugs out for a thrill and free food. Fellaghas would have protected themselves better and put up a fight."

"Well, Lieutenant, whoever they are, they won't bother anybody for a long while."

I had one more thing to do. I walked back to Amin's farm to give him his grain back. When I got to the farm, Aisha ran to me and took my hand.

"I'll be back, Aisha."

"Thank you again," Amin said to me.

The prisoners and the dead rebel were loaded on a truck and the platoon headed home.

On the way back, I thought, more wounded, more blood, more pain. There'll be more tomorrow.

What a waste.

Chapter 8

Halfway to Tiaret, the site of the regiment headquarters, the easternmost part of my zone of responsibility was the least populated and the most rugged. The rebels used a long series of hills which ran west to east to get to the central plain and the northern cities. Ill-defined paths crisscrossed the steep slopes on the northern side of the hills; the southern side was almost vertical. Rocky and inhospitable, the bare terrain of the top of the range followed the crest from summit to summit. It looked to be the ideal environment for the rebels to build a fortified stronghold as well as using it as a route for fighters.

After a morning at the firing range, the Captain called me to his office.

"A light aviation pilot reported that he spotted rebels moving east on top of your favorite crest. He estimated the group to be at least a strong katiba. The report has not been confirmed, but you have to try to find them."

"Yes, Sir. Do you think they're just passing through?"

"I've no idea. They could be or they may want to set up some relay station. It's also possible they're trying to lure soldiers to go after them and destroy the patrol because they let the pilot see them. It's a delicate and dangerous mission, but you have to go find them and wipe them out."

"Thanks for the warning. I'll be ready for an ambush. Can this pilot look for them and radio me if he sees them?"

"Yes, but they'll probably hide during the day."

"I'll do my best, Sir."

"Get going early in the morning. They might be a day ahead of you, or waiting for you some place."

Because it was so remote, the most effective way to patrol this wild area was to plan on a four-day foray. I would get resupplied on the second and third day.

I gathered the sergeants. "Fells have been spotted on zone eight. We're leaving on search-and-destroy at five tomorrow morning. We'll be gone four days. Your men must start with enough water and food for two days."

Sergeant Clavery added, "All the squads must carry as many cartridges as possible. Make sure the clips are fully loaded. The trucks will bring more ammo."

That was my fourth patrol in that area. Unlike the first three, which turned out to be just walks in the wilderness, it looked like this one would likely be a tough outing that would involve a confrontation with the enemy. I knew the terrain, but in spite of my experience in running patrols, I knew how difficult it was to lead the troops when the platoon ran into an ambush. The first bullets would hit without warning, and thereafter everyone had to fend for himself. I could also be the first one to get it.

I trusted my men; we worked well together, but combat is chaos after the first seconds. If the insurgents wanted to kill as many of us as they could, it would be one of our most dangerous missions. I feared potentially high casualties, but at least I had been warned and would be ready. Definitely apprehensive, I did not get much sleep that night.

Trucks transported the platoon to the foot of the western end of the trail going up to the top of the hills. Places suited for an ambush were around the rocky summits. The rebels would post one or two lookouts to find out the strength of my patrol. But I thought it unlikely these sentries would open fire. They would run back to their line to report. I hoped we could spot them.

So I decided the best way to approach this mission was to have two squads advance side by side, one following the trail on the top of the range, the other on the slope on the northern side of the hills, which was less visible from the top of the hills. The south side of the arête was too steep to hike on, or for rebels to hide. The rest of the platoon would follow a hundred yards behind. I had to keep the soldiers alert and decided it was much too hot to wear helmets all day. The soldiers would have them attached to their belt until they were close to an area of potential ambush.

Once deployed as I planned, I led the platoon on a cautious walk. We moved slowly, because I had no idea where the dissidents were. We had to search every tree, rock, hole in the ground, or shallow cave that could hide a dissident. I was not even sure whether they would fight or not. They might flee when they detected the soldiers; that would be nice; or they might think they had a chance to surprise us and cause a lot of damage. I had no way of knowing the answer to that question, so I had to assume they would attack the platoon some time.

I acted as if rebels were over the top of every hill or that a sentry was hidden among the next block of boulders. I had conducted many patrols, and my mind focused on the task at hand. My stomach got a little tight, but I displayed calm and confidence.

I usually enjoyed the mountains; their wilderness and emptiness brought some peace to my mind. It was hard to explain, but probably my way of coping with tension and suppressed fears. But today I had no time for reveries. I had to stay sharp, and keep my men the same way.

After a couple of hours, we came in sight of the first hill. There were only a few sand-color rocks, but the far side of the top was not visible from where I stood. I stopped the platoon.

Sergeant Clavery, who led the rear with the third and fourth squads, came next to me.

"What do you think, Sir?"

We were close to the beginning of the range, midmorning, and the rebels knew that my troops were fresh and alert.

"There's probably no one hiding up there, it's too open, but let's go take a look."

I took two soldiers from the first squad, and asked Sergeant Lupin to cover me. The round summit was a hundred-fifty yards away. The three of us ran, bent over, ready to hit the ground. No shots were fired. Within twenty feet of the crest, I dropped to the ground. "Stay here," I told the two soldiers. I crawled on my knees and elbows, got behind a rock and peeked around it. I couldn't see anyone in the distance either. The next summit rose a couple of miles away. I stood up.

To fight the dangerous monotony, I switched the squads around every two hours, so they would occupy a different position and as-

---

sume a different role. Three more summits were cleared and no rebels were sighted. At the end of the afternoon, I decided to stop for the night on the hill that we just searched. The view was unobstructed in all directions, and the southern slope too steep to hide any danger. It should be a safe enough place. Sergeant Clavery organized the sentries. I wanted them doubled. I did not want any surprise, and it was easier for the lookouts to have a buddy with them. At night the sense of danger increased, and nerves were tested. Every little critter foraging for food sounded like dissidents crawling to surprise the soldiers.

Moonlight provided visibility so that would help minimize undetected assaults. We had done the first of the four-day patrol. I tried to relax, my head on my pack, my carbine across my chest. The temperature dropped when the sun went down. It was less miserable. I enjoyed the deep silence of the dim-lit scenery. I closed my eyes, enjoyed the scent of the shrub relinquishing the heat of the day, but never really went to sleep.

I went over my plan and could not think of any way to improve it to minimize the risk of high casualties. Unless they left the area on their way to the northern plains, the rebels would follow our moves and undoubtedly set up an ambush.

The next day, the agonizingly slow and scary progress continued. This part of the range had a few low juniper trees that required a careful approach. We cleared summit after summit. The round tops were not likely to hide many rebels. There were not enough rocks or escarpments for them to hide. Not finding any of the dissidents became monotonous and, I knew, dangerous. One could easily get lulled into a false sense of security. With no breeze, no animals scurrying around, and no birds flying, the soldiers were the only creatures moving under the torrid sun. In addition to worrying about our enemies, sweat poured down my face and got into my eyes; I fought the unbearable heat, the rugged terrain, and the stress of waiting for that first bullet. My neck and shoulders ached from the tension.

I stopped at the end of the day at the trail where the trucks were to bring us our supplies. I sent a squad to meet them and bring the food and water. No ammo had been used so the magazines did not have to be replenished.

Like the night before, I doubled the sentries. We had to be closer to the dissidents, but how close? So I warned the pairs of lookouts. "You have to stay awake and watch your partner's back. You don't want to be kidnapped by a couple of dissidents. They'd cut you up in pieces."

Nothing happened during the fitful night. The third morning, I called Sergeant Clavery.

"I think today is the day. The terrain is rougher. Some of the hilltops are perfect for ambushes."

"You're probably right, Sir. My guess is it'll be in the afternoon. As you know, the hills further east are steeper and the red rocks are chiseled into perfect hiding places."

"I think so too. I won't rotate the squads today. I want to have the first squad with its automatic weapons up front with me."

"Yes, Sir."

I was tired, and I could see from the way the soldiers walked, a little hunched forward, that they were too. The little magic pills that were supposed to replace sleep made everyone nervous and jittery. They kept us awake, but they did not suppress fatigue. The troops had to fight the long march, the heat, and the ever-present fear of the sudden tack-tack-tack of an assault rifle discharging lethal bullets into their body. The physical weariness made the situation more dangerous. Lapses of concentration were likely to happen. I decided on a change of rhythm. I had each squad send three pointmen ahead while the rest of the soldiers waited, protecting them if they were fired upon. After a hundred-fifty yards, the point men stopped and the rest of the squad caught up with them. The pace became slower, but less monotonous, and the stop-and-go kept the troops more alert.

Hours and miles went by without any incident all morning.

Early afternoon, I stopped the platoon before the top of the last hill before the one I thought was the most likely to harbor the dissidents. Where we were, the platoon was not visible to the east. The men rested, ate some food, and drank water. I scanned the hazy, next hill, about eight hundred yards away, with my binoculars. I could distinguish some of the features of the red rocky promontory and the steep southern face. The mess of rocks, boulders, juniper trees, and brushes provided many hiding opportunities. I looked intensely, but I could not see any movement anywhere around the hill. That did not mean nobody was there.

I called the second squad sergeant.

"Take your squad on the lower trail on the northern side of the range. Keep your men low enough on the slope so you can't be seen from the top of the ridge." I pointed to the distant hill. "If the rebels are there, they'll never see you. You can get on the other side of the next summit without detection."

"How fast do I go, Sir?"

"I'll have one of Sergeant Lupin's men walk on the edge of the slope. He'll be visible to you. Keep pace with him. When he signals you, continue a couple of hundred yards ahead of him, past the summit, and position your men so that they can stop the rebels if they flee to the west. They won't expect you there."

"When do I commence firing?"

"Use your judgment. I'll attack the dissidents and Sergeant Clavery will cover me. When I rush them, they'll be focused on me. You can move up and observe. Open fire to stop the Fells if they try to escape."

"Yes, Sir."

I went back to look at the hill one more time before I moved. I saw no movement on top of the hill. Then, about five hundred yards from where I looked, the glitter of the sun hitting a piece of metal caught my eye. I focused on the area. A head appeared over a rock; it had to be a lookout for the katiba; this had to be the hill.

I went over the plan in my head. This was the best I could come up with. Within the next few minutes, the first volley of lethal bullets would hit one of us. It could be me. Fear burning my stomach, I crawled back to the platoon and calmly said, "I saw a sentry. That means the rebels are waiting for us on the next hill. The second squad will proceed on the down slope."

"We're on our way, Sir."

I turned to Sergeant Clavery. "Sergeant, take the third squad and the B.A.R.s and follow me fifty yards behind the first squad."

"I'll cover you, Sir. If they pin you down, stay down, I'll open fire with everything I have."

I turned to Sergeant Lupin. "Have your men check their weapons and ammo, and put your helmets on. We're on our way."

The War Inside His Mind

With everybody ready to move, the first platoon spread out across the width of the top of the range. Bent over, ready to dive on the ground, the troops' eyes were on the promontory. All my senses on alert, I walked slowly, the two point-men level with me about thirty feet on my right and left. We saw no movement, but I had seen a sentry. I knew they watched us, and waited for the squad to get closer. Every soldier in the front lines anticipated the firing of that first bullet. Which chest would stop it? Would it be mine? My head was ready to explode.

Signs of my rank were on the lapel of my fatigues and on the back of my helmet, not visible to the enemy, but I led up front, an obvious target. I tried not to think about it. I had to be ready to hit the dirt the minute I saw a flash. Light traveled faster than sound, and faster than bullets.

I stopped within a couple of hundred yards of the red rocks and dropped to the ground. The first squad did the same. I listened, looked, and waited for any hint that someone would start to shoot. They had to be there. After a long two minutes, I gave the sign to crawl forward.

The point-man on my right lifted his head. A burst of AK47 bullets hit him. He fell back to the ground. Then from seemingly everywhere, a hellish fire erupted. Assault rifles were pouring bullets directed at the first squad. The rebels saw the squad come toward them, so they knew exactly where everyone was. Although I heard the sharp crack of the bullets narrowly missing me and the whistle of those not so close to my head, I could not determine where the gunfire exactly came from.

The first squad and I were pinned down. I could not give any hand signal. Sergeant Clavery, the old-timer, knew that, and opened fire above our heads. The two BARs and the rifles from the third squad poured deadly bullets onto the rebels who had shown themselves so they could hit us. That forced the dissidents to take cover and to hold up their shooting.

I had to move. The rush of adrenaline propelled me to my feet; I signaled to charge up the rocky area. Sergeant Clavery stopped firing. I fired my weapon, got up, zigzagged, and, like the rest of the squad, threw grenades over the natural rock wall that protected the Fellaghas. It was chaos.

Yells from the rebel area told me that our fire and grenades were doing the job, but the dissidents who were not down returned fire and hit some of my soldiers. I could not see how many. Half crazed, still standing, I threw more grenades and poured fire in the direction of the Fellaghas. Some of my troops were able to do the same. The situation became too confusing for me to try to direct them. Every man had to use his experience of months of fighting.

A bunch of rebels got up and started to run toward the other side of hill. What was left of the first squad and I fired and stopped some of the running Arabs. The others ran into rifle fire from the second squad. A few were able to continue to run toward the east and escaped.

Sergeant Clavery had started already to disarm the rebels who were still alive. He found nine dead insurgents and seven wounded. On our side, the point-man who had been hit in the head, was dead. Another soldier was down, and had probably been killed too. Nine other troops, six from the first squad and three from the second squad were hurt, two severely.

The second squad sergeant said his squad killed three dissidents and wounded five. Two of the rebels who ran to the east were hit too. He estimated no more than three escaped.

The medic attached to my platoon for the mission stabilized the two seriously wounded men.

"Sir, we need urgent medical evacuation if these guys are going to make it."

"I'll call for it," Sergeant Clavery said. He called for quick removal of the gravely wounded men, insisting there was much urgency. "Three men are critical, urgent evacuation is absolutely necessary. There are also five others who need to be treated."

I heard the calm response. "Okay, Sergeant, keep your hat on. We'll be there in ten minutes."

"Roger, see you then."

I went to the man who was not conscious; he had died. Another had been hit in the neck and bled profusely. It pained me to see it was Private Vidal who rode on my jeep that first day in Sidi Bel Abbes. I felt responsible for this devastating wound. The medic worked with him, but there was not much he could do.

"How is he?" I asked.

"I can't tell if anything vital has been hit. All I can do is protect the wound from infection and slow the bleeding. I'll monitor his vital signs. His heart seems to be working okay... so far."

Sergeant Lupin gathered the dead rebels and lined up the wounded ones who were now prisoners. Some were in pain. I did not feel sorry for them. I had eleven casualties among my troops.

I went to talk to my men, who were wounded but not critical. The medics had given morphine to the ones who were hurting.

One of them said, "Sir, I'll get a few cushy days in the hospital before I get back to the platoon. I hope the nurses are nice."

"Thanks for your courage, soldier. I'm glad to see you're in good spirits."

My hands were sweaty. Still in high gear, but I called the Captain and told him what happened.

"Those are good numbers, Lieutenant. It's too bad about your casualties, but it could have been worse, considering the number of rebels you were up against."

I did not say anything for a few seconds. *Damn it, Private Vidal is more than a number. He is a vibrant young man who may die soon. That's what we are, young men, not numbers!*

"What are my orders now, Sir? Do you want me to pursue the ones who escaped?"

"They'll never let you catch them. Your mission is done. You did the job. You can come home. I know where you are. There's a trail down from that hill, which connects to the road. I'll send trucks and a couple of ambulances to pick you up. Can your wounded walk on their own?"

"Yes, Sir, the critical ones will be picked up by helicopters. But some of the wounded dissidents can't."

"I'll send a few stretchers up your way. The convoy should be down from your hill in about three hours."

"Thank you, Sir."

The roar of the three helicopters broke the silence of the afternoon. Sergeant Clavery directed them to land on the top of the hill. Nurses jumped out. They strapped Private Vidal, who was still unconscious, to a stretcher. One of the choppers took him off right away. The nurses were able to stop the bleeding of the seriously wounded ones and took them out in the helicopters.

Two soldiers, who were hit in the leg and hip, were evacuated too. The three others would ride in the trucks with us.

I asked the medics to check the wounded dissidents. "Any of them critical?" I asked them.

"No, Sir, they'll make it."

"That's too bad," one of the corporals said.

"Okay, no evacuation for them. We'll bring the bastards back in the trucks."

The soldiers who were not wounded sat around, their heads down, some smoking. In the aftermath of the battle, they were exhausted; I was too. Once the adrenaline level drops, the energy level drops also. I walked toward them. "I'm sorry about our casualties. We were up against a well-armed and well-trained Katiba, and you wiped it out, an outstanding job. Once again, the platoon distinguished itself."

Indeed it had, but the cost was high. How many more months of combat? How many more battles? How many more killed? How many more wounded? I had no answer, and dreaded the next ambush.

The trucks came. Soldiers from the support platoon came up with stretchers to carry the wounded rebels down. The platoon gathered weapons and ammo and walked to the road. When I got back to the base, Sergeant Clavery and I went to talk with the Captain for a debriefing.

"Sir, I'm mad at myself, I suffered too many casualties for one day. What's infuriating is I knew it was the perfect spot for an ambush. I thought I did the right thing, but I lost all these guys. I guess I still have a lot to learn."

"Lieutenant, ambush is one of the most difficult situations to handle, because, as the word means, it is set up so that the location of the fighters is a surprise. You can't know when or where the enemy will strike until he does. How did you approach the hill?"

I told him how I deployed my squads.

"Sounds like a good plan."

Sergeant Clavery added, "Sir, it was a perfect maneuver. I wanted to come to the debriefing, because I wanted you to know that Lieutenant Alain is now a seasoned infantry commander."

The Captain said, "Thank you Sergeant." He looked back at me. "Lieutenant, you accomplished your mission one more time. You have nothing to feel guilty about."

"Well, I do. I didn't get hit, my men did."

"Lieutenant, I know it's hard to have men hurt, but that's part of the job."

"Yes, Sir."

I needed to be alone; I went back to my room. The more my platoon did, the more I hated the merciless, endless war. I knew I would have to run that patrol again, and others too. I would lose more men, like Private Vidal. After weeks of patrols and the mounting losses, what happened today changed me forever. Almost twenty percent casualties in one battle was a high price to pay. Gone was my squeamishness about shooting human beings; gone was my hesitancy to destroy the enemy. I wanted to kill more of them. I felt guilty. I was angry. I had the urge to fight. I hated these rebels. I swore I would pursue them relentlessly and have no mercy. I was ready to kill.

I never thought I would, but today I had become a ruthless warrior.

Chapter 9

I was no stranger to death. When I was a child, innocent civilians strafed by German planes died on the road before my eyes at the outset of World War II. Later, during the occupation of Paris, I saw people shot at by German soldiers, I witnessed in horror my two Jewish schoolmates taken forcefully from my school by the Germans and French police, never to be seen again, and I stared at busloads of people, enemies of the Reich as they were called, being taken to concentration camps. In my childhood, when I saw a stranger killed, I felt sad, angry, sometimes happy it was not me, but I got used to the fact that it's what happens in war, and nothing much can be done about it.

When my uncle died, it was a different story. I loved him. He raised me and made me the man I am. He encouraged me and guided me into being accepted in the top engineering school in France. I would never forget how after three grueling years of study and long exams, I burst into his office while he was dictating a letter to his secretary.

"It's official, Uncle Raymond, the results are out. I'm ranked seventy-five out of the twenty-five hundred who took the exam. The top two hundred and seventy are accepted. I'm in!"

I turned to Simone, who sat across the desk from my uncle, a pad on her knee. "Hello, Simone, sorry to barge in like that, but I had to tell him."

"It's all right, Alain, I'm happy for you."

My uncle got up from his chair. Tall, trim with short black hair, he came to give me a hug. "That's terrific. You worked long and hard, studied day and night, and it paid off. You should be proud of yourself."

"I made it, thanks to you. You were there for me all that time and you took care of me whenever I could take a break."

He put his hand on my shoulder. "Well, I'm glad I could help."

"You've done that since you got back from the war. You remember the summer of nineteen-forty-five? You and I spent three months in that little village, *La Chartre sur le Loir*, to recover from the war. You are my real father. I don't know what I'd do without you."

But he died of lung cancer the following year. I was devastated. I knew of people who became sick, some passed away, but it was not supposed to happen to him. Although letters from Ms. Rooth helped me with my sorrow, rudderless, I drifted until the dean of study with whom I had a great relationship called me into his office.

"Alain, your school performance is abysmal. A good student like you is getting the lowest possible grades. The death of your uncle has been hard on you, but that does not make it right to give up on your education."

"Sir, I've no idea what my grades are."

"That's part of the problem. I'll be blunt with you. Your uncle encouraged and sustained you through hard years of study, because it was the right thing for you to do. You succeeded. Do you think that he would be proud of your performance today?"

I could not look at him. My eyes were focused on my feet. "I guess not."

"Well, you have to get out of your funk. I understand your pain, but you're gifted, and you have a bright future. It's now time to stop feeling sorry for yourself."

His words shook me up. I looked at him. "You are right. My uncle wouldn't have wanted me to do that to myself."

He locked his eyes into mine. "I'll make a deal with you. I'll talk to the professors with whom you had these atrocious grades. I'll ask them to give you a make-up exam in a couple of weeks, because of your traumatic loss. Study and get your grades up. It will get you out of the rut you're in. Do it for yourself, Alain. You're worth it.

"Thank you, Sir. You woke me up. I'll do it."

The dean gave me the jolt I needed at that time. I grew up a lot that day. I studied and took the exams over and did much better. I realized I had to grow out of my sadness and accept my uncle's death. I went back to see Mr. Boucheron to thank him. "I'm grateful you took the time to shake me up. I needed it." When I found myself in difficult situations, there seemed to always be someone, a teacher, a doctor, a principal or a friend to help me out, and ... somehow, I got tougher and wiser.

Today was different. The death of my soldiers was not that of total strangers; neither was it like the loss of someone I loved dearly as I did my uncle. They were young men I knew and respected, and I had a responsibility in their demise. They followed my orders.

I got to know my platoon well. I not only knew the soldiers' names and where they were from, but also how strong they were physically as well as mentally. I needed to know who to call on if we got into a nasty situation when lives were at stake. Physical strength did not mean much most of the time. The ability to keep cool and to execute orders in a fire fight was at the top of my requirements for these guys.

At the firing range, Sergeant Clavery and I discussed the soldiers' performance in combat. A few of them used their weapon sparingly and were not always aiming at specific enemy targets. I had to know who they were. I could not use them as point men. Even steady, reliable soldiers could be unpredictable. When one of their buddies was hit, even seasoned troops could freeze, or worse, go crazy and rush the enemy without any regard for their own safety. Sometimes, someone snapped at the wrong time. I could not predict when it would happen. That was part of being in constant danger. I had to lead these men regardless.

Higher level officers deplored the losses of soldiers, but dealt with numbers. The rebels lost twenty-seven to our eight casualties; a good count, they would say. But the numbers meant little to me. My losses had names. Yesterday I lost Sergeant Picard, shot dead in his third month with the platoon; Privates Vidal, who rode in the back of my jeep on my first day with the platoon; Romeo with a shattered leg; Delon, Laurent, Raynaud, Joffre, Lemeland, and Harmon with that unforgettable smile. They were not a number with a minus sign. Every violent end of their lives and each devastating wound to their bodies hurt me and made me tougher. I could not afford to get in a funk as Mr. Boucheron said; I did not have the luxury of feeling sorry for myself. I had to suppress my emotions and keep the platoon going. Killing enemies was my job, a tough one, but I had gotten good at it and getting better as time went on.

I steeled myself and did my utmost to accomplish my goal of eliminating more rebels, while hoping Private Boole, Corporal Gaston, Ser-

The War Inside His Mind

geant Lupin, and all the others who still fought alongside me would make it home. At the same time, I struggled with the guilt of losing soldiers while coming out of the same battles unscathed. Some days, I thought I might survive this terrible conflict, but somehow it did not seem to matter to me as much.

The company had trucks going every four days to Sidi Bel Abbes to get supplies of food and ammo. Captain Dufour ordered me to get in the next convoy, and take a three-day leave there. "You can stay at the officers' quarters in town, which has a nice swimming pool, take your meals at the Foreign Legion Officers' mess, which serves good food, and forget about combat. You need a break. I can't afford to have you break down."

'But what about my platoon? Sir?"

"Sergeant Clavery will run it. Believe me. It'll do you a lot of good."

So two days later, I got a nice room in the Sidi Bel Abbes officers building, went to a nearby café and had a cool beer. I had no responsibility except to rest my mind and my body.

For a few days I walked around the town parks, read books on a lounge chair by the side of the pool, and had great meals. Slowly, my body slowed down, my muscles rested, and although I carried a side-arm, I did not have to be within inches of a rifle. The rhythm of my life slowed down. Re-energized, I got on the next convoy and rejoined the platoon.

"Thank you, Sir," I told Captain Dufour, "I never realized how much I needed that; I'm ready for the next year."

"You're welcome. Actually, I knew you had to have that rest, but I mostly thought you were ready to have a mental collapse which would have been catastrophic in a battle. So it was a bit selfish of me to send you on leave."

The military service was open-ended. No one knew when they would be released from the army until they were told one hundred days before the date. One day, some of my soldiers got the good news. They were going home. They chatted happily outside their barracks. I went to talk to them. "How long will you have been in the army, Private Martin?"

"Sir, that'll make it twenty-nine very long months. I'll be so glad to get back to Brittany."

"I'll be sorry to see you go. You saved my life my first week here. But I'm happy for you to go back to a normal life."

"I'm looking forward to that. Thank you, Sir."

I received replacements for the soldiers who had been released, and for the casualties the platoon suffered. I did not know anything about the new men, what kind of soldiers they would be. I wanted them to be fit, competent riflemen, and more importantly a part of the team. That seemed to be the best way to keep the new recruits safe. The older soldiers helped me integrate them into the tough unit we had become.

The first three months were the most dangerous for them. I took them to the firing range and walked them back. The first patrols I took them on were not in the most arduous terrain or the most dangerous areas. Yet no training could prepare anyone for being shot at, and until the first time it happened, I never knew how they would react. They did not know either. Bravado does not work in combat.

The rebel activity seemed to be picking up. There were more attacks on civilians in northern Algeria, both on Arabs and on French people. I ran into more dissidents in my patrols, although a lot of times they fled and refused to fight, probably determined to reach the north of the country where they could do more damage to people than in the mountains.

There were twelve ranches and several farms in my zone, and I knew all the families. I stepped up my visits to keep an eye on them. I loved George, Thérèse and their two sons. Another of my favorites, Tom, also ran a French farm. He stood in front of the house when I went to see him.

"Hi Tom, how are you doing? Everything going well with the business?"

"Yes, Lieutenant Alain. The grapes look good. We'll have good wine this year, and a lot of it. Get your guys to pick some oranges if they want. It's on the house. The figs aren't ripe yet."

"Thanks, Tom. No unwelcome visitors lately?"

"No. As you know, I have weapons and ammo. My three helpers and I keep watch as soon as it gets dark. My wife is a good shot too."

"How is Francine?"

"She went to town to get some provisions. She's doing well. It's nice of you to keep an eye on us, Lieutenant. We feel less isolated."

"You have a radio. Call me if there's anything suspicious."

"I won't hesitate, Lieutenant. We're well armed, but we can use help."

In spite of their weapons, I had no doubt they would need my platoon if attacked. They could not sustain a prolonged battle. They were not professional soldiers.

All the ranchers and farmers welcomed my troops' support.

While patrolling my area, an incident heightened my contempt for the rebels. A reconnaissance helicopter made an emergency landing in the mountains near Sidi Amar. The repair unit needed an escort to retrieve the aircraft. Although it was outside of my zone, the Captain assigned me the job because I could respond immediately. My orders were to meet the salvage team in a small hamlet on the way to the crash site.

When I got to the village, I dispatched the second squad to protect the pilot, while the rest of the platoon waited for the aircraft mechanics. The trucks were parked in the large plaza in the center of the village. It was mid-afternoon and hot. There were a few Arab men around, smoking and talking. Then I noticed that one or two at a time, the Arabs disappeared from the square. Something was up, but what? I immediately doubled the sentries.

I scanned the buildings on the other side of the plaza. I could see a store and a row of stark white houses. The village looked empty. The door of one of the houses on the far side of the plaza opened. Nothing happened. What was that all about? Then a little girl, about five years old, came out of the house and started to walk toward me. She held her hands together in front of her. I walked toward her. She smiled at me. She was as cute as could be and reminded me of Aisha. She got close, looked at me, and said something in Arabic I did not understand. I smiled back at her and said, "Salaam Alaykum."

She lifted her hands to give me what she held, and when she opened her precious little white palms, the grenade she held did not fall on the ground, but the handle released. It would explode within seconds.

"Grenade," I yelled. I grabbed the device and threw it as far as I could in the direction the little girl came from. I took the child in my arms and dove to the ground. I protected her with my body. The explosion came as we hit the dirt far enough away so neither of us got hurt.

I stood up. Frightened, the little girl cried; she did not understand what happened, but I could not console her. I was shaking too hard. I had to put her down.

No one in the platoon was hit. Sergeant Lupin ran to me. "Are you okay, Sir?"

"Yes, Sergeant."

I had been seconds from death. My legs almost buckled under me. I asked the sergeant to take the little one back to the house she came out of. "Take a couple of soldiers with you, just in case."

The sergeant got to the house; a woman grabbed the little girl, pulled her inside, and closed the door. When he came back, he shook his head. "She said nothing, and I didn't see any Arab men anywhere." Whoever gave the little girl the grenade was long gone, for sure. The cowards had vanished. I hoped the little girl would not be punished and suffer because she had not killed me. What a terrible thought.

I could not calm down. I went to sit in my jeep and held my head in my hands, still in shock from delayed fear. I was angry; I could not talk. Sergeants and soldiers knew to let me be.

The aircraft people came into the village; I led the escort to the crash site. It took the salvage crew a while to load and to secure the helicopter on their truck. By that time, I had regained control of myself.

I was sitting in my jeep. Sergeant Clavery came to talk to me, "Are you okay, Lieutenant? You looked shaken up for a while."

"Sergeant, that scared me to death."

"Well, that was close."

"You're right, and it makes me mad. I can't understand how these insurgents can justify sacrificing an innocent little child, just to kill me."

"I can't understand it either, Lieutenant. These people are ruthless; they have no conscience."

When the aircraft was loaded on the special truck and ready to go, I led the platoon back through the village, but I did not stop. I did not see anyone. The villagers probably expected me to come back through the same route and did not want any confrontation. I

　　　　　　　　　　　　　The War Inside His Mind

stopped beyond the hamlet. The helicopter-rescue people thanked me and went on to their base. I took the platoon to our quarters. I was still fuming.

Back on the base, I told the story of the little girl to the Captain who shook his head in disbelief. Then I asked him, "Sir. Who are these people who tried to kill that little girl? There's no cause on earth which justifies this. How can they murder their own children? Is it in their culture? Their religion? Or are they just miserable criminals?"

"Lieutenant, I've never seen anything like that. Not during World War II, not in Indochina. Not even here, until now. It makes me mad too."

I went back to my quarters with only one thought: *These despicable rebels must be exterminated like vermin.*

Chapter 10

Mascara. July 1960

Barely up at five in the morning, expecting another scorching day at the end of July in the Atlas Mountains, an orderly told me Captain Dufour wanted to see me immediately. It could not be good news so I ran to the command post.

"Lieutenant, I just received a message from one of the old men from the Sidi Boussaid village. A French ranch may have been attacked last night. It's George's place, in your sector."

My heart sank. No, not George.

"Yes, Sir. I stopped by the farm less than a week ago. I know the family, nice people."

"Any children?"

"Yes, Sir. Two young boys, Michael and René, five and two; the mother, Thérèse, is expecting number three. What happened? Who could possibly want to harm them?"

"I don't know Lieutenant. Get out there fast and find out what's going on. Give them help if they're in trouble, then report to me."

"I'm on my way, Sir."

I felt like I received a blow to my stomach. This was not the way I thought of combat, like honor, courage, and valor. This was about a peaceful farmer's family, and hopefully not potential mayhem.

I got the platoon ready in a few minutes. "It's George's ranch. The Captain heard they might have been attacked last night. I have no idea what the situation is. It could be a false alarm; they may have been robbed; they may be held hostage, or worse. Whatever it is, the job is to fix the problem."

Many of the troops felt the way I did. They boarded the trucks in a hurry.

Before six in the morning, it was already hot. I got in my jeep, and we sped out of our base. I did not want to announce our arrival if rebels were in the area, so when I got close to the ranch, the platoon jumped from the trucks and started on foot. I took the lead. "On the double. Let's go." We ran until the vineyards and the orange grove came into view. When I could see the farm, I stopped and scanned the area. I saw no sign of activity around the building but the door was not totally closed. Not a good sign.

I called Sergeant Clavery. "Sergeant, secure the perimeter."

I turned to the platoon. "I need two volunteers to go in with me."

Two old-timers, Private Boule and Corporal Gaston, came up to me.

"Reporting, Sir."

"Corporal, you only have two months left before you go home. Are you sure you want to do this? It's a dangerous mission."

"Sir, I like that little guy, Michael, and I like Thérèse too. I'll be mad as hell if the Fells have harmed them."

"Fine. Let's go."

The sergeant deployed the squads on each side of the farm.

I had my heart in my throat like Corporal Gaston. Actually, I had a sense that something terrible had happened. The three of us ran to the wall of the farm and stopped by the door. Nothing stirred. I kicked the door open. Still nothing, no movement. I went in, the two soldiers behind me. The large room was empty. Chairs were thrown all over the room. A bottle of red wine lay on its side, the red liquid all over the tablecloth and on the floor. Half-eaten lamb chops were left on plates, a couple of them on the ground. Couscous grains were scattered all over. Glasses were broken. The remnants of the meal and pools of blood everywhere bore witness to a violent struggle.

On the ground behind the table, the rancher's body had been dumped on the red tiles, knife wounds all over his hands, arms, face and chest. George must have put up a fierce fight. We did not need to check if he was dead.

"What a terrible death. Corporal, cover his head with some cloth. We've got to catch whoever did this."

"Yes, Sir," the corporal replied, holding his weapon tightly, ready to fire.

"Check the kitchen and the rooms on the right," I told the soldiers.

I went to look into the room on the left. I opened the door. I gasped. The reek of death and dried blood was overwhelming. The bodies of the two young boys were on the bed. Their throats had been slit with a sharp blade, probably a razor. Their eyes were wide open, frozen in death, flies all over their faces. I wondered if they had been conscious when they were killed.

I almost threw up. I went further into the room. The mother lay on the floor behind the bed, the blood drained from her mutilated body. I was not dreaming. This was not a nightmare. I kicked the bed. I punched the wall. I had never seen any sight as shocking as what I was staring at.

The two soldiers had finished checking the kitchen. They heard me and came to look into the bedroom. They saw the kids and ran out. I came out of the ranch, overwhelmed by the sight of the little boys and their mother. The soldiers were both crying. Once outside, I gave the signal for everyone to hold their positions. I called for my radio man.

"Get me the Captain."

My Senior Sergeant, a crusty old warrior, came next to me. We had gone through a lot together, and we trusted each other. He did not have to ask. He looked at me, and he knew it was bad.

I could hardly talk. "Get a sentry to guard the door. I don't want anyone to go in. Make sure the perimeter remains secure, although I don't think the bastards will dare come back; only cowards would do what they did."

The Captain came on, "Lieutenant Alain, what did you find out?"

"Sir, they are all dead."

"Damn. So the old man was right, they shot them all."

"No Sir. They were not shot."

"What do you mean?"

"They were slaughtered with knives and razors."

"The ranchers did not defend themselves? They were armed, weren't they?"

"They had weapons and knew how to use them, but they did not get to. The attackers must have taken them by surprise. The family was overconfident." I fought back tears, because I knew I should have insisted they be prepared for the unexpected, but I did not. "They told me they trusted the villagers."

The Captain said nothing for a while. Then, "Damn it. How could we have prevented that? Lieutenant, did the attackers leave anything we can use to track them down?"

"I don't know, Sir. I'll go back inside and look for signs. Sir, I want to go after these rebels, real bad. I want to go to the village. I want to talk to that old man who warned you about the ranch. How in hell did he know about the attack? He could not have heard anything; there was no gunfire."

"Hold on, Lieutenant. I don't want your platoon to go there and manhandle innocent people."

"No, Sir. You know me better. I've been in this fight too long. I know most of those old men, and they know me too. They have a pretty good idea of what's going on. They're not innocent. They're just scared to talk."

We said nothing for a moment. I had to get hold of that old man. He had to know something, and he had to tell me what he knew. Then I had an idea, "Sir, could you stop in the village and bring this old guy who told you about the attack? I'll have him look at the kids and at the mother. Then I'll ask him some questions. I can be pretty persuasive."

"Not a bad idea. I'm coming right now to help and to take care of the bodies. I'll bring Abdullah. Stay put, Lieutenant."

"Yes, Sir, I'll be here."

I had to make Abdullah talk. How? Trying to think of a plan, I looked at the sergeant, "The Captain is bringing some help. In the meantime, I have to look for clues. I'll go back to the farm with the two men who went in with me. I don't want anybody else inside. It's bad enough to know what they did; seeing the carnage adds another dimension. I don't want anyone to go crazy, certainly not the new guys."

The sergeant's face tensed up. "Sir, you should know that when these Algerians cut someone's throat, it is also meant as an insult. If they cut the carotid artery, death is painless. If they cut the front of the throat, bleeding is as endless as the pain."

"How despicable." I saw little blood on the boys' chests. I hoped they did not suffer.

"Sir. We should look for tracks around the farm?"

"Yes, get a few men and look at the terrain and bushes; you may see something useful. Look for traces of blood. They must have been covered with it. They may be in the caves, up in the short hills, a few miles from here. You know the ones I'm talking about?"

"How many guys would you guess did that?" The sergeant asked.

"I don't know, Sergeant, probably less than a handful. It had to be a small group."

The sergeant nodded. "They must have left a trail. I'll find it."

I called Corporal Gaston and Private Boule. Both were livid.

"The three of us have to go back inside and look for clues. I have to know who did this. You take the big room and the kitchen. I'll take the bedroom."

"Yes, Sir," Corporal Gaston said. "I got to know who the murderers are too. I'm going to kill them."

I went back to search the bedroom. I figured that Thérèse tried to get to the closet where the guns were when they caught her. Of course, the guns were gone. I could not help looking at the horrid sight of the ravaged remains of the poor young woman. I grabbed a bed sheet and wrapped it tightly over her. I found a piece of paper. I wrote on it DO NOT REMOVE THE SHEET and put it on the covered body. No one but me had seen how Thérèse had died. I planned to show her to Abdullah, but nobody else should see her. She had suffered enough.

The attackers had not left anything except footprints on the dried blood. It was not dry when they walked on it. I left the room; the two soldiers had finished their search too.

The corporal said tersely, "No clue that could identify who the bastards are or where they came from. What about you, Sir?"

"Nothing. They walked all over the pools of blood. There has to be a trail."

Is this what they called war? I asked myself.

The three of us went back out. "This is plain murder. The cowards who did that probably don't belong to the organized rebellion."

The sergeant came back from his search and told me there were blood stains on bushes on the trail leading to the caves. I ordered my vehicles to come up to the ranch. Once I got information from the old man, I wanted to be ready to go. The murderers had a few hours' lead on me, but they had to walk.

Waiting for Abdullah, I had time to think. I had heard of families being slaughtered several times, although it never happened in my assigned zone. It always revolted me to hear how innocent people were subjected to horrible fears and suffering. I could not comprehend it. I could not believe any ideology in the world could warrant that kind of cruelty. But today I saw the aftermath of such a crime. I witnessed with all my senses the ugly side of war. This was not like hearing about it on the radio or reading a dispatch that one's mind can dismiss as another terrible event. I saw the horrible mutilations, I smelled the coagulated blood, I heard the flies buzzing around the dead boys, I touched the cold bodies, and I tasted the hot humid air which carried the scent of death. This was engraved in my brain and would live inside me forever. The hatred for those who committed this horrible crime would stay in me for the rest of my life.

The Captain's convoy stopped in front of me, and the Captain jumped out. "Lieutenant, you know Abdullah."

I looked at him, peering into his eyes as if I could read his mind. "Abdullah. What do you know about this?"

"Me? I know nothing."

"Abdullah, you have grandkids and one of your daughters is expecting a child. Am I right?"

"Yes. What does that have to do with anything?"

"Come with me." I pointed to the farm.

The two of us walked to the farm. I told the sentry to let us in. I took Abdullah to the bedroom door. "Open it," I told him. He did and saw the boys on the bed. He stopped.

I pushed him inside. "Go on, Abdullah."

He went into the room. "Look at them." He stared at the two small boys. Then I said, "Come around the bed." I lifted the sheet.

He gasped and turned away.

I grabbed his arm to bring him back in front of the body. "Abdullah. You have to look at her."

Abdullah's face turned white. He opened his mouth and shook his head. He turned his head away.

"Look again, Abdullah. Your people did that."

I put the sheet and the sign back, and we left the room. I sat him on a chair, and I towered over him. "Abdullah. These people are innocent victims. She could be your daughter, and the child she expects, the boys could be your grandsons."

He could not speak.

"Do you still want to protect the ones who did that?"

His lips quivering, his face turned white,. "They'd kill me, if I tell you who they are."

I exploded. "Abdullah, if you tell me, I'll find them and they won't ever bother you. If you don't, I might kill you myself. Nobody would blame me. You knew about it. You are responsible for this."

Abdullah hesitated. Then, he said, "It was Mohammed and his three sons."

"Why did they do it? Are they religious fanatics?"

"No. No one in the village is devout. They are artisans, they make tools. Mohammed told me they hated the French family because they used land that belonged to the Arabs. "

"Who told them to do that, Abdullah?"

"Fellaghas rile up people when they pass through. Mohammed swore he only planned to scare them, so they would leave the ranch. That's why I didn't say anything at first." Abdullah was shaking, his eyes avoiding me.

"Are they back in the village?"

"No, Lieutenant. When they didn't come back, I realized something must have gone wrong. That's when I sent the message to the Captain. After what they did, they probably went to hide in the caves for a couple of days."

"Abdullah, next time you hear something like this is about to happen, you have to alert me before anybody gets hurt."

He started crying. "They'll kill me if I do."

I stared at him. "You keep saying that, but you are responsible for this family's death. Do you think I care if they do?"

Abdullah looked at me and shivered. He knew I meant every word I said. He found himself in trouble whichever way he went.

I knew where the caves were, about fifteen miles from here.

Outside, I told the Captain, "Sir, he told me who did it, and I know where they're hiding." I looked the Captain in the eye. "The men who did that are not warriors. They're criminals, sexual deviates, and sadists. I'm going after them. Can you keep an eye on the old man, so he does not talk to anyone?"

"I will take him to our camp and keep him until you are back."

He looked at me with fire in his eyes. He said, "Lieutenant Alain, your orders are to find the assailants, and don't bring back any prisoners."

I saluted him. "Yes, Sir."

That would be an easy order to execute. I was not myself; I wanted revenge. These murderers did not deserve to live. I got the platoon on the road. We drove toward the caves, but not close enough to be detected. There were many hills so we could get close. After a half-hour, we left the trucks and walked.

"Sergeant Clavery, I'll take the first squad. Position the rest of the troops where they can stop these bastards, if they run away from me. Keep out of sight."

I skirted the big boulders which marked the beginning of the trail leading to the caves.

I gathered Sergeant Lupin and his soldiers and said, "My orders are not to take any prisoners."

Clenched jaws, clutching their weapons, they nodded. "Yes, Sir."

I took the lead. We got close to the caves; I positioned the squad to cover the entrances to the three openings.

Corporal Gaston came next to me. "I'm going in with you, Sir."

I knew he would, and I was not about to argue. He followed right behind me. Without making any noise, the corporal and I neared the ledge where the entrances to the three caves were. I did not know which one they were in. The first cave was close, a bit to our right, the other two, further out on the same path. The challenge was not to give ourselves away if they were in the last cave.

I grabbed a grenade in my right hand, a submachine gun firmly held in my left one. Corporal Gaston did the same. "Okay, Corporal. Let's move."

We crawled toward the first cave. If the Arabs were in there, they could not see us. They did not know we were close. I could see the opening of the cave, although not the inside, so I threw a small rock inside. If the men were in another cave, I did not want to announce my presence by having them hear a grenade explosion. The rock landed, I heard no movement.

I turned to the corporal. "Let's look inside. Careful, cover me."

I put my submachine gun into the opening, my body still shielded by the side of the cave.

Nothing.

I ran across the opening.

Nothing.

Corporal Gaston said, "My turn." He repeated my action in front of the second cave.

Still nothing.

"They better be in the last one. If not, we've lost them," I told the corporal. Again I threw a pebble in the third cave. Immediately a shot rang out.

"That's it. We got them." Corporal Gaston exulted.

I threw a grenade into the opening. When it exploded, there were screams. The corporal got closer to the entrance and threw his grenade deeper inside. The two of us ran to the opening, our sub-machine guns firing. Shots were fired at us. A bullet went through my left sleeve, but luckily I did not get hit. We ran to the other side of the cave opening and the corporal threw another grenade.

After the explosion I couldn't hear any more screams. I went in cautiously. Four bodies were on the ground. The corporal kicked them to verify they were not alive. Two of them moaned. He shot them both.

Now, the four murderers would never harm any more women or children.

I called the rest of the squad. They dragged the bodies back to the truck.

I got on the radio. "Captain, this is Lieutenant Alain. Mission accomplished, Sir."

"It had to be done, Lieutenant."

"Sir, could you tell Abdullah what we did? I want the villagers to know that the killers did not get away with it."

We threw the bodies into one of the trucks and drove back to Mascara. On the way back, I could not stop thinking about George's family. I would never be able to erase the images of the maimed bodies, certainly not the one of Thérèse. The ranch was in my sector. It was my job to protect them, and I had not. I felt guilty. They had been careless and trusted men they should not have, but they did not deserve that fate.

We had killed four men who slaughtered a mother, a father, and their children with incredible cruelty because they wanted their land. The murderers could not have tilled it if their lives depended on it. They were not farmers. Why did they do it? The villagers must have known about it. Why didn't they stop them? I guess it did not really matter. None of it made any sense.

I was fuming. I hated the whole village. I hated the rebels, I hated the war.

We pulled up next to the barracks. I told the platoon to stay in the trucks and went to see The Captain in his office. "Sir, I'm going to take the bodies of the Arabs and dump them in the middle of the plaza in the village for all to see."

"That won't be necessary. Abdullah will tell them what you did. It would serve no purpose. You are seething. Your men are too. It's understandable. But, Lieutenant, you have to keep your cool. I know it's hard, but it's part of your job too."

"Yes, Sir."

I went back out and told the platoon to get off the trucks. "You are angry. I am too. This has been hard on all of us. Your afternoon is free. Write to your loved ones. But there will be no passes to go into town tonight. You'd get in trouble. The people in the village did not do the killing. We took care of the ones who did."

I went to my room and stared at the walls. The images of the dead family kept flashing in front of me. I had a hard time getting hold of myself. Full of hatred and guilt I did not know who I was anymore. I would never be the same. I had not been able to prevent the death of innocent people, of children. I could not close my eyes because of the images in my mind, and I could not keep them open because I saw their faces on the wall.

Savagery had replaced war. Would I lose my mind?

What was going on in my world?

Chapter 11

Troubled by the senseless killings, I hardly slept. I could not imagine the pain and the fear the young boys had endured, not knowing why it had to happen. I could not erase from my mind the image of Thérèse.

I knew little about razors, knives, or any blades. These weapons were not commonly used by westerners, but were by the Arab world. Although I never experienced the pain of being hit by a bullet, or flying shrapnel, I saw it happen many times and witnessed the agony of those who were hit. Blades were different. The images of the two boys and Thérèse bothered me because I did not comprehend the terror and the pain of having one's body cut open. I shivered at the mere idea of it. Because of the way they died, George's family's death had hurt me deeply. I remembered when I was issued the regulation army knife on my first day in Mascara; I did not know what to do with it and hoped I would never have to use it. I had not. Seeing the mutilated bodies heightened my sense that I did not want to.

I had great difficulty understanding and coping with the brutality of this war. There were no front lines. My adversaries blended in with the local population. I did not know who the enemy was. It was not that little girl with the grenade, but she almost killed me. Were the Mohammed family enemies, or were they out on a personal vendetta? Atrocities and murders maimed and victimized more people than battles between trained soldiers. Nobody was safe anywhere. It was a horrible, confusing mess.

Ms. Rooth had told me that, once in a fight, one does not worry about the reason for it, only about getting out of it alive. The way George, Thérèse and the children had been murdered haunted me. It may have little to do with the "why" of the war, but it had to do with the "how."

I thought it would be helpful to me to write to her and tell her about the murders. I related the events, without too many details. *I need your wisdom. I am seeing too many atrocities. I don't like what this war is doing to me. I am good at what I am asked to do. Yet, I no longer know why I'm doing it. I'm angry. I'm angry at the war. I'm angry at the dissidents who started it. I'm angry at the French who escalated it. I'm angry at the ones who wage it today. I'm angry at the senseless violence, I am angry at myself. I wish there were a way out of this horrible conflict, but I know there is none to be found.*

I could not let another massacre happen in any of my ranches. I had to come up with a plan. Turning and tossing all night, I came up with some ideas.

Early the next day I went to talk with Captain Dufour.

"Good morning Lieutenant. What's on your mind?"

"Sir, I'll never know what made these killers behave the way they did, but I have to change the way I protect the farmers and their families. There can't be another ranch massacre in my area."

"You are right. I talked with the Colonel, who's quite perturbed about the incident, and how it happened. He wants to make changes to avoid another devastating attack."

"What did he suggest, Sir?"

"He said we cannot detach soldiers to protect every ranch. He asked me if it made sense to plan to help the farmers set up stronger security for themselves and train them to better handle their weapons. I said we could do that."

"That can be done to a certain extent," I said, "But did he have any other suggestion?"

"No he didn't."

"Sir, I thought about the murders all night. I was close to George and to his family. I failed them. I don't want any of the other farmers to suffer the same fate. I don't want to ever have to look at the body of a George, a Michael, or a René, or at another Thérèse. I can help set up or improve security procedures, and I can do some training, as the Colonel suggests. It'll make the ranchers safer, but that's not enough. They're not soldiers. They can't sustain a fight for long."

"What do you think they should do? They can't become soldiers."

"Sir, I have other ideas. Actually, I have a plan."

"Let's hear it, Lieutenant."

"Sir, some farmers have a radio and can communicate with us. Others don't. They all should, so they can call us the minute they smell trouble. All ranches should have a watch at dusk every day, so they won't be surprised, like George was. We should also go to the village every day and talk to the people. Abdullah knew what was going to happen. We should find out what they know."

"That could help, I agree."

"There must be a detailed plan for every ranch and family in case they are attacked."

"That's harder to do, but we should try."

"I will do it, Sir. I know the ranches and their surroundings. So do my soldiers. I'll rehearse the counterattacks so that each troop knows exactly what to do. But that's not enough. When I hear that a particular ranch is a target, in the evening, the next day, or in the next thirty minutes, I want my platoon to be on standby. I want to have helicopters bring us there in minutes. Trucks are too slow. Flying in, we'd get there before the attack is over, and kill the bastards instead of looking at the dead bodies of the ranchers the next day."

The Captain had a nervous laugh. "That's quite a program, Lieutenant, but we have no helicopters."

"Sir, my plan makes sense. You and I could go see the Colonel. He's in charge of the security in his area. He wants to do a good job of it. What happened to George is not helping his reputation. We can propose my ideas to him. He can get us helicopters. What do you say, Sir?"

"Lieutenant, the Colonel is a senior officer. He's busy. It's not our job to tell him what to do. He's not always easy to talk to."

"Sir, the ranches are his responsibility as much as mine. My platoon and I have been on more operations than any other in the company and, I bet, in the regiment. I know more than the Colonel about the terrain and the rebels in this area. I may not know the big picture like he does, but I know what's happening in my sector. I know how the dissidents work and how they think. He does not. Innocent lives are at stake. I can talk to the Colonel, Sir. I won't get intimidated."

"Well, he knows your reputation. He thinks you're great. Let me see if we can try him on your ideas."

Early afternoon, a staff helicopter came in to take us to the Colonel.

"Wow, Captain, you do fast work," I said.

"We'll see if we are still captain and lieutenant at the end of the day," he said.

I teased the Captain, "If the Colonel doesn't like what I say, he can send me back to Paris." Tapping his fingers on his thighs, Captain Dufour looked nervous. I was not. It was his career. It sure was not mine.

We flew to Tiaret, the regiment's headquarters, about eighty miles east of Mascara. When we got there, a jeep drove us to the command post. We were shown into his office. We both saluted. Tall and trim, strong and fit, the Colonel looked me in the eye and gave me a firm handshake.

"Lieutenant, I have heard only good things about you and your platoon. You have quite a few Fellaghas to your credit."

"Thank you, Sir. My guys are good."

"You're their leader, Lieutenant. Now, your captain tells me that you have ideas on how I should run my business."

"Not at all, Sir. You suggested that we train the farmers to better defend themselves. It's the right thing to do. I'll do that for my ranchers. I also think every ranch should have a radio to call us. We would be able to respond more quickly."

"That's a good idea. What else, Lieutenant?"

I took a deep breath. This was my chance to sell him my plan. "Sir, I've been in the area for over a year. I know all the ranches I have to protect. For each of them, I know the terrain, the trails, the hills and the places where the dissidents can hide. I also know how they can sneak in, and how they can escape. My soldiers and I have spent days learning that while meeting the farmers."

"I believe you. What can I do to help you? You are in control of your zone."

"Sir, I'll refine and rehearse a detailed plan for each ranch. The farmers with their new training and their new radio can call me when attacked. My platoon would be on stand-by. As soon as I get the call, we'd be dispatched by helicopters, and get to the ranch in minutes. The farmers would have been trained enough to hold off the assailants for a short time. I'd know exactly where to land and how to deploy my troops and my soldiers would know exactly what they have to do. No rebel would escape. If we foil one attack on one ranch, we might discourage raids on other farms. That would be the best way to protect the families I'm responsible for."

"How would you know when to be on alert, ready to scramble? You can't be ready to jump day and night."

"Sir, they always attack shortly after dark. It gives them time to make their escape undetected when they are done. They won't do anything during the day; the farmers are scattered outside."

"That makes sense."

I added, "Also, by talking to the old men in the village, I could get a warning that something is brewing."

"Why would they talk to you, Lieutenant?"

"Sir, I know some of these men. One of them, Abdullah, is afraid of me. He and I had a tough talk after the massacre at George's ranch. He'll let me know if something is up."

The Colonel turned to the Captain. "What do you think, Dufour?"

"Sir, the Lieutenant has great instincts. He knows the area and his people are tough. I think it's a sound plan. It might work."

The Colonel thought for a moment. He looked at me and said, "Lieutenant, I like your ideas. Let's make it happen." He turned toward Captain Dufour. "Captain, there are some political developments that might motivate the rebels to raid more French properties to further their cause. I'll work on helicopter support. I'll let you know what assets I can commit in that regard. Work on the details of the plan. Keep in touch daily."

He turned to me. "Lieutenant, your reputation preceded you. You did not disappoint me. I am impressed by your command of the situation. Make that plan work. I'm counting on you."

"Thank you, Sir. I won't disappoint you."

The Captain and I saluted the Colonel and went back to the helicopter.

"Lieutenant, you did well. You spoke your mind in a way that the Colonel could hear. Now let's set everything in place. How many radios do we have to give out?"

"Sir, I'm not sure. Probably less than ten."

"I'll get the supply sergeant to get them," he replied.

"Sir, I'll start going to the ranches tomorrow. I'll begin with the ones which are already equipped with radio communications."

I gathered my sergeants and told them what had happened in

Tiaret and explained the new plan. Everyone thought it was great.

One of the new sergeants said, "Sir, I may not be battle-tested like the old timers, but I was at George's ranch. I'm as angry as everyone; I'm all for the plan, Sir."

Corporal Gaston came to see me once he knew about the new approach. "Sir, I'll be going home in two months, but I hope I get to go on one of your raids before I leave." He grinned and continued, "But I'm not going to re-up if I don't."

"Thanks, Corporal. It'd be nice if there were no raid, and we didn't have to ever execute the plan, but it's not likely."

The next morning, I took the platoon to Tom's ranch. I knew he had a radio and several weapons. I told him how the platoon's reaction capability had changed. He was thrilled.

"Tom, do you need additional training for you and for your helpers?"

"I have enough weapons. Everyone knows how to use them, including Francine."

"Tom, if you are attacked, which way do you think they'll come and which way will they try to escape?"

"A few came up the front of the house once and were chased back, but look at the end of the vineyard, Lieutenant, there's a little knoll. On top of it is a trail you can't see from here because there's a natural three-foot dirt wall in front of it. From there they can observe us and sneak in through the vineyard. A path goes up there from the village. Past the mound, it goes down. It gets steep and rocky."

"I know the area, Tom. At the bottom there are a few trees and bushes. Then the trail veers east toward the mountains. That's got to be their escape route."

I got back to my guys. "Let's go to the front of the farm where we'll land and rehearse what we'll do when we are called."

Once there, I went down the field to where the helicopters would drop us. I said, "This is where we start. Squads two and four will jump from the chopper landing here. They'll combine and deploy on the right and the left of the ranch and cover the vineyard. So, there'll be an automatic rifle on each side of the house. That'll keep the dissidents down." I turned to Sergeant Clavery. "You and the third squad will go around the right to the bottom of the ravine and hide. Be ready to cut down anyone trying to escape that way.

It'll be dark. The rebels won't know you're there. They'll walk into the ambush." I continued, "I'll take the first squad, run up the hill, and attack the insurgents from the village side of the path. We'll hopefully get there before they make their move toward the ranch. We'll be in great shape to mow them down."

"Good plan, Sir," Sergeant Clavery said.

I said, "Let's time how fast we can get to our positions." The squads went where the helicopters would let them off. When everyone was ready, I signaled "Go."

Everyone scrambled. The second and fourth squads reached their line of attack in less than two minutes. They would pin the rebels down. Sergeant Clavery reached his position in place in a bit over five. The first squad and I reached the slope going up to the path in three minutes. We would be the most exposed, but we would be able to inflict the most damage. I told everyone, "Remember the terrain around you. Next time, it'll be dark and you'll be under fire. You'll have to move fast."

I went back to Tom. I said to him, "It should take us around ten minutes to fly in, after your call. That's how long you have to hold out. Call me the minute you see rebels going up the trail. It'll take them a while to reach the knoll and get set. Don't shoot first. Let them do it. Don't worry. It'll work. I'll get here in time."

Similar scenarios were crafted for all remaining ranches. Some were short on manpower. I suggested they hire a couple of men to help them with the watch. My radio guy trained the ones who were getting new sets, and the sergeants helped them with their rifle handling.

It took a couple of weeks to get all ranches ready. I documented all the plans so that any officer could run the attacks if something happened to me.

I had Abdullah come to see me at the base. The reason I gave him was to talk about Mohammed, and his three sons. I persuaded him to help me. "Abdullah, you have to alert me when something is planned. If a massacre happens, and I didn't know about it ahead of time, whether you were aware of it or not, I'll personally kill you. So keep your ears open and talk to me."

He did not protest too much, but he said, "I will help you, but I don't want the villagers to know I did."

So I devised a scheme whereby each ranch would be identified by a signal. When I went to the village, all he had to do was raise his right hand, and nod his head one to six times, same with the left hand. Each ranch was identified that way.

I was all set. All I needed were helicopters.

Chapter 12

A couple of days later, the Captain received word from the regiment that three helicopters, H 21 - we called them bananas, because of their shape - would be stationed in our barracks area every day from four in the afternoon to midnight. The Colonel had done his part.

Several days went by; then one late afternoon at about six, Tom called me on the radio. "Lieutenant, two armed Arab men walked toward the ranch house a few minutes ago. They looked menacing. My helpers asked them to stop. They did not. As they got closer, I fired a warning shot. They didn't back off, so I shot one of them. I hit him in the arm and dropped his rifle, but both were able to flee back to the village, cursing me. They may have been testing us. I'm afraid they'll come back with more manpower to take revenge."

"Tom, nothing's going to happen tonight. They can't react that fast. Once they get organized, they'll probably try to retaliate. That'll be tomorrow or the next day. Be extra careful. Don't let Francine and her brother out of the ranch. I'll be ready to jump in if something happens."

Two days later, late morning, I rode to the village and chatted with a couple of the old men. As I walked by Abdullah, he raised his right hand and nodded his head three times. That was the code for Tom's ranch. Something was up for tonight. I went back to camp and told the Captain that Tom's farm would be attacked that evening.

"I'm not surprised, Lieutenant. Now, don't leave until Tom calls you. I'm sure the rebels mean to punish him. They'll want to kill everyone and destroy the ranch to set an example. Expect fifteen to twenty armed men. You want them to be in place when you get there. You don't want any of them to be able to turn back before you close your trap."

"Yes, Sir. I'll send the fourth squad with the two Browning Automatic Rifles crews early this afternoon. They'll hide next to the building and they'll provide covering fire when the helicopters land."

"Smart idea. Good luck, Lieutenant."

I called Tom. "Tom, I'm sure a group of dissidents will attack your ranch tonight."

"Really, Lieutenant? What should I do?"

"I'll send a squad to take position at the bottom of the vineyard this afternoon. They'll be able to protect you in case you need it, if the rebels come before the choppers arrive. Just go about your business and call me when you see the Fells walk up the trail."

"Okay, Lieutenant. I'll call."

When the choppers came in, I showed the pilots on the map where I wanted them to drop every squad. The platoon was ready to go. Dusk was around six-thirty.

Around seven, Tom called. I gave the sign to board the choppers.

Tom was excited. "Lieutenant, there must be more than a dozen of these guys moving up the path. They're cautious. They walk slowly, bent over so I can hardly see them. They know what happened to their buddies the other evening. They are coming for me for sure. They will be at the top of the vineyard in about five minutes."

"Okay, Tom, keep your shirt on. Let them get settled and make the first move. Don't start firing until they do. I'll land in less than ten minutes."

The platoon took off and got to the drop-off spots. Each squad jumped out, all greeted by an intense barrage from the rebels' AK47s and rifles. Our B.A.R.s responded immediately to suppress their fire. There were no casualties when we jumped off, and the helicopters were able to get off the ground and return to base with no damage. The second squad ran to its planned positions on both sides of the farm and added rifle fire to that of the B.A.R.s. That allowed Sergeant Clavery and the third squad to get around to the right undetected. The rebels were still on the knoll, exactly where I wanted them.

With the first squad close behind me, I scrambled up the side of the vineyard. The rebels saw us coming and poured heavy automatic fire on us. Bullets hit the dirt near our feet and blew by our ears. The second squad continued firing on the knoll with their automatic and semiautomatic weapons to force the rebels to hide behind rocks. It helped us charge up the path. One of my soldiers yelled. He had been hit, but he continued to run a few steps before he fell. Another one stumbled. When I got to the top, I threw myself on the ground and cut my left hand badly on a sharp rock. I cursed. It hurt, but I could still hold my carbine and pull the trigger.

We attacked the dissidents. Several of the rebels went down. Their fire became less intense, so I gave the sign to run at them and shot a flare; the second squad ceased fire. The Fellaghas realized they had fallen into a trap. The ones who were still able to run fled toward the ravine. I and several of the troops got to the top of the hill and shot the rebels running down the trail. We did not run in pursuit. We held our fire, and stopped before going down the rocky path to let the dissidents rush unknowingly toward the third squad.

On top of the knoll, in the midst of smoke and the smell of powder, the soldiers checked the Arab bodies that were spread all over the ground and disarmed those who were still alive. Seven dissidents were dead and four wounded. Three of my men were hurt. Joffre, the soldier who had stumbled, had been hit in the chest and had already been wounded a couple of months before. I went to talk to him. Medics had flown with us. One of them knelt at his side, "Don't let go, soldier. Stay with me. Don't close your eyes. Talk to me. You'll make it." I looked at the other one. Dupont, a new recruit, had a mess of flesh and broken bones where his shoulder should have been. The medic had shot him with morphine to keep him from excruciating pain, but he still hurt. Neither could talk or listen to me. It hurt me just to look at them.

Noise from a furious exchange of gunfire came from the bottom of the ravine. Sergeant Clavery was doing his job. When the firing stopped, I went down to meet him.

"Lieutenant, we got the seven guys. Nobody escaped. Four of them are wounded; three are dead. We suffered two casualties: One hit in the lower leg, the other in the shoulder. Both need to go to a hospital."

I went toward the ranch. There were three minor injuries in the second platoon. I needed air evacuation for four soldiers. I got on the radio. The medical support crew would send two choppers. A medic saw my hand. "Let me take care of that, Lieutenant."

"It's just a scratch."

"It's a nasty cut, Sir." He cleaned my hand and put a dressing on it to protect it. There were blood stains all over my fatigues.

Inside the ranch building, Tom, Francine, her brother, and their three helpers greeted me. They were excited.

"It's over, Tom, you can relax."

Tom came to shake my hand. "Lieutenant, thank you. You saved our lives. There must have been fifteen of these guys attacking us."

"Actually, there were eighteen of them. They're all accounted for."

Francine, her face still tense from the fear of the last hour, frowned when she saw my hand and the blood. She said, "Lieutenant, you are hurt."

"I'm fine, Francine. It's just a cut. Thank you."

"Do you think we'll be safe for the rest of the night?" Tom asked.

"Tom, they have been beaten up twice coming here. There can't be many Fells left in the village. If there are, they'll find easier targets."

The medical helicopters took away the wounded soldiers. I radioed the Captain. "Sir, it's over. No one escaped; the Fells lost all their guys, dead and wounded. Tom and the family are shaken, but okay."

"Congratulations, Lieutenant. Any casualties on our side?"

I told him about the wounded, and the several minor injuries. "Sir, we need transportation back to base."

The Captain replied, "The choppers are gone. The trucks will be there in under an hour."

Tom came out with bottles of his Mascara wine for the soldiers. "Thanks, guys. We could have ended up like George's family."

I gathered the team together. Their fatigues full of dirt, the soldiers stood outside the ranch, still alert. They had not yet relaxed from the intensity of the fight. Some had lost their best buddies, at least for a few weeks; their clenched jaw showed their anger. "Men, you fought well, your execution was perfect. We annihilated a well-armed outfit. They deserved what they got. They were out to murder a French family. I thank you for a job well done."

Corporal Gaston, who fortunately had not been hit, a month from going home, came to me, "Sir. I'm glad to have been part of this. It'll not bring back George's family, but it almost makes up for the tragedy."

The trucks came. The troops loaded the prisoners and the dead bodies and piled in, and the platoon drove home.

When we got there, the special unit took care of the Arabs. The Captain was waiting for me. "Lieutenant, we have kept hot food for your soldiers, but I would like to talk to them first.

"Men, your accomplishment tonight speaks for itself. The Fellaghas failed to hurt the ranchers. Your leader was the architect of this. You fought bravely. I am proud of all of you and I thank you."

The Captain added, "The Fellaghas will think twice about attacking any farm in your area. They won't want to fall into a trap like they did today. That's good news for the other ranchers. They'll go attack farms in some other sector."

A soldier came to get the Captain. "Sir, The Colonel is on the radio."

The Captain went to take the call. He came back and said, "Lieutenant, the Colonel is pleased. You made him look good. He made the right decision to go with your plan."

He looked at my hand. "Your hand okay?"

"Yes, Sir. I can still hold my rifle."

The next day, the Colonel flew in. The company assembled and stood at attention outside the barracks.

He said, "I want to commend the second platoon for their success last night. A ranch and a French family were saved. You wiped out half a katiba with minimal casualties on our side. I am awarding this regimental award for gallantry to the second platoon. Lieutenant Alain, please come and receive the award."

After the ceremony Captain Dufour, the Colonel and I went to the Captain's office and talked. I said to the Colonel, "Thank you, Sir. My troops appreciate the recognition."

"Lieutenant, I appreciate what they did."

"I also thank you for the helicopters. That's what made the difference."

"It made sense to me to have them on stand-by for your troops."

I sent a message to the four wounded soldiers in the hospital to tell them about the award. They sure had earned it. They would get the ribbons later.

The next day, I was scheduled to be the duty officer in Mascara. The Captain called me.

"Lieutenant, you're off duty tonight."

"Well that's good news; I'm never looking forward to visiting the brothel. I'm not going to miss it for sure. What happened?"

"Lieutenant, I had to pull you off. I received intelligence that the rebels have put a price on your head. You killed Mohammed and his three sons, and with the ranch operation you just led, you caused serious damage to the local Fellaghas. They lost twenty-two men to be exact."

"How did they know it was me?"

"Lieutenant, do you think you're the only one Abdullah talks to?"

"I get it."

"Be careful, poor Arabs can get some money by taking you out. The word is the dissidents also believe someone tipped you off. They're searching for who it is."

"I'm not afraid of these guys. I can go with an escort."

"No, it'd be too easy for them to get you at night in the dark streets. Stay on the base. It's an order."

"Yes, Sir."

"Also, be aware of it when you go in any village, even during the day."

"Yes, Sir."

Later in the week, the Colonel sent for the Captain and me. When we got to his office, the Colonel talked to me. "Lieutenant Alain, the regiment will soon redeploy to the south. Your company will go near Aflou, a hundred miles south of Tiaret. The new zone of operations is the tough mountains of the northern Sahara, the Amour Range. The move will take place in about two months. In preparation for that, Captain Dufour has requested that your platoon get additional training and better weapons. I agreed to it. The people in the commando school scheduled a six-week program starting next Monday. Your unit will be an even greater asset to the regiment."

"Thank you, Sir. I welcome the additional training, and frankly, my platoon can use a break from combat."

The next day I received a letter from Ms. Rooth, a response to my request for help after the massacre at George's and Thérèse's ranch. *Alain, I can feel your distress. You are unfortunately involved in a war which has the elements of a civil war, a guerilla war, and a political war. Each of these has its own players, its own agenda, its own passions, and its own savagery. The result is uncoordinated chaos and devastation. The destruction extends to lives, to property and, as you found out, to the human mind.*

I am proud when I hear of your accomplishments as an infantry leader. I had told you that this war would change you. I had no idea of the extent to which it would. Indeed, I cringe when I think of what you are going through. I long for your return.

I welcomed the letter. It touched me. It was like peeking through a little window into my former life. Somebody still loved me, Alain, the person. I had changed, but Ms. Rooth's love for me was unshakable. To her, I would always be Alain.

Later that day, the Captain said, "News came that General De Gaulle is preparing to open negotiations with the insurgents."

That came as a shock. Outraged, I said, "That comes from the same man who two years ago promised that Algeria would remain French."

"That's right, Lieutenant."

I remembered nineteen-fifty-eight. The French government did not seem to be able to deal with the North African rebellion. The rumor was that, after almost ten years, General De Gaulle was going to attempt to seize power again. Lots of people did not want him. Yet, mid-year, he managed to be appointed into the government and maneuvered to take power and run the country. He gave a resounding speech, saying that France went from Dunkirk in the North to Tamanrassett, at the southern border of the Sahara desert. He promised Algeria would remain French. "Algerie Française, Algerie Française," he shouted.

"De Gaulle increased France's military commitment and sent me here for who knows how long. Then, waging war was the right thing to do."

"Well, Lieutenant, he may be prepared to change his mind."

"Sir, it's betrayal. I don't profess to know what the right solution for Algeria and its people is. But, since his first talk promising the continuation of the French state, thousands of soldiers and civilians have been killed or wounded on both sides. He has blood on his hands."

"I don't think the general is concerned about public opinion."

I thought of George, Thérèse, and their children, and it made me furious. They died a dreadful death because De Gaulle had decided to play soldier to regain power for himself. Like George, Tom and all the other farmers and their families brought prosperity to this beautiful land. What would become of them?

I welcomed the respite from combat, and now from politics. The platoon was going off the line. The next few weeks would be a welcome change in the daily routine. Advanced training and better weapons would make it safer for my men. I had been told about the Atlas Mountains in the northern Sahara. They were rugged. Fellaghas were using them as a route to the east. It would be a tough assignment, but we'd be better trained and better equipped. The training took place in Arzew, a beautiful spot, right on the Mediterranean, east of Oran. It lasted six weeks. The training was intense and physically demanding, but a nice break from the stress of patrols and combat, and no one would be shot at. The new weapons the platoon trained with were Thompson submachine guns. The army wanted to test them in the desert. We practiced with them and learned how to dismantle them and to put them back together in record time. They were heavier than the MAT49 French submachine guns, but they were more reliable and had a longer range. They also had larger magazines.

All of us also became proficient in handling the new knives we had been issued, a new experience for me. They looked like the ones the platoon was issued in Mascara, but these new blades were razor-sharp and perfectly balanced. I learned how to throw mine accurately at a target fifteen feet away. The instructors also taught me how to fight with it. After hours of repetitive and exhausting mock fights, I mastered the skill of disarming a man attacking me with a knife, using only my bare hands. The thought of knife wounds was still revolting to me, but it was comforting to know how to deal with a knife-wielding attacker. The Special Forces instructor said, "This is not for the fainthearted, for sure. But if you are ever jumped by a man trying to stab you, you'll be glad you had this training."

I told him, "I hope I'll never have to get into one of those man-to-man struggles. What a nightmare."

"Lieutenant, if you ever have to, it won't be your choice. I know the training is rough, but it might save your life one day. As you know, the Arabs like to use any kind of blade at close range."

I shivered. "I know."

We were assigned no guard duty because we were in training, and we had a little free time to swim and relax. When the six weeks were over, although we did not go through the full three months of *Commando de chasse* training, we were awarded the black berets. The platoon was a seasoned unit and passed all the tests with flying colors. It made me proud of my men. It distinguished the combat second platoon from regular infantry. I hoped the rebels would know not to tangle with my troops, but it was unlikely.

I did not enjoy participating in a war, but I felt proud to wear the beret and to lead a well-trained unit. The military fostered that kind of pride. I felt strong, almost invincible. That was the dangerous part. We may have been deemed elite troops, but we were still flesh and blood when bullets came our way.

Vehicles came to take the platoon to its new quarters in Aflou. There, the company was housed in tents. On the way, I had to stay overnight in Tiaret, the regimental headquarters. The trip to Aflou could not be done in one day. The road was not safe to use at night. I had dinner at the officers' mess. The Colonel saw me and invited me to his table.

"Lieutenant Alain, I see you now wear the black beret. Congratulations."

"Thanks for the opportunity, Sir. My men are better soldiers."

"You were pretty effective before that. The regiment is happy you're returning to the line. I'm sure your captain will be relieved to have you back."

"Sir, my platoon has new skills and a great sense of pride and capability."

"You'll be more effective, that's what I'm looking for."

"Sir, has anything changed since the negotiations speech?"

"Lieutenant, don't get me started on this. The answer is, not really. The generals in Algiers are angry, and the army feels betrayed. There's talk of a referendum early next year to ask the French people if we should negotiate for Algerian independence and for the end of the war."

"Colonel, all the sacrifices made by so many were in vain. What a waste. If he was going to give the country away, why not bring the French people back to France two years ago?"

"At the time, he needed the army to grab power in France. Today he thinks he does not need us."

"Why not stop the killing today?"

"Unfortunately, the killing is far from over. The rebels are going to be encouraged."

When dinner was over, The Colonel said, "I'm counting on you for continued good work."

"I'll do my best, Sir."

"That's good enough for me, Lieutenant."

The next day, we got back on the road through the Atlas Mountains. It was magnificent and picturesque, but also dangerous. I trusted we'd not have a problem. As we were driving, I reflected on my life as an officer.

It was late October. I had been in Algeria for over a year. It felt like a lifetime. I liked the country, the heat of the days and the cold of the night, the arid mountains and the endless vistas. I was strong and fit. The army had made me an elite officer, a title I would never imagine would apply to me. I was an expert at waging war and was focused on my job, day and night. I was protective of my soldiers, I had confidence in them, and they trusted me.

A new page, and not an easy one, was about to be turned in my military life. The Colonel talked about the tough mountains of the northern Sahara, and my captain had requested that my platoon be better armed and better trained. What lay ahead? Would I survive?

Chapter 13

Aflou, Fall 1960

My new military chapter began in the northern Sahara, east of the village of Aflou, in the foothills of the Amour range of the Atlas Mountains. The company's camp was set up on a little sandy and rocky hill that was easy to defend.

The Captain's new command post was in a large tent.

"Lieutenant Alain reporting, Sir."

"Welcome back. How was the training?"

"Rough, but effective, Sir. We worked with grenades, knives, and our new Thompsons, which are great weapons; the platoon's ready for anything."

"I'm glad to hear that, Lieutenant. This is a tough area. Your new combat skills will be put to good use."

"Thank you, Sir. I won't let you down. The men are sharp. Also, thank you for getting me out of the bounty zone in Mascara. Do you know if the rebels found out Abdullah was the one who tipped me?"

"I don't believe so. Now, Lieutenant, to conclude the Mascara era, I have good news. Private Vidal sent word he will fully recover from his neck injury and will soon return to civilian life."

What good news. I usually never heard from the wounded soldiers who did not come back to the platoon.

"Thank you for telling me, Sir. That makes me really happy."

From our camp, one could see forever. The immense sky stretched to the fuzzy sandy horizon. I rated a large individual tent on a flat graveled area. Inside were a table, a chair and a large box with a lid, so the sand and insects would not get into my clothes.

The cot had its legs in cans full of water. I ask Sergeant Clavery, who showed me my quarters, "Why the tin cans?"

"Sir, there are venomous black scorpions on the ground. Without the cans, they can climb onto your bed, and they have a nasty sting. The way it is, if they try to get up, they'll fall into the water and drown. If you use a blanket at night, make sure it does not hang down to the ground."

"I guess I should put my boots on the bed too."

"No, just shake them down before you put them on."

I groaned. "Any other threats out there, Sergeant?"

"Yes, Sir. There are sand snakes; they're called horned vipers. They're not much more than a foot long. They hide in the rocks during the day and come out at night looking for food. Don't walk barefoot. They're sidewinders and not aggressive, but if stepped on, they'll strike. Their bite is not lethal, but it's painful."

I shivered. *Vipers! I hate snakes*, but I had no choice. "I can deal with that," I said.

Later that evening, looking at the starlit sky and the barren landscape, I stared at the desert; I already liked the barren nothingness of a nature I had never seen before.

Now in the desert, in charge of an elite infantry platoon, I stood ready to face a determined enemy on difficult terrain. Things were not going to get any easier for the second platoon in the next few months; we would lose more men, but would annihilate more of the rebels.

I was responsible to patrol the mountains north of the camp. The Amour Range peaked at about five-thousand feet, and it had steep slopes. I had to learn the unfamiliar territory, but I enjoyed the arid slopes and the rugged landscape of complex rock formations. It was dry wilderness, hard ground with a few shriveled trees and bushes. I also loved the vastness of the northern Sahara, its emptiness and magnificent red and ochre colors. I did not mind the heat during the day or the cold once the sun went down. The starry night sky nurtured my soul.

The Captain briefed me on the second platoon's mission.

"The dissidents use the mountain trails to travel from Morocco to the northern Algerian plains where the population is dense. There are no farms or any kind of structure or any family to protect on the mountains. Your job is to hunt the rebels. You can use trucks to bring the platoon to trail heads at various points of the range; from there, like the Fellaghas, you have to walk the hard trails, day or night, looking for them or for tell-tales they had been there. When you find them, destroy them."

"Do you know if they stop and stay anywhere for a few days?"

"They might, in concealed high areas, but only for a day or so. They're in a hurry to get to the cities where they can do damage to French people and their Algerian sympathizers."

We started to run daily routine patrols. The rebels tried to avoid confrontations, so most days and nights we did not see anyone, sometimes only evidence they had been there. But when I caught up with them, they defended themselves fiercely. With our superior Thompsons and the special training we had, the platoon always got the upper hand. The rebels suffered heavy casualties, but sometimes at a high cost to my men.

I still hated it when any of my guys were hurt. Some of the wounded were treated in faraway hospitals and did not come back. Some returned after a few days; others with less severe injuries stayed with us. Our medics kept their bandages clean to stave off infection. Sulfa drugs and morphine were their main tools.

After a few weeks, my soldiers and I became tense and weary, but we had to keep alert and sharp on patrol, day after day. The safety of every man depended on strict discipline. I demanded that soldiers keep their distance from one another and held their weapons at the ready, so they could react instantly if fired upon. It was my job to enforce it, a lonely one.

The end of the year was approaching. The Captain got the lieutenants together for a briefing. "Last Christmas, the insurgents attacked French ranches and army posts, hoping to catch the settlers and the soldiers with their guard down. This year, the brass told me to expect more trouble."

"Sir, there are no ranches around us, do you think they'd try to jump us?" I asked the Captain.

"Well, here is what I know," he replied. "There are intelligence reports that the rebels are planning a massive break through the electrified fence which separates Algeria from Morocco. They want to bring more well-trained fighters into this country. Our military operations have depleted their ranks. With the talks about independence about to start, they want as many men in Algeria as they can get."

That seemed puzzling to me. "But, Sir, the border is far from here, isn't it?"

"Yes, but, as you know, the Fellaghas can walk long distances. The information is that the break is imminent. They could be here in a week to ten days. That would be around Christmas."

"Sir. There are troops between here and Morocco; won't the dissidents be intercepted before they get here?" I asked, shaking my head.

"Some will, but these rebels are swift, and as you know, they're experts at camouflage. At night they're hard to see."

"Which route will they take, Sir?" The first platoon lieutenant asked.

"Nobody knows. The best guess is that most will go through the Atlas Mountains. It's their favorite way because it's easy to hide there. If they do, they'd go through Lieutenant Alain's area, north of us. He'll have to stop them in one of the narrow passes."

I reacted in a second. "I sure will, Sir."

The Captain went on, "They could also hug the Sahara and come around south of our camp, in the third platoon zone."

"Sir, how and where can I stop them?" The third platoon leader asked. "There's a lot of space around us."

"If they come through the desert, we'll have to see what kind of intelligence we can get. People in the village of Aflou are likely to know something. Someone might be willing to talk."

In mid-December, the dissidents made a fifty-yard break in the deserted south end of the fence. Ten to fifteen katibas, about three to five hundred men, were assumed to have gotten into the country. Nobody knew the number for sure. In the next few days, a small number of dissidents were stopped in the desert south of Aïn Sefra in the northwestern desert, but most katibas went undetected. They were thought to have taken the mountain route, and would be coming through the Amour range that I started to know well.

The Captain called me to his tent. "Lieutenant Alain, it's your job to stop them. You'll have to set up an ambush and wait for them as soon as we get word of their whereabouts. The first platoon will stand by in reserve."

"Yes, Sir. If there are more than one katiba, it might be more than I can handle. I may need help."

"Lieutenant, they'll space themselves. Their objective is to reach the cities in the north. They don't want too many of their men entangled in a single gun battle," the Captain said. "I'm sure you won't have to fight more than one katiba at a time, thirty to thirty-five guys at most."

A few days later the Captain had news. "Lieutenant, we got word the Fellaghas were sighted a couple of days from here. They're getting close. You're to set up an ambush in the western pass tonight. The information came from an old man in Aflou. You and your men will have to walk from here in the dark to reach your ambush spot. I don't want any of the local people to know your platoon has gone to the mountains; they could warn the rebels."

"Sir, I'd like to go to the pass this morning to look over the terrain in daylight, so I can make my plans. I can also hide ammo and food. We might be there a few nights."

"Good idea, Lieutenant, but make sure you return during daylight. You need to be seen coming back to camp."

I decided to take the second squad with me. Its sergeant just joined my platoon and had not experienced much combat. I wanted to settle him down. I suspected he was scared, and it would help him to know the terrain. We drove to the bottom of the trail and walked up to the top of the pass. I decided where I would place the squads.

The terrain rose higher on both sides of the pass. There were rocks and a few shriveled bushes. "Sergeant, your squad will occupy this area," I pointed to the right. "You'll be well protected and have a clear view of the slope. I'll position one of the two Brown Automatic Rifles with Sergeant Clavery with your squad. Think about where you'll place your guys."

"Yes, Sir. Thank you, Sir."

The experience of Sergeant Clavery would be a stabilizing influence for the new squad leader in his first combat. I decided to put the third squad on the left side, with the other BAR so the slope would be covered by crossfire, Sergeant Lupin's first squad in the middle, on the flat part of the pass. We hid ammo, water and food

The War Inside His Mind

supplies behind rocks. They were in metal containers so no animal could get to them. We returned to camp.

As soon as I was back, I said to Sergeant Clavery, "We'll leave at ten tonight. We have to walk to the top of the pass tonight. There'll be no talking until we get to the top. Inspect all weapons and have the men load their packs with food, ammo and warm clothing. We might be there three or four nights."

"Yes, Sir. I'll also make sure they all carry full clips."

It was cold and dark. We went up the same trail we did in the afternoon, but it proved to be more treacherous in the dark. It took over eight hours from the camp to our positions. When we got to the pass, I showed the sergeants where they were to set up their troops.

We had about twelve hours to wait till sunset. Sergeant Clavery placed look-outs, but I did not expect anyone to come through during the day. Men and sergeants would take turns sleeping, while the others kept watch.

I did not know where the dissidents were, but I made sure we could not be seen. "Don't let any soldier show himself to the west," I told the sergeants.

I tried to get some sleep, but I could not. My whole self was on high alert. So I went to look at the west slope from behind a thick little bush. With my binoculars I scanned every rock, bush, and shriveled tree. I memorized where they were because in the half-moon light they would be hard to see. I was nervous and anxious to get started. When the Fellaghas showed up, they would not run back; they would fight and there would be casualties. Damn! How I hated this war.

Late afternoon, everybody got food and water and took the assigned positions behind rocks, the open sandy slope in front of them. I inspected everyone's post and told the soldiers. "Men, I'll be at the top of the pass. As soon as I detect the dissidents, I'll raise my hand. The soldiers close to me will pass on the signal to the rest of the platoon. When the dissidents get closer, I'll send a flare up to illuminate the terrain. That'll be the signal to open fire. Keep your eyes open. And good luck."

I sensed everyone's apprehension. Even with the dim moon-light, one could hardly see beyond a few yards, and it was scary.

If they detected us, the Arabs, who were experts at handling their knives, would try to sneak around and jump us. We had to see them first. Once we spotted them, we would react fast.

For hours, we waited and listened intently for any sound that would betray the rebels' approach. Staring into the dark, I had trouble keeping my eyes open. Everyone kept quiet, afraid that their own breathing would give them away. That made the night even more spooky. I battled the cold which grew more intense as the night went on. I could not stamp my feet, so I tried to wiggle my toes. I wore mittens so I could pull the trigger on my Thompson, but my fingers got really cold. Blowing on them did not help much. After a while, I wished the rebels would show up tonight; I wanted to get the battle over with. The wait was excruciating. The night went on. I did not fall asleep. Nothing happened.

The next day, we stayed hidden as the day before. I posted a few sentries. If the dissidents were to come during the day, the lookouts would spot them early and the platoon would have time to take their ambush positions. The rebels had to be getting closer by now. I peered into the west slope again, hoping to detect some movement, but nothing stirred as far as I could see. I began to hate these guys. Where were they? They were going to try to kill us, and they made us wait?

The War Inside His Mind

Chapter 14

The day dragged on. It became stifling again. There was no shelter from the blazing sun. The men tried to catch some sleep. When they moved around, their heads were down. I was tired too. The evening finally came and promised a night just as cold as the previous one. The soldiers took their positions. The agonizing wait resumed, and it became harder to stay awake than the night before. I kept hoping the damn rebels would show up, but the night went on, and it just got colder by the hour.

My fingers were numb. I had to keep moving them and rubbing them against my fatigues so I would be able to pull the trigger when the time came. I scanned the dark slope for insurgents, but the cold made my eyes water. I had to be able to see, so I kept wiping them with my icy hands.

Around five-thirty in the morning, I heard a metallic noise, that of a weapon hitting a rock. I peered into the night and barely made out shadows moving up the slope. I raised my hand; the soldiers passed on the signal. All my senses were at a peak. The flare gun in my hand, I held my breath and waited. Then, not far down the slope, I heard one of the insurgents kick a rock and curse. I shot the flare.

Thirty or forty Fellaghas were spread over the slope, some bunched up, a few as close as a hundred yards from our line. They had come closer than I expected. The light caught them by surprise and blinded them for a few seconds. The crossfire of the two automatic rifles sprayed the whole width of the slope. Troops fired their Thompsons and threw grenades. Many rebels were hit in the first few seconds of the fight, but quite a few had time to hide behind rocks and bushes, and to return fire. Out of the corner of my eye, I saw one of the guys from the first platoon get hit and fall. He did not scream, not a good sign. One of his buddies crawled to him.

The exchange of fire went on, seemingly for a long time. The rebels were hard to see. They went from rock to rock, firing a few rounds at a time before moving again. The smell of powder, the noise of the explosions, the screams of pain, and the shouts of anger from men from both sides magnified the madness of the moment. The dissidents kept fighting, and so did we.

For what seemed to be an eternity, the rebels were quiet, then resumed firing from different hiding places. A faint movement made me look to my right where Private Boulot had fired rounds after rounds, protected by a boulder. On the other side of it, I saw one of the dissidents, a knife in his teeth, crawl toward him. I shouted at the private, but in the thick of automatic fire and explosions, he did not hear me. I stood up, aimed at the rebel, and fired a couple of shots. I hit him before he could lunge at my soldier. The private realized what had happened. He looked at me and put his thumb up.

At that instant, a bullet bounced off my head. The strap of my helmet broke. It rolled to the ground. Thrown backward, I fell, and I dropped my weapon. One of my men rushed to me. "Are you hit, Lieutenant?"

I shook my head, dizzy. I touched my skull. No blood. "I'm okay, thanks."

He replied, "I thought you bought it, Sir."

"No, I'm fine." I retrieved my Thompson, put my helmet back on, and went back behind my rock, but my eyes would not focus, and my hands were shaking. I could not aim. My fingers were stiff, and I could hardly pull the trigger. I closed my eyes. After a few seconds, I recovered and tried to figure out what was going on.

All of a sudden, a grenade exploded right in front of the rock I hid behind. The explosion was very close, the noise of the blast deafening. For a short time, I could not hear anything. A piece of shrapnel nicked my arm, but neither I nor any of the soldiers near me got hit. The rock saved us.

It was a bad miss for the rebels, but I wondered if I had been targeted. My lieutenant bars were invisible, but someone out there had tried to hit me twice in a short time. I must have been spotted when I shot the flare. I had not moved after doing it, always a bad idea in combat. Next time, I had to remember to move right after I shot a flare. I had been lucky, and I learned something which might save me another day.

The War Inside His Mind

Within a couple of minutes I recovered enough of my senses to see what was happening on the slope. A few Fellaghas got up and started to run back down. The troops mowed them down. After a short while, we received no more incoming fire. I sent a flare up to give the signal to cease fire and moved to my left, just in case. I saw a couple more rebels fleeing down the slope. The faint light of dawn showed bodies strewn all over the hill.

I called the third squad leader, "Sergeant, go after the guys who are trying to escape. Stop them if you can."

I turned to Sergeant Lupin. "Sergeant, take your squad and go check the dissidents. Disarm the ones who're still alive. Watch out, some may still have fight in them. Bring the prisoners to the top of the pass. Then give me a count."

I called the second squad sergeant and complimented him on his first firefight. "You did well, Sergeant. You did your share of the fighting. Thank you."

"Thank you, Sir." He appreciated the good words, but his trembling hands and his ashen face covered with sweat were signs he was shaken.

I asked Sergeant Clavery to report on our casualties and went toward the soldier I saw being hit. Private Leblanc had a big bloody hole where his left eye had been. His buddy, Private Gautier, cried as he held the body in his arms.

"I'm sorry, soldier," I said, "He was hit in the first seconds. He had no chance to escape the bullet."

I turned to Sergeant Clavery who came back with the casualty list. In addition to the dead soldier, seven men were seriously wounded: one in the face, three in the chest. The three others had shattered arms or shoulders. The medics shot them with morphine and tried to stabilize them. All needed to go to the hospital. I got on the radio and asked for urgent medical evacuation. The field hospital was in Aflou, a few minutes away by helicopter.

Sergeant Lupin reported on the rebels' casualties. "Eighteen Fells are dead, Sir, and thirteen wounded, some severely."

I went to look at the prisoners. Indeed, a couple of them looked badly hurt. I ordered the medics to tend to them. Private Gautier went to look at the prisoners too. He kicked one of them who moaned on the ground, in visible pain. I saw the soldier lower his gun. I ran and yelled, "Private Gautier, secure your gun immediately. It's an order. These men are prisoners."

"Sir, they killed my buddy. I'm going to shoot this one in the stomach, where it hurts."

"Private, if you lower your gun, I'll shoot you in the foot. You'll be crippled for life." I stared at him.

He stared back. "Sir, are you protecting these bastards?"

"Private, they're not the murderers we killed after they butchered innocent civilians. They're soldiers. They fought. They lost. They're hurt. They're our prisoners. We don't kill defenseless people."

All the soldiers watched the confrontation. Private Gautier hesitated but did not move his rifle. Private Bernard, a soldier from the same squad, went behind him and put his powerful arms around Gautier's upper body. "Take it easy, Buddy," he said to him. He held him, and one of the sergeants grabbed his weapon. The private returned to his squad, mumbling.

Sergeant Clavery said to me, "The problem with being in a war is that the rifle is the swiftest way to solve problems. That's what we all learn through combat."

The sun had come up. Helicopters came and landed on top of the pass. Army nurses jumped out and tended to the injured men. At that time, AK47 fire aimed at the choppers came from down the slope. I sent the third squad to take care of it. The six nurses, in their fatigues and white helmets with a red cross in front, did not even blink. They went about their work. They worked fast, cutting pieces of uniform to bare the injured areas, securing the wounds, stopping the bleeding and injecting more morphine to dull the pain.

Lieutenant Danielle was the head nurse.

"Thank you for coming so promptly, Lieutenant," I said to her.

"Lieutenant, I know these men are in pain. We'll take care of them, don't worry." She looked at my arm. I had blood on my torn sleeve.

"Were you hit, Lieutenant?"

"Just a scratch. I'm okay."

"Let me see." She cut my sleeve, cleaned the blood off, and put a dressing on it.

"Here you go." Then she added, "You look a bit shaken. Are you all right?"

The War Inside His Mind

"I'm fine, Lieutenant," I showed her the dent in my helmet, "I almost got hit in the head."

She said, "You were lucky. Are you dizzy?"

"No, Ma'am, I was for a while when I got hit, but I'm okay now."

"You should take it easy for a couple of days."

I chuckled. "Sure. Do you want to write a note for my captain?" She laughed too.

I smiled and added, "Lieutenant, I'm not sure what the rules are, but there are two badly-hurt dissidents. Can you take care of them too?"

"Yes, I will. It's good of you to ask me to do that. They almost killed you."

"If I don't send them with you, they'll die for sure. They're helpless. It'd be like murdering them."

She looked at me intensely for a second or two. "I respect you for that, Lieutenant," she replied.

The nurses stabilized all the wounded, wrapped them in blankets, loaded the stretchers on the helicopters, and took off for the field hospital.

The third squad came back with another prisoner.

"Sir, we killed the one who fired on the chopper. Two Arabs escaped down the slope."

I called the Captain. "Sir, it's over." I gave him the tally on the thirty-five rebels. "They did not expect us to be there. They were sloppy and bunched together. The ambush turned out to be a total surprise." I told him about our eight casualties and the minor scratches.

"Sorry about your losses, Lieutenant, but you wiped out a katiba. That's the kind of result the Colonel hoped for."

"Thank you, Sir. Do I come down now? Or should I keep guarding the pass?"

"The pass has to be watched. There are other rebels out somewhere near. I'm sending the first platoon to relieve you."

"Thank you, Sir."

"By the way, Lieutenant, Merry Christmas."

"Is that what today is? That must be why the rebels were not in attack formation. They did not take the usual precautions. They didn't think we would be waiting for them on this day. It cost them. Merry Christmas to you too, Sir."

Like my men, I had trouble keeping my eyes open, but I had to set up sentries, just in case. I told everyone, "I feel bad about our casualties, but it could have been worse. You did well. You eliminated an entire fresh, well-trained Katiba."

The soldier who had run to me when I was hit in the helmet said, "Yes, Sir, and we almost lost our Lieutenant."

Private Boulot, who came close to having been knifed, came to me. "Thank you, Sir. You saved my life."

I nodded and smiled. "I'm glad I saw the guy."

"One more thing, guys. Captain Dufour wishes you a Merry Christmas."

"That's what I always wanted," one of the sergeants said, "Spend Christmas on top of a f... desolated rocky place in the middle of f... nowhere. Merry Christmas to you, Sir."

Early morning, the men from the other platoon arrived and took over our positions. The contrast between my soldiers and the fresh troops was amazing. We looked like tired old men. We were.

The prisoners were helped down the pass and loaded in the trucks. The men piled in. Gautier's sergeant made sure that the private did not get in the same truck as the Arabs. When we got to camp, I went to see the Captain in his command post. I told him what had happened with Private Gautier.

"Sir, can you have him transferred out? I don't want him in my platoon. I don't want to get hit in the back by friendly fire. As far as I'm concerned, this guy is no longer fit for combat."

"I'll take care of that. We have supply trucks returning to Tiaret today. He'll be in one of them. I'll write the order."

I called for Private Gautier. "Private, I'm sending you to be reassigned to headquarters. You have done enough. I don't want you to lose another buddy."

"Thank you, Sir. I don't mind getting out of this bloody mess. Sir, May I ask you a question?"

I nodded.

"Would you have shot me in the foot?"

"Close enough to scare you to death."

He shook his head and said, "You are tough. Thank you, Sir."

I went back to see the Captain in his command post to complete the debriefing. Then he looked at my sleeve. "What's with your arm?"

The War Inside His Mind

"A grenade shrapnel grazed me, Sir." Then I showed him my helmet.

"Well, you are lucky too."

"Yes, Sir. I am, but I wish I were not responsible for so many dead people. I hate these rebels, but still ..."

"Lieutenant, you and your platoon have saved hundreds of lives. You saved the lives of soldiers that the dead Fellaghas can no longer attack, the lives of Europeans farmers they can no longer surprise and murder, the lives of Arab civilians who no longer can be punished for favoring our side."

"I know, Sir. But I wiped out over thirty young men."

"Lieutenant, the men you and your soldiers have shot were going to the cities in the north to murder Arabs and French people alike, even children, as you know. They were murderers, ready to kill. You've seen their work. Don't feel bad."

"You're right, Sir. I know they are dangerous men. I'm glad we got the job done, but I lost too many of my guys."

"Go get some sleep, Lieutenant, you earned it."

I had not slept for four days and three nights. I went to my tent and fell asleep instantly. This year, Christmas would have to happen without me.

The first platoon had been guarding the pass where we had the fight on Christmas morning. They had not seen any rebels in the past couple of nights. At the morning briefing, I told Captain Dufour, "Sir, there must be more dissidents in the mountains. They'd have been detected if they had moved away from the Atlas Range."

"I think you are right. There's that other pass, five miles west. It's much wider than the one where you fought on Christmas Eve. As you know, at the top, there are two promontories separated by a narrow trail. Both have caves and a lot of huge rocks. There are many hiding places."

"I know the trail, Sir."

"Many katibas may be stacked up there because of the one you destroyed last week. "

"That makes sense. Should I attack them?"

"No, Lieutenant. I don't know how many rebels are hiding there. When the brass gets intelligence, they'll draw a plan and tell me what they want me to do."

I dreaded it, but we had to relieve the first platoon, and went back to occupy the old ambush positions. Again, the cold and more endless hours of waiting frayed our nerves. We stayed there for three nights. No rebel showed up. Early in the morning of the fourth day, the Captain called me, "Lieutenant, Fellaghas have been spotted on the west pass, as we suspected. There might be a hundred or more men hiding up there. I need you to run a patrol and find out what you can about their strength."

"Yes, Sir. I'm on my way."

"Lieutenant, take your whole platoon. Locate their positions, but don't engage them. I don't want you to tangle with too many dissidents by yourself. Take a prisoner. I need to know their strength, their weapons, and how they're deployed."

When I got to the bottom of the trail, I stopped and called the Captain. "Sir, we are ready to start moving up the pass. I'll call you when we make contact."

"I have new orders, Lieutenant," the Captain replied. "I'm bringing the rest of the company. I'll be at the bottom of the pass in less than one hour. A company of the Foreign Legion will be going up on the west side of the hill."

"Do I wait for you, Sir?"

"No, proceed with your patrol. It's now even more important to get that prisoner. I'll brief you when we meet up there."

"Yes, Sir."

The French Foreign Legion, the toughest branch of the French Army, was run by French officers, but the ranks were foreigners who enlisted for five years. The discipline was extremely harsh. All their units were well-trained, fearless, and deadly to their enemies. They would attack the rebels on the west summit of the pass.

I called my squad leaders. I said, "We're going up. We won't attack the rebels until the rest of the company joins us. This battle is going to be a big deal. The Legion will be on the other side of the pass."

One of the sergeants said, "We're short nine men."

"I know, Sergeant, but that's the way it is. We'll head the attack for the company. We're the elite platoon."

I reflected for a second or two, that once more I would lead my soldiers in a frontal assault and lose more men.

I looked at my guys. "We have a tough task ahead of us. We're not at full strength, but we'll avenge the ones we're missing today. The first mission is to get a prisoner without being detected. Let's go."

Chapter 15

The trail was about two and a half miles to the top. I called the squad leaders. "Rebel sentries might be anywhere. We can't afford to be detected, so we'll walk up slowly. Spread out, keep your eyes open and your head down."

I went first, a point-man on my left and one on my right. We did not see anything suspicious for the first couple of miles. We reached a false summit, less than half a mile from the top. The platoon was hidden from the crest. The slope ahead of us was a maze of large rocks, small trees, and acacia bushes with their nasty thorns.

The rebels had to be close. I signaled for the sergeants to come to me.

"Now, no more walking," I said, "We have to hug the ground. We'll move forward squad by squad, in hundred-yard increments. I'll take the first squad with me. Sergeant Clavery will take the third squad and go last. We should locate a sentry within the next three or four hundred yards, so be vigilant."

On my hands and knees, my Thompson in my left hand, we proceeded cautiously up the trail. If their lookouts saw us first, they would not hesitate to shoot. My men had superior fire power, but it did not help until we knew where they were. I inched up the slope as silently as I could. As we got closer to the top, further up on my left, I saw a patch of green under a bush that did not match the ground or the foliage around it. I raised my arm to stop the squad.

I pointed toward it and told Sergeant Lupin, "Can you see the rebel under that bush?"

"I can't see anything, Sir."

"There's something that's not of a natural color. It must be part of his uniform."

The War Inside His Mind

"I still can't see anything. If there's a guy up there, I'd walk right into him."

"He's about a hundred yards away. He hasn't seen us yet. We have to get around the side and capture him before he gives us away. You hold the fort right here, sergeant." I took Private Bernard with me. He was strong and did not get rattled easily.

The two of us started to crawl toward the side of the trail. We made no noise. The look-out showed no sign he knew we were closing in on him. We got within a few feet of him. We caught him dozing; that's why he never saw us. The private looked at me. I nodded. We both grabbed our knives and lunged. Private Bernard immobilized the rebel and put his knife on the man's throat. The rebel woke up and his eyes almost popped out of their sockets. I put my hand on his mouth. "You yell and you're dead," I said, right in his ear. He blinked to indicate he understood me. Private Bernard dragged him back to our line.

Sergeant Clavery told him in Arabic that we would not harm him and asked him about the Fellaghas up at the pass. Shaking, still terrified, the young man was eager to please, and replied that there were four Katibas, evenly divided between the two summits. Over a hundred and twenty men were scattered over the one half-mile top.

"Why so many men in the same place?" I asked him.

"A katiba was wiped out a few days ago in the next pass. French soldiers are still guarding it. We're checking every day. We'll go once they leave, one katiba a day. Most of the men are resting, holed up in the caves or behind the rocks. Only a few lookouts man the crest. We didn't expect anyone to surprise us."

Sergeant Clavery said to me, "They're backed up because of us. That's to our credit."

I told the sergeant to ask him about the terrain beyond the crest. The prisoner said that there was over a hundred-yard open area between the crest and the caves.

"They'll see you coming and wipe you out if you attack them," he boasted.

"Were you going to leave tonight?" I asked him.

"No, tomorrow. The chief is sure the pass will be open."

"That's New Year's Eve," one of the soldiers said.

Then the prisoner told the Sergeant, "I'm due to be relieved. When they find out I'm no longer at my post, they'll know something is up. That means trouble for you. We have mortars and machine guns."

I called the Captain, told him about the prisoner, the number of dissidents, and the kind of weapons they had.

"Thanks. I'll pass it along to high command."

Then I asked, "I'm less than two hundred yards from the ridge, well hidden from the top. Do you want me to hold here, come back down or go further up, Sir?"

"Stay where you are. The rest of the company is less than thirty minutes from you."

Suddenly, mortar rounds exploded, not too far from where the platoon was hiding. The rebels had probably found out the sentry was missing. They may have wondered if he deserted, but they were firing rounds if he did not, guessing French troops might have taken him. Obviously, they had no idea where we were. That was a waste of their supply. Rounds came down at random; they fell everywhere. Bushes and trees were shattered, broken branches, shards, and rock fragments turned into deadly missiles. The noise of the explosions was deafening. There was no place to hide. Nowhere was safe. All one could do was to hug the dirt and hope not to get hit. Fortunately, because the dissidents had to carry the rounds on their back, they had a limited supply. Soon the shelling stopped. No one had been hurt.

The Captain arrived with the rest of the company. I went to greet him at the rear of the platoon. Standing, hidden from the top by huge boulders, he asked, "What was that mortar attack about, Lieutenant?"

"They must have found out we took the sentry prisoner. No casualties."

"Good. We'll seal the trail so that they can't escape. The legionnaires will do the same on the other side."

"We're not going to attack?"

"We are, but not now. With your information about the four katibas, the brass decided to call for an air strike to soften their defenses before we storm the enemy positions. It would be nice to have some of the dissidents sidelined before we go after them."

"Yes, Sir."

My platoon was dug in. Nobody would be able to get through

our lines. The Captain said to me, "You'll lead the assault on the caves after the air raid. The first platoon will be behind you to support the attack. I'm going to position the other platoons where they can best support you."

We put colored markers in front of our lines to show the pilots where we were. The rebels did not fire at us. They did not want to reveal their positions.

Then I heard the sound of a chopper. An Alouette helicopter came to the rear of my platoon. A general got out. I was surprised.

His uniform was impeccable, his helmet shiny, obviously unused in battle. He was accompanied by the Colonel in charge of our regiment. *What the hell is a general doing here? This is a combat zone, not a parade ground.*

I went to greet the General and saluted him. He glared at me, and said, "Lieutenant, is what you're wearing supposed to be your uniform?"

"Yes, Sir."

"It's a disgrace for an officer to look like you do."

I had been up for four days and three nights, lying on the ground or walking and crawling in the mountains. I was unshaven and covered with dirt. My left sleeve was torn, because it had gotten caught in an acacia bush. I had my dusty, bullet-dented helmet on my head, my knife strapped to my left leg, and a couple of grenades hanging from my belt. My pockets were full of ammo for my Thompson, which I was holding in my left hand.

"Yes, Sir."

He replied, angrily, "Don't you respect your rank? Are you one of those soldiers who crawl in the dirt to hide from the enemy?"

"No, Sir."

At that time, the Colonel stepped in, "General, Lieutenant Alain is my best platoon leader. He has more dissidents killed or captured to his credit than anyone in my regiment. He decimated a whole katiba just a week ago. He's a fine soldier."

The General grumbled and stared at me. "Then brief me on what's going on, Lieutenant."

I told him about the rebels' strength and our plan of attack and added, "And, General, Sir. This is not a safe area. The rebels have light mortars. They must have located your helicopter by now. You don't want your chopper to get hit."

I was hardly finished with my report, when a couple of mortar rounds fell a few hundred yards from where we were, not really close to the chopper. The General told the Colonel, "Let's go, I've seen enough." He turned around and hurried to his chopper.

The Colonel said to me, "These katibas have to be eliminated. It's an important assignment. Good luck, Lieutenant."

The Captain came back from deploying the support troops below the top, further west, where they had a clear view of the enemy positions. He said, "Lieutenant, you got to meet the General."

"Yes, Sir. I didn't understand what that was all about. All he said was that I shouldn't look dirty. Then he got scared and ran away. I've no idea why he came here."

"Lieutenant, when a general flies into a combat zone, he wants to understand what's happening on the ground. Also his record shows he was there. It's input for his resume."

"Sir, I was glad the Colonel was with him. He stood up for me."

"The Colonel does not want you to get in trouble. He needs you."

Every soldier waited for the air strike, hoping it would disable many rebels. Soon, two T6 fighter planes flew in with thunderous roars. They were low, just high enough to clear the cliffs, each targeting one of the summits. They came three times and strafed the caves and the surrounding area. It was an ominous display of power and a relief not to be on the receiving end of the strikes. I remembered being strafed and missed when I was a kid, and I recalled the people on the road who were slaughtered in front of my eyes because they could not hide in time. Today the targets were armed soldiers, but the noise of the plane engines and of the machine-gun fire sounded as frightening as it did twenty years ago.

I did not know what kind of damage, if any, the strikes had caused to the rebels' positions, but I would launch the attack at the same time as the Legion, three minutes after the planes left.

The Captain said, "Get your men ready."

I reminded the sergeants, "Remember, after the ridge is an open area. It is fully exposed to the rebels' fire. The faster we get close to the caves, the lower the casualties. Keep your men moving."

I got up and yelled, "Let's go get them." We ran toward the top. At first, we only received light automatic fire. The first line of defense on the crest had little punch and was overrun quickly. As we

The War Inside His Mind

cleared the summit, we received heavy AK47 and machine-gun fire from the caves and from behind the boulders. The defenders poured showers of bullets on the men running at them. The air strikes may have softened the dissidents, but they had not shut them out. Covering fire coming from the third platoon helped, but after a while, I had to get everyone moving. I gave the sign to jump up. Bent over, we ran and zigzagged. Every twenty yards or so, we threw ourselves on the ground, fired toward the caves, rolled over a couple of times, and stood up a few feet from where we were seen last, hoping the rebels were still aiming where we were seen last.

I had to keep everyone going forward, using signals, yelling, pulling some soldiers by their fatigues. Some of the men got hit while running and did not get up. The medics would tend to them. As I got up after one of the rolls, a bullet grazed my left thigh. I felt a burn. A patch of blood tainted my pants. It hurt, but I could run, so I knew no bone was broken. While we received only automatic-weapon fire, I could hear mortar rounds hitting the legionnaires' zone, no more than five hundred yards from where we were. The rebels were more afraid of them than of my men. Good for us.

When we got near the caves, the covering fire had to stop, so we would not get hit by our own people. Rocks and boulders protected the rebels, but they offered some shelter for us too. I sent Sergeant Lupin and his men to take care of a machine gun hidden behind the boulders on my right. It caused much damage to my guys. The second squad covered the Sergeant and his squad as they moved forward. There was a furious exchange of fire between the machine gun rebel crew and my troops. Finally, a soldier was able to throw a grenade that exploded close enough to the gun to silence it.

The first squad continued to attack the dissidents shielded by the big rocks. The second squad could now move. I gave the signal for the final rush. I got up and felt another sharp pain, this time on my lower right leg. It bled quite a bit, but I could still move. Almost deaf from the cacophony of the fight, the firing of the guns, the explosions of the grenades, the screams of those who were hit, and the yells of soldiers on both sides, half crazy with fear and hatred, suffocating from the smoke and the smell of gunpowder, I used all my senses and my combat experience to direct my troops. Continuing to zigzag, the second squad got close enough to the caves to throw grenades inside. Men fell. A few Fellaghas came out of the caves firing. They were mowed down. A few tried to flee down the slope. The first platoon caught them. A couple of rebels stood up with their hands up. A soldier shot them both. I gave the ceasefire signal.

It was over.

I ordered the third squad to clean up the caves. "Throw grenades before you go in. Make sure no one stays hiding in there." The second squad disarmed any rebel who was still alive on the ground.

The aftermath of the battle was chaos. Soldiers carried their wounded buddies and called for medics. Others just sat on the ground, dazed. Bodies of rebels, dead and alive, were strewn all over. I was out of breath; my head throbbed. I was still tense with fear, my hands were shaking. I tried to stay focused to take care of the men.

I called Sergeant Clavery. "Sergeant, give me a count on our casualties."

He reported we had three men killed and ten wounded, six pretty severely. "We need urgent air evacuation," he added.

"Thanks, Sergeant. I'll call for it."

He looked worried when he saw the blood on my fatigues, and asked, "Sir. Are your legs okay?"

"I'm standing, can't you see? I'm fine."

"Yes, Sir."

I checked on the wounded who had been carried to a triage area. I was distressed to see that Sergeant Lupin was one who had been hit, but relieved to find out he was not one of the most serious cases. Since I had been fired at for the first time, when I had taken over the platoon, a year and half ago, he had been by my side every day. I trusted him with my life. I had the utmost admiration and respect for his competence, his courage, and his determination.

"How are you doing, Sergeant?"

"I got hit in the chest, Sir." He was having a hard time breathing and talking, but he continued, "The medic said nothing vital has been touched. The bullet went in and out of my upper right lung." He grimaced. "I guess, in a way, I got lucky."

"Don't talk, Sergeant. Take it easy. The nurses will take care of you. You are probably done with the war. Thank you for knocking down the machine gun. It was a turning point in the fight."

"I knew we had to take it out."

The War Inside His Mind

"You're my top squad leader. I'll miss your skills and your support. But soon, you'll be back in Menilmuch with your family where you belong." I patted him on the head. "Say hi to Paris, and good luck to you, Sergeant."

"Thank you, Sir."

I turned away. I was angry ... and I felt like crying.

Some of the wounded were in great pain. Just looking at them was difficult. I was responsible for their agony. I was the one who led them on the assault. They trusted me, they followed me, and they paid for it.

The Captain sent word the legionnaires had suffered severe casualties, but all sixty or so rebels who faced them had been killed. No Arab was wounded or taken prisoner on their side of the pass.

The medical helicopters came. Lieutenant Danielle, who had helped me on Christmas Day, jumped out. Her dark hair showing under her helmet, she saluted me, a broad smile lighting her tanned face, "Hello again, Lieutenant. You're keeping me busy."

"Yes, Ma'am. I'm glad to see you, but I wish I didn't have to. Take care of my guys. They fought well." Her nurses hurried to tend to the wounded men.

"Don't worry, Lieutenant, we'll fix them up." She looked at my bloody pants. "What's wrong with your legs, Lieutenant? You're bleeding and you're limping."

"I'm okay, Ma'am. It's just a couple of scratches."

"What's your name again?"

"Lieutenant Alain, Ma'am."

"Lieutenant Alain, don't you know that where blood comes out, infection goes in? Do you want to lose your legs?"

"No Ma'am. But I was just grazed by bullets."

"It there's blood, there's a wound. I have to take care of it."

She grabbed a pair of scissors and cut the right leg of my fatigue pants below the knee, and the left one above the knee. The skin was burned and blood was coming out of both places where the bullets had hit. It looked ugly.

"It's not as bad as it looks. You were lucky again, Lieutenant." She cleaned the wounds with some stinging liquid and secured them with a couple of dressings. "You're all set."

I felt some relief. The pain had eased up. "Thank you, Lieutenant."

"You're welcome. Have your medics keep an eye on it. The climate is not good for any kind of wound. They tend to fester."

She was young but tough. I admired her courage and her ability to deal with wounded and confused soldiers. I asked her, "Lieutenant. Can I visit my men in your hospital?"

"Most of them won't be there. All we have in Aflou is a front-line support unit. Most of them will have to be transferred to the military hospital in Tiaret, some to Algiers. They need more treatment than we can supply. But you can come and visit me any time."

"That'd be nice."

Soon, the wounded were loaded in the choppers and air-lifted. She was gone.

The clean-up crew took the final tally for the dissidents. I sat on a rock. The Captain came to talk to me. "Thank you, Lieutenant. This is a great victory for our side, four crack Katibas eliminated. We had limited casualties."

I did not feel that way at all. "Sir. Last week, I had forty-five men. This morning I started with thirty-six; I've twenty-three left. Half of my platoon's gone."

"I know it's tough for you and for your men, but, overall, those are good numbers. The Colonel can tell your friend the General what you accomplished."

The company, with what was left of the second platoon, went back down the trail to get to the trucks. My legs hurt and I was limping, but I managed to walk; somehow it was important to me to make it to camp with my soldiers. From the bottom of the hill, we rode back to camp. Weapons had to be cleaned and oiled, but my soldiers would be exempt from guard duty tonight.

I went to see the Captain in his tent for the usual debriefing.

"Lieutenant. You lost thirteen men. Are you okay?"

"Not really, Sir, but I don't know what else I could have done."

"You didn't ask them to do anything different from what you did. The high command wanted the assault because they knew the Fellaghas had four of their best units cornered up there. They wanted them annihilated."

"Sir, the air strikes didn't help much. The rebels had a lot of fire power left. We made it easily over the ridge. The Fells were still dazed from the air strike, and you were delivering intense covering fire. There was confusion among them. I didn't want to give them time to recover. I rushed at them in the open. That's when many were hit."

"Yes, and you and your men fought bravely."

I shook my head. "Captain, I don't know about bravery. When we rush an enemy position, the soldiers execute orders, your orders, my orders. When the fight is over, to be called brave does not make any of us feel any better, nor does it do anything for the ones who didn't make it. We're relieved to be alive. We mourn our buddies who died or were hurt, and we have to live with the knowledge of what happened to them. People who have never been in combat can't possibly imagine what it's like. You know, Sir. You've been there."

"You and your soldiers accomplished the mission at great personal risk. I watched your platoon. No one cowered. Everyone followed you and ran forward. I want you to know that the Colonel and I respect the courage that you and your men have shown."

I shrugged. "As you know, Sir, in combat, it's better to move than not to. My job is to minimize casualties and to complete the mission. You may call it courage, but rushing the enemy was my only choice. I made my men run at them. Some of us made it, others were hit." I paused for a second. "I need to say something else."

"Go ahead, Lieutenant."

"When I was drafted into this bloody war and came to the company, I knew nothing about combat. Thanks to my men and to Sergeant Clavery, I had some initial successes, learned my job, and the platoon became a tough fighting unit. We were able to execute the missions we were sent on. We had special training and got better weapons. But we're in harm's way more than anyone else in the regiment. The more we do, the more we have to do. That's why I have so many casualties."

"Lieutenant, I'm aware your ranks are depleted, and so is the Colonel."

"Unlike you, we're not professional soldiers, nor do we plan to be; we're creating a heavy baggage for ourselves, memories we'll take to our future lives. My men are tired, Sir."

"I know your platoon is far from being at full strength." He smiled at me, and added, "Even you can hardly walk. Go get some rest, Lieutenant."

"Yes, Sir."

I had given the fight all I had. My legs hurt. I got on my cot with my boots on and my legless pants. I was asleep before my head hit the pillow. Tomorrow would be another day.

At least there would be a tomorrow for me.

Chapter 16

Still troubled when I woke up, I sat at my desk to write letters to the families of the men who gave their lives for their country. I led them to their death while bullets only tore a bit of flesh off my legs. After so many casualties, I was tired of the war, and had no fight left in me. I wanted to go home, but I could not; I had no place to go to anyway.

I wrote to Ms. Rooth and, without too many details, mentioned the high toll of the last two weeks. I knew I could share my distress with her. *The last few days have been a test of my resolve. My concern is for the young men who obey my orders and trustingly follow me. It is unfair I always get out unscathed or with minor scratches while my soldiers get gravely wounded or worse. I have no choice but to lead them into battle. This useless war is killing people, day after day. I am in the middle of it, but I can't stop it. I don't like to feel helpless.*

Guilt and anger were on my mind all the time, like demons eating at my sanity. I decided to talk with Sergeant Clavery. He was an old-timer and might be able to share with me some of the wisdom he acquired after years of war in Europe and in Indochina. I asked him to come to my tent. He sat on my cot, his eyes open wide; I could see he wondered why he was there.

"Sergeant, during World War II, you fought big battles. You must have lost many buddies."

"That's right, Lieutenant. I did. I even got hit in the foot myself in Italy and missed six weeks of the war. But the number of men involved in a fight doesn't matter much to the soldier.

One bullet or random shrapnel can kill him whether his squad fights five rebels or his division battles an enemy corps of thirty-thousand men."

"But that's not what we do."

"That's right. What is different with the war we fight here is that our battles last minutes, maybe hours, but not days or weeks. They're short but relentless, almost daily occurrences. In the big wars, soldiers were bombed by warplanes, fired at by heavy artillery and tanks. We have to contend with machine guns, and grenades, but in the end if one gets hit, it does not much matter how. The Algerian war has already lasted four times as long as my campaigns from Italy to Berlin, and there's no end in sight. The stress on the soldier is different, but it's really the same."

"How did you manage to keep your head together?"

He tilted his head, looked far away and said, "That's a good question."

"More than not losing your head, you had to keep going. Did you steel yourself to suppress your feelings?"

He looked down at his feet and shrugged. "No, not really. In a war, after a while you look at the battles as chores. Soldiering is a job, a thankless job, a dangerous job, and a dirty job. You might have instincts, gain experience, but destiny does its thing. You have to become fatalistic. You can't think about going home. It's too depressing."

Somewhat uncomfortable opening up to him, I fidgeted a bit and said, "I'm not worried about myself anymore, but I can't stand seeing these young men getting injured or worse."

The Sergeant smiled. "That's what I mean about doing your job. You have to keep focused on the mission and do your best to limit losses. I know you're down, Sir. This last week was hard on all of us."

"I'm trying to minimize casualties, but when the battle is over, I feel guilty."

"I know it. Your whole platoon is aware of it. If we get hit, we know it's not your fault."

"But I make the decisions. I give the orders."

"You do the best that can be done. This is war. There are risks. Soldiers are hurt, they lose their lives. You can't let it get to you. I know how you feel, your soldiers know it too, but you're our platoon commander." He rose from the cot.

"I hear you, Sergeant. But we go over the same terrain day after day. We're making no progress. We eliminate dissidents, but more come back to the same hills to do the same harm to more of my soldiers. In your first war, you landed in Italy, and eighteen months later you got to Berlin. I've been fighting in place for almost two years."

Then his face darkened, like I saw it many times before a fight. He looked at me, his eyes riveted to mine. "Sir. Your men respect you. The platoon can't afford to have you fall apart. You're a professional soldier now."

I took a deep breath. "I know, Sergeant."

The conversation with Sergeant Clavery was a turning point. Like the dean of my engineering school who told me to get out of my funk after my uncle's death, the Sergeant told me in his own way to stop feeling sorry for myself and to get on with the war. Indeed, I was now a professional soldier. What a depressing thought.

With my platoon about half-strength, the Captain made sure that our duties were light. He assigned the second platoon to patrol the desert in vehicles at the bottom of the hills. The first platoon replaced mine and guarded the range.

One day, about fifteen miles from camp, I heard an exchange of fire. It happened behind a little hump in the desert. I hastened the platoon to a spot where I could look over the crest at the firefight. A bunch of Fellaghas hiding behind rocks and piles of sand were firing at an ill-equipped group of nomads who fought back with old single-shot rifles.

There were no more than ten rebels. We drove right at the dissidents, the Thompsons showering them with lethal bullets. We hit several of the dissidents; a few tried to return fire without much conviction. When I got close, I jumped out and shouted, "Put your arms down. Surrender."

One man stood up and aimed his AK47 at me. One of my soldiers took him down before he could fire.

"Secure the Fells," I told the second squad Sergeant, and I went toward the encampment with my Senior Sergeant. The nomads had camels and goats.

The Sergeant said to me, "They must be Berbers, but it's odd. The men wear the indigo face veils of the Tuaregs, and the women are bare-faced and their dresses colorful. That's what Berbers wear in the southwest, not here."

Whatever their ethnicity they were friendly and came to meet me with big smiles.

"Thank you Lieutenant, we were in trouble. The rebels were determined to get our animals."

"I'm glad to help. Anybody hurt in the compound?"

"No, Sir. You showed up right in time. Everyone is okay."

"I would not camp so close to the mountains if I were you. The rebels use them to travel east. Go fifteen or twenty miles further south into the desert. You'd be safer."

"Thank you Lieutenant. We just got here, but we're leaving right now. I know where there's water two days south of here. That's where we'll go."

"I'll protect you until you're on your way."

They packed their belongings and loaded them back on the camels. The women and children left with the goats, and a few moments later the slow-moving caravan went on its way. We went back to camp and gave our prisoners to the fourth platoon.

After a couple of weeks, I went to the support hospital in Aflou to retrieve the lightly wounded soldiers who were ready to come back to the platoon. I was disappointed to find out that Lieutenant Danielle was away on a mission. My legs were healing well, and I wanted to thank her for taking care of me.

Replacements for the casualties, including the Sergeant who would take over the first squad, had been assigned to the second platoon. Most had just graduated from the camp where we trained a few weeks before. Like my men, they had earned the black berets. For some reason, another three recruits, fresh from basic training in France, completed the group. They would not have the same skills. I would have to deal with that.

The Captain decided to send me to bring them back to Aflou. "Go pick them up, Lieutenant. It'll be a little break for you."

"Thank you, Sir."

With a light escort, I drove to Oran. We had to stop in familiar Tiaret overnight, and reached Oran early afternoon the next day. There, I went to the officers' center. It was luxurious compared to my tent in Aflou, or to my quarters in Mascara. My room had a real bed with sheets, and a shower. Luxury! I must have spent an hour getting rid of months of Saharan dust. What a treat! I could see from my window that the complex had a pool with a bar next to it. It was late afternoon. I went to have a beer and relax. A woman in a swim suit sat in a chaise, reading a paperback, an almost-empty glass on the table next to her.

"Good afternoon, Ma'am, I'm Lieutenant Alain. I see your glass needs to be filled. May I get you another drink?"

"No thanks, Lieutenant. I'm okay." She gave me a radiant smile. "My name is Chantal; what brings you here?" She had short blond hair, a toned body, and a captivating smile.

"I'm stationed near Aflou. I'm in Oran to pick up replacements."

"Where in the world is Aflou? I've never heard of it," she replied, raising her eyebrows.

"It's in the northern Sahara, a hundred miles south of Tiaret . . . which is way east of Sidi Bel Abbes. . . It's a small village in the middle of nowhere." I chuckled. "No wonder you haven't heard of it."

"I see that you wear a Special Forces beret. Have you seen much fighting?"

"More than enough, Ma'am. What do you do here?"

"I work at the Oran military hospital. I am in charge of the nurses. I have the rank of captain, that's why I live here in the officers' building."

"Nice to meet you, Captain." I saluted her.

"Lieutenant, let's cut out the military stuff. Call me Chantal. Does that work for you?"

"That would be great, Chantal. Call me Alain."

"How long are you here for?"

"I'm just here for the night. I'll get my fourteen guys early tomorrow and go back to the line."

"You lost that many men in your platoon?"

"Actually, I lost two dozen guys around Christmas. Some are already back, a little banged up, but ready to keep on going."

"You weren't kidding when you said you saw more than enough fighting. You've seen combat indeed."

"You may have some of my guys here. A few were seriously wounded."

"Possibly. I treat wounded men. I pay little attention to what unit they come from."

"I hate losing any of my troops. Frankly, I hate the war," I said.

"I do too. And it's hard for me too when my patients don't make it."

"Let's not talk about that. Are you free for dinner by any chance? I don't know Oran at all."

She beamed. "Yes, I am and I'd be delighted to show you the town. I know a couple of nice restaurants. I bet you've not had a good meal for a while."

"That's an understatement. Social life in Aflou is less than stellar. I was in Mascara before, and it wasn't much better. That has been my life since I came to Algeria." Then I asked her, "How's your life here? Is it hard to see wounded soldiers day after day? Is it lonely?"

"Yes and yes, but I'm sure that your life is much tougher than mine. Any interesting women in Aflou?"

"Not really. There is a nurse, Danielle. But she's busy and so am I. We only meet on battlefields when she picks up my casualties. That's not too romantic. There are no civilian European women in Aflou. To tell you the truth, I've not had a drink, a conversation, or anything else for that matter, with a woman in over a year."

She tilted her head, looking at me, a cunning smile on her face. "That could be changed," she replied.

"I'd welcome it, "I replied.

"Let's go have dinner. Wait for me, I'll go change."

She came back wearing a crisp khaki uniform with red crosses on her sleeves. She got a staff car to drive to the restaurant she had picked, Chez Laurent. We had a nice dinner of delicious local fish and drank French white wine. I had not had either since I had come to Algeria.

Sitting across the table from me, Chantal said she came from Amiens, north of Paris. She had been in Oran for twelve months, and had six more to go before going back to France. She had enlisted for four years, with one more to go.

She said, "Three years ago, my brother was wounded near Algiers. He lost his left arm. I decided to come and help relieve the pain of the soldiers who get hurt in this stupid war. That's why I'm here."

I told her about the nurses who evacuated my wounded soldiers. "The other day, they received fire when they were tending to some of my guys. They went about their job as if nothing happened. They have guts."

She took my hands in hers. "We're here to relieve suffering."

We chatted about the future. She would go back to the Amiens hospital where she worked when she left for the army.

"What about you, Alain, what will you do after the war?"

"I've no idea. All I want is to be Alain again and drop the Lieutenant bit. I'm tired of the killings and of the atrocities."

After the lovely evening, she asked me to come to her room.. Chantal pointed to the one armchair. "Have a seat; I'll get a glass of wine."

She returned with two glasses of white Sancerre and sat on my lap. I groaned.

She got up. "I'm sorry. Did I hurt you?"

"I have that light wound on my thigh. It's almost healed. I didn't expect you to sit on it. It surprised me, but I'm okay."

She said, "I need to see what's hurting you." She helped me take off my pants.

"Lieutenant Danielle cut my fatigues to get to my wounds. I'm glad you didn't."

She chuckled and looked at the wounds on my leg. "Did your friend Danielle fix those up for you?"

"Yes, she did. She said I could get an infection if she did not take care of it."

"She did a good job. Nurses are good at treating wounds. They are also good at other things. Let me show you." She pulled me toward her bed.

Chantal was beautiful. She had active hands and voluptuous lips. Her body, including her breasts, had a golden glow from her light tan. What a delight to be able to touch and to caress her silky skin. I had almost forgotten the wonderful feeling of the softness of a woman's body.

Chantal had to be at the hospital early the next day and I had to return to Aflou. It had been a short encounter. Yet, Chantal had been Chantal, and I had been Alain for a night.

There was no captain, no lieutenant, no war, and no tomorrow. It had been good for me, and I hoped for her too.

I met Sergeant Lemoine and ten privates, all looking very fit.

"Nice to meet you, Sir," said my new sergeant.

"Welcome to the second platoon, Sergeant." Then, with my new men, I went to the port of Oran to get the three replacements from

France and headed back to Aflou. We had to stop in Tiaret overnight. The Colonel welcomed me.

"Lieutenant, I'm recommending you for a medal to recognize your bravery in your recent successes in the mountains."

"Sir, I lost men, four of them killed in those two fights, several wounded. They should be the ones honored with a decoration and thanked by the French government for their sacrifice. They deserve it and it would mean much to them and to their families." I paused for a second. "Could you give the award to the whole platoon instead of to me?"

The Colonel was surprised. "But you should be proud to receive the citation you have earned with your courage and your leadership."

"Sir, the trust that my troops have in me and the respect that you and the Captain have for me are my true rewards. If I make it, I'll be a civilian in a few months. I don't need ribbons on my chest."

"You're right; I will make the citation a Unit Military Medal. They earned it." He looked at me. "You should know that I have a son who is seventeen. I hope he grows up to be someone like you."

"Sir, I trust that he won't have to do the sort of things I have been doing. But I appreciate your kind words."

Once back in Aflou, I noticed that one of the three new guys who got off the ship, Private Simon, was timid and did not look strong physically. He also wore thick glasses. I worried that it would be hard for him to fit in the platoon and not to be an early casualty. I could see that some of the veterans were already ignoring him. They probably thought he would not carry his weight like the buddies they had lost.

I called him. "Private, how much firing practice have you had?"

"A few sessions, Sir. With my glasses I'm not too bad. Without them, I'm as blind as a bat."

"We'll see how you do tomorrow; you have a new weapon to learn." Private Simon should never have been assigned to an infantry company, let alone a black-beret platoon. Yet I had to give him the best chance to make it through the next few months.

The next day, I watched him when he fired his Thompson. He was not a sharpshooter, but not as bad as I feared. I decided to work on his morale and his attitude.

"Private Simon. We are going to run a lot of sweeps, some on foot, and some in vehicles. When we ride, I want you to sit behind me. Your job will be to watch my back."

"Sir, I'm sure there are other soldiers better equipped than me to do that job. I would be afraid to be responsible for something happening to you."

"I've seen you at the range. You can do the job."

One of the sergeants said to me later, "Lieutenant, you don't want to trust this guy with your life. Do you?"

"He'll do fine. When he sits in my jeep, the other guys will have more respect for him too."

We ran daily patrols, some on foot, to get the new people used to walking in the heat, and some in vehicles. We had a few encounters with dissidents. One day, my jeep was leading the platoon down a mountain trail when gunfire erupted. It came from the slope on our right. I stopped. Private Simon immediately returned fire toward the area where the shooting had come from. We all jumped out of the vehicles and he ran next to me toward the assailants, firing his Thompson. The platoon captured a couple of rebels. When we got back to the jeep, I thanked him for his quick reaction. He beamed. As the days went by, he became more alert and more sure of himself. That could save his life.

One day, in the desert, a low, dark red cloud appeared to the west and moved swiftly toward the platoon. I stopped the convoy. Sergeant Clavery came next to me.

"What's going on, Sergeant?"

"It's a sandstorm, Sir. The desert people called it the Sirocco, the word for warm wind. We need to prepare fast."

We were about twenty miles from camp. The ominous cloud was getting close. Sergeant Clavery knew what to do.

"Park the vehicles next to each other. Hide under the tarps. Close your eyes, and put any kind of a cloth, a handkerchief, your shirt, anything over your face. You don't want sand in your lungs or in your eyes."

It grew dark. I could not see anything. The storm hit us. It was unbelievably hot and stifling. Without any air to breathe, we almost suffocated. We only had to hope it would end soon. Indeed, less than an hour later, the worst of it was behind us. The Senior Sergeant had predicted it. Now we had to clean up.

The sand was everywhere. Regardless of the precautions I had taken, it went into my clothes, my mouth, my ears, and eyes. I wiped my face the best I could. More importantly, the platoon had to be ready to defend itself.

"Clean your weapons. Disassemble them and wipe out every single part and oil them. There's sand everywhere. There's not much danger of a surprise attack. If there are any rebels around, they'll have gone through the same storm, and they'll have to clean their weapons too."

Some of the engines would not start, so the drivers worked on them. They cleaned filters, fuel lines, and I'm not sure what. They finally managed to get them going. It took a couple of hours to get started again. Such storms were frequent in the desert. I was glad I spent most of my time in the mountains.

That evening, because of the particles of sand in the air, the sunset colors dazzled me. Bright and dark red, gold, and orange made the sky look like a gigantic furnace. It was a grand spectacle. I hated the Algerian war, but I loved the country. I knew now how warm and bright the sun could be, and how incredibly blue, or sometimes almost white, the sky could get. I discovered the trees bearing exotic fruit. I walked up and down arid but beautiful mountains. I experienced the desert, its heat and cold. I spent my life close to a nature I had not known before. That was a great contrast with the destructive job of waging war.

Chapter 17

One morning, the Captain called me to his command post. "Lieutenant, do you know what a *raima* is?"

"No, Sir."

"Sit down, Lieutenant. Let me tell you."

I pulled up a chair and sat across from the metal table which was his desk.

The Captain splayed his large hands on his desk top. "It is a temporary tent village. The Berbers usually roam around the desert and survive in the harsh environment. They find places to grow food and keep cattle. But lately, the Fellaghas have been stealing their food, and killing their animals. Because of that, many families got together and created temporary camps to better protect themselves. They're the raimas."

I knew about the nomads. I nodded. "Sir, I rescued a group of Berbers who were under attack not long ago. I happened to be there at the right time; so I got rid of the Fells and sent the nomads further south into the desert. They were nice people, very friendly. I gathered they hate the dissidents and are on our side."

He nodded. "That's right. Several families have recently set up a camp south of here. As they're within the Colonel's area of responsibility, it's our job to see they're safe. The Colonel and I decided to take your platoon off the line, and give you the job. It'll give you time to integrate your new troops with the old-timers."

"That's sounds good to me, Sir. Does that mean no patrols, no ambush, no fights, and hopefully no casualties?"

"You're right. Sentries and watches. That's all you'll have to worry about. The rebels won't want to tangle with your platoon. There are easier targets for them to get food. You'll be re-supplied once a week with whatever you need."

I wanted to know more. I sat up and asked, "How long is the mission and where do we have to go?"

The Captain got up and went to his chart hanging on an easel in back of him. "You'll be there ten weeks and be relieved by another platoon." He pointed at a dot on the map. "The raima is about fifty miles southeast of Aflou, in the middle of the desert. There's not much going on there. It'll be hot and quiet."

"When do I go?"

"You're due the day after tomorrow."

"Thank you, Captain. It sounds like a soft assignment to me."

I called Sergeant Clavery to my tent and asked him to get the platoon together. The men assembled as usual in the flat bare area outside my tent. Their worried eyes and the frowns on their faces told me they were apprehensive.

"We've been assigned to protect Berbers in the desert for the next two and a half months. We'll be in the middle of nowhere, south of here, with not much to do but guard duty. Prepare your gear. We leave the day after tomorrow at six in the morning. Beware that with nothing to do but write letters, you might get bored."

Private Bernard, one of the old-timers said, "Lieutenant, being safe is not boring."

I chuckled. "You're right, Private, no crawling or snatching of prisoners."

He smiled at me. "I won't miss that, Sir."

Our trucks set out for our new quarters and got to the raima early enough to have time to set up camp. We established the defense positions we needed to protect ourselves and the Berbers. There was a well and a couple of ponds with murky water, shriveled bushes, a few trees, and a scattering of rocks. The small trees provided some shade, and the green bushes added some color to the sandy little place. The tents were barely up, a quarter of a mile from the Berber camp, when a group of young men, all carrying rifles, came toward our camp. I knew that the nomads were armed, so I was not alarmed. Unlike the ones I had rescued earlier, these men did not wear Tuareg clothing or turbans; their free-flowing dark hair framed their tanned faces.

One of the young men asked who was in charge. I stepped up to him, smiled, and said, "I'm Lieutenant Alain."

The War Inside His Mind

He smiled and extended his two hands, palms up. "My name is Habib. My father, Ramiz, is the elder of the compound. He invites you to share a welcome meal with him tonight. Please come."

That was a nice welcome. I smiled at him. "Thank you, Habib. Tell your father I'll be there." He and his friends went back to their camp.

Sergeant Clavery told me, "So you know, in Arabic, Habib means *beloved* and Ramiz means *respected*. This invitation is an honor for you. In the desert, the rules of hospitality are sacred. You'll be safe inside his domain. You must not carry any kind of weapon. You have to show your host that you trust him."

That night, in a clean uniform and unarmed for the first time in months, I went to the Berber encampment. The large tent, made of goat hair, that they ushered me into was high and spacious. Inside, colorful rugs hung from the top to separate different rooms. Others adorned the rough ground.

Ramiz, wearing a long dark Djellaba, came to greet me. His face was leathered by years of exposure to the elements. He displayed his two upper front teeth in a welcoming smile. I saluted him; he bowed his white-cloth-covered head. "I'm Ramiz, Salaam Alaykum."

I said, "I'm Lieutenant Alain," and repeated the greeting. His son Habib brought a cup and a pitcher of hot green mint tea, which from his extended arm, way high up, he poured into the cup. He gave it to his dad who took a sip and offered the cup to me. I drank from it. That was his way of telling me I was safe in his home. He was not going to poison me. It was my way of showing him that I trusted him. My sergeant had told me about the wonderful old custom.

The old man and I sat on low cushions on the ground, face to face. Other old men sat in back of us. Younger ones brought out dishes from behind one of the rugs. There was no woman to be seen. It would have been improper for me to see any of them. They had cooked the meal, but stayed inside, behind the rugs.

The welcome meal was a feast. Using our fingers, we ate stewed lamb and spicy chicken, flatbread and grains, vegetables and many desserts, figs, dates and sweet pastries. At the end of the meal, we drank Arak, a strong anise liquor.

The elder spoke excellent French. "Lieutenant, why do your troops wear black berets?"

"Sir, we had special training. My men are good soldiers."

"Good, I feel safe with them around. You have nothing to fear from anyone inside the compound. We do not hide rebels. We do not support or agree with them. Before the war, the French let us live with our traditions. We know the desert and how to survive in it. Once the insurgency started, the dissidents became our enemies. That's why we keep trying to find a safe place. With your men around, I know I have found it. I don't want the Fellaghas to win the war."

"I feel the same. My platoon has done well in fights with the rebels, but I'm afraid that the politicians have other ideas. Have you ever seen a representative from the French government?"

"No. They don't even show up in the big cities like Oran. I know. I have family there."

"Well, they don't know anything about you and your people; yet, they think they know what's best for you."

"Lieutenant, I welcome you. I like you."

"Thank you, Sir, I like you too, and I'm happy you feel safe with the second platoon. You are." The evening ended on that cordial note.

Our new lives started the next day. It was very hot, and the terrain arid. Our small tents did not provide much protection from the sun. The Senior Sergeant organized the guard schedule. I had one of the Sergeants set up a firing area about a mile from the camp.

The terrain around us was a monotonous plain of light ochre sand and sparse dry grass. Mild undulations made the desert look like an endless ocean of still waves. I loved the bare landscape. That was where I took squads on maneuvers to train the new troops to handle the hot sun and to cement the bond between the old-timers and the replacements.

There were not many distractions. We used several piles of rocks as shields behind which sentries would stand guard. We found out that sand vipers hid there during the day. So, periodically, soldiers poured gasoline on the rocks, lit a fire, and used their submachine guns to kill the escaping reptiles. That made it safer for the night watches, which was when the snakes searched for food.

There were firing practice sessions in addition to the walks in the hot sun. To pass the time, troops would also have scorpion-fights. They made a circle of fire with fuel, put two scorpions inside the circle and watched them fight each other.

Those distractions were not very civilized, but they helped provide a change from the daily boredom. Otherwise, the soldiers played cards or wrote to their families.

Free time was nice, but lonely. As much as I admired and respected my men, they and I could not be buddies. I had responsibility for their lives and they had to follow my orders when they were in harm's way.

The first supply truck brought mail. I received a letter from the Countess.

The news of the impending negotiations is probably good and bad for you. Good, because this horrible war might end soon, if the negotiations do not drag out too long; bad, because they come two years too late. The useless sacrifices you had to make and the atrocities you have witnessed will haunt you and be more difficult to accept under the new circumstances. I welcome the news because it tells me that you are less likely to be in danger. I am looking forward to your return.

Her letters always gave me news of the current mood in France, and gave me a sense of still belonging to the world I used to live in.

One day, a few weeks later, the elder sent for me in the middle of the day. I had no clue why he would do that.

I walked over to the camp to see him in the big tent I liked so much.

"Lieutenant, there's trouble in your army. Generals in Algiers want to fight the peace process and decided to rise against your government. I thought you would want to know."

"Thank you, Sir. This war is becoming more incomprehensible day after day. Whatever happens, I'll do my best not to let you down."

As I walked back to my tent, I wondered if I had made a promise I might not be able to keep. When I got to our little camp, I called the Sergeants and told them what I had just learned.

"How in the world did he hear about it?" One of the young Sergeants asked.

Sergeant Clavery said, "We call it the desert telephone. Somehow, news travels and it moves fast."

The next day, The Captain arrived unannounced in his jeep. He sat on the hood, and the Sergeants and I stood around him. He said,

"A few generals in Algiers have rebelled against the government. They are questioning the validity of the referendum and the decision to negotiate with the rebels."

I said, "We know, Sir. The old man told me yesterday. Don't ask me how he knew, but he did."

"These folks are good people. They are amazing. I'm afraid we are going to let them down. What a shame."

I replied, "I admire their way of life and their ability to survive in the desert. I talk to the old man now and then. I respect him and I like him."

Then the Captain said, "Why don't you guys sit down? This is important. There's great confusion in the military chain of command. There are two factions: the De Gaulle faction and the rebel generals. General Salan is their leader. The Colonel has started to receive conflicting orders from both sets of leaders. Some orders even go to the company or the platoon level."

"How would I get these orders, Sir?"

"They could come through your radio, or a special courier could bring you written instructions."

"I see."

"Now, I want you to know," the Captain continued, "our chain of command is not part of the upheaval. We are loyal to the French government, even though some of us may not agree with the decisions that were made. We only take orders from the Colonel. If you receive orders which are not from me or from my boss, do not execute them, no matter what the threat might be. Just let me know. You have a little over three weeks on this job. Stay put."

The Captain went back to Aflou.

Sergeant Clavery said, "What a mess. Now we have not only Arabs against French and Arabs against Arabs; now the war will also pit French against French."

"The good news is that here, we are isolated from the turmoil," I replied.

The Captain had given me a letter from Ms. Rooth. As usual, I rushed to open it. It was the reply to mine telling her about my losses in the last battles in the mountains. *Alain, I understand how you feel about your losses. First, I must say, selfishly, that you may feel guilty not to have been hit, but I'm relieved that you were not one of the casualties.*

I trust that I should not worry about the minor scratches you mentioned. I have renewed hopes that the end of the war is coming. It'll be hard for you. You'll feel betrayed. You were. But you can't change what is happening. Stay away from the controversy as much as you can. Write often and come back to see me soon. Love to you.

I always treasured her letters. It felt good to be reassured that she loved me. I cared for her even more deeply here where normalcy did not happen. Nicole mentioned in her forwarding letter that her brother Thierry came back to France. He had been selected to work on De Gaulle's program for nuclear weapons.

Alain, I'm not in support of constructing a French atomic bomb, but although Thierry has never seen combat in Algeria, I am relieved he is back safely in France. I hope the same will happen to you soon.

On the last day of our mission, the people in the raima treated us to a feast to celebrate my platoon. All my men and the ones from the Berber families had been invited. The main part of the meal was called a *mechoui*, a lamb roasted for days in the sand, protected by hot rocks. The cooks basted the meat frequently with a special Berber sauce. The barbecued delight was a welcome change for my soldiers. They enjoyed the celebration and got to talk with the young Berbers. They would have preferred to meet the women, but that was out of the question.

I felt sad to leave the friends I had made here, but another platoon would relieve us, so the Berbers would still be protected. At the end of the feast, the elder and I drank Arak from the same cup. Then, he kissed me on the forehead. I did the same with him. This ancient custom made Ramiz and me friends for our lifetime, the Berber way. I treasured that friendship.

The next day, the second platoon broke camp and headed back to our base not knowing what the news would be. Arab unrest? French unrest? Military confusion? All of the above?

Back in the old camp, I went to be briefed by the Captain on the political and military state of affairs.

Sitting behind the familiar table, the Captain greeted me. "Welcome back, Lieutenant. Sit down. I'm sure you're anxious to know what's going on. We have a bit of a messy situation here. Let me tell you what I know."

I leaned toward him, my elbows on my knees. "Thank you, Sir. I'm sure that things have changed since you last talked to me three weeks ago."

"They have indeed. The rebel generals took over the city of Algiers for a few days and threatened to take over Paris, too. A regiment of Foreign Legion paratroopers was ready to jump over the capital. A tank regiment loyal to the government moved to the city, supported by several infantry companies, so the jump never happened."

"Sir. The rebel generals must be insane. That was nonsense."

"Yes. Fortunately, no civil war started. These generals have no more official function now. Some were arrested, but others are still in Algiers, protected by troops which are loyal to them, but that's temporary."

"So, it's over?"

"Unfortunately, it's not. The rebel generals have inspired, and organized a secret organization. It's called OAS, for *Organisation Armée Secrète*. It is attracting the *Pieds Noirs*, the local civilians who do not want to leave and surrender their country to the Arabs. So, now we have another set of rebels. Most French people in Algeria are sympathizers; some are active members. They have vowed a campaign of terror, whatever that means."

"How's that going to impact my platoon and the job we have to do?"

"I'm not sure, Lieutenant."

I got up to leave. Then I looked at him in the eye. "Sir, will my troops have to fight the OAS?"

"No, Lieutenant. No one is talking about that."

I shook my head. "That's good. I could not order my platoon to fire at French people, even if they were part of that secret army."

I went back to my tent, called the sergeants and updated them on the new developments. They and I wondered what the French secret rebellious faction meant when they promised a campaign of terror.

A few days later, the Captain called the officers to his command post and briefed us on the first agreement reached in the Geneva independence talks with the dissidents.

He said, "All our offensive operations are to cease immediately."

"Is it some kind of a truce, a ceasefire?" The first platoon leader asked.

The Captain shook his head. "Not really. It's a one-way street; the Fellaghas can continue their attacks as before."

We could not believe it.

I was incensed. "Do you mean that they can come here, attack our camp and, until they fire at us, we can't fire at them?"

"That's right, Lieutenant."

"Sir, we should invite those idiots who do our negotiating in Geneva to come here. I'll have them sit for a few days and pee in their pants while they wait to be assaulted by the rebels. This agreement is ridiculous, outrageous and it puts the troops in grave danger."

"Hold your horses. The Colonel is coming later today. I'm sure he'll have ideas on how to cope with that. He's not going to let your people be assaulted without any defense."

The Colonel flew in early that afternoon. He gathered the officers and Senior Sergeants in the mess tent.

"Men, I understand that you have been told about the change in offensive operations. I'm sure you don't like the new rules of engagement. No more offensive operations. Any questions about that?"

"Sir, does that mean that we have to sit here and wait for the dissidents to fire at us before we can respond?"

"Lieutenant Alain, my plan is to establish a comfortable perimeter around all our installations and to consider any trespassing to be an attack. I'm not going to let you be sitting ducks."

"Thank you, Sir. Sorry if I'm a little hot about the new rule."

"You don't have to be sorry, we all are." The Colonel got up and hung a map on an easel he had brought with him. "Now there have been substantial troop reassignments which affect our regiment." He put a finger on a spot in northwestern Algeria. "The regiment will be moving to the Sidi Bel Abbes area."

Some were pleased to hear that. One of the lieutenants pointed at our tents. "No more canvas roof and no more sand. Hurrah."

Then another said, "Great! We'll be near a real town for a change."

The Colonel chuckled at the reaction of seasoned officers. "I'm glad you like the new orders, but it's not clear what our responsibilities will be in a more urban environment." He turned to me. "Lieutenant Alain, your job is the only one that has been identified precisely. In our new territory, there's an airstrip five miles east of Sidi Bel Abbes that the Fellaghas may attack because of the confusion caused by the movement of troops. Your assignment is the protection of the light reconnaissance planes and helicopters stationed on the base. You'll pack your gear immediately and get there by tomorrow morning. Once there, you're allowed to fire at anyone you think might intend to violate the perimeter of the base. I have written the order." He gave me the folded piece of paper which allowed me to use my weapons.

I got up. "Thank you, Sir. We are on our way."

"Hold on, Lieutenant. One more thing. You are due for an automatic promotion to first lieutenant in a couple of months. As a reward for the brilliant way you've led your platoon, I'm moving the date up. You turned down the medal I wanted to award you. You can't refuse this."

"Well, that's a nice surprise. Thank you, Sir."

"Don't thank me. I thank you for what you have done for the regiment and for your country. Congratulations, First Lieutenant Alain." He saluted me and gave me my new two-gold-bar insignia.

Captain Dufour shook my hand. "Well-deserved, Lieutenant. You earned it many times over." There were numerous handshakes and pats on my back to congratulate me.

The recognition pleased me greatly. Although not of a military mind, I felt honored and proud. I never aspired to be an elite infantry officer, but it felt good that military professionals recognized my contribution. My uncle would have been proud of me. I served well, like he did.

I went back to the platoon. I had to get it ready to leave as soon as the gear was packed. I assembled the men in front of my tent, and explained our new assignment to the men. They were all happy to get close to a larger town. When the Colonel had announced the move, Sergeant Clavery had jumped up and down. His wife lived in Sidi Bel Abbes; he would be able to go home at night when he did not have evening or night duty. I was so happy for my reliable number two. Courageous, experienced, always willing to help and to contribute, never complaining, he finally got a nice break.

The soldiers noticed my shiny new bars. A corporal asked, "Should we congratulate a new First Lieutenant?"

"Yes, Corporal, as of today."

The War Inside His Mind

All the troops cheered and shook my hand. It gave me goose bumps.

"Okay, guys. We have to move on the double. We have four hours to pack all our gear except the tents."

Later that day, I left Aflou, ready to face unknown challenges.

Sad, in a way, that I had to say good-bye forever to the Sahara I loved.

Chapter 18

Sidi Bel Abbes, Spring 1961

Having driven all night, the second platoon arrived in its new quarters early the next day. I could see the base five hundred feet from the road, in the middle of a barren plain. Beyond several rows of perfectly-spaced white one-story structures parallel to the road stood a couple of hangars, and then the airstrip. The sentries at the gate directed me to the command post where I met Major Rostand. I saluted him.

"Lieutenant Alain, reporting, Sir." I showed him the paper signed by the Colonel. "My orders are for my platoon to protect your planes and helicopters."

Red in the face and pudgy, the Major welcomed me. "I'm glad to have Special Forces guys here. My duty officer will show your men their barracks. You and I will get in my jeep and I'll show you the defense emplacements we have around the perimeter. You may decide to add new positions."

I asked Sergeant Clavery to come with me. He was the master at organizing sentries and guard duty. We went around the hangars and crossed the long air strip with its red and white windsock. The perimeter of the base had a six-foot fence with barbed wire on top which was located quite a distance from the air strip and from the tarmac where the planes were stationed; it gave my troops room to maneuver. The existing machine-gun emplacements and observation towers provided an adequate defense infrastructure.

The Sergeant placed soldiers in the towers, established a watch schedule, and a communication protocol, using field radios. The duty officer room, my new domain, had a great view of the airstrip and the fence. I liked the setup. I went to inspect the men's and the Sergeants' lodgings.

Well-kept and clean, they were much nicer than the tent camp we had in Aflou. My hosts assigned me a simple room, which had walls, a roof, a sink, and a shower at the end of the hall. I spent the day getting my bearings, walking the perimeter, and staring at the terrain beyond the fence. I talked to my troops; our morale was high. Protecting the base was a welcome assignment. In the evening I had dinner in the officers' mess with the base doctor and a few of the pilots. The food tasted a step up from the Aflou fare. Tired after the night drive, I turned in early. It seemed that being exhausted was my normal way of life.

The next day, the major called me to his office. I stood at attention across from his desk.

"Lieutenant, I have intelligence that legionnaires may want to use this facility to land planes to fly to Algiers. I want your men to prevent them from taking over my airbase."

I could hardly believe what I heard. "Sir, do you mean you want my men to fight the Legion?"

He raised his voice. "I want you to stop them from using my airstrip. That's an order."

Did he think he would intimidate me? "Sir, my orders are to protect the planes and helicopters. There are no provisions for me to have anything to do with controlling what troops use the base. Sorry, Sir. You can't change my orders. I don't report to you."

"We'll see about that."

"Yes, Sir."

I saluted him and left. I had no way to communicate with the Captain, who was in transit on his way here, so I called the Colonel in Tiaret. I told him what the Major said.

"I'm not sure what chain of command he is part of, but I don't believe I have to follow the Major's orders."

"You are correct. I'll take care of him. Imagine, fighting legionnaires. This guy must be nuts!"

The legionnaires never showed up and the Colonel must have made sure the Major understood my chain of command and my orders. He never mentioned the incident again.

In the next couple of weeks, the regiment established its headquarters in town. The various companies were stationed on or close to the airfield. Captain Dufour established his command post on the base too.

I had spent a week in Sidi Bel Abbes when Captain Dufour had sent me on a four-day leave a year ago—it seemed like a century. I liked the town and was glad to be back. The beautiful city with wide tree-lined avenues and a few open-park areas harbored the headquarters of the Foreign Legion. On the impeccably maintained grounds, a vast compound, with many stark-white buildings, housed two regiments of legionnaires and support companies.

Today, because of their support of the rebellion, most of them had been assigned to different areas of the country, and the garrison was a skeleton of what it used to be.

Members of the Organization Army Secrète hid in the European quarter. Next to it, the Arab section was made up of many narrow smelly alleys like the Algiers Casbah; the Algerians were nervous about their newly aroused European neighbors. Overall, the city did not remotely resemble a peaceful place. Both the Fellaghas and the OAS were active. Bombs would explode in markets, cafes, anywhere crowds would gather.

One day, my platoon received the order to set up a road block on the road from Sidi Bel Abbes to Mascara, not far from the air base. We had to search cars and trucks for hidden arms and ammunition entering and leaving the city. All cars, with Arabs or Europeans, driving in either direction, had to be stopped and inspected.

An old dusty Renault heading toward Mascara came to a halt at the checkpoint.

"Out of the car," one of my soldiers told the driver and the man sitting next to him. The two Arabs got out, fidgeted, and mumbled a few words to one another. They looked around as if trying to find an escape route. I was suspicious of what they were afraid of, so I gave the prearranged signal to move jeeps in front and back of the cars we suspected of doing illegal transport so they could not drive away.

Two Arabs, a man and a woman, were sitting in the back of the car. I opened the door on the man's side. He stiffened. He had a big scar on his right cheek, and he would not look at me. The woman wore the traditional Arab dress and veil. I could not see her face. She also had a light blue scarf on her thighs which hid her forearms and hands. Was she hiding a weapon? I remembered the little girl with the grenade, so I went carefully to her side of the car and opened the door.

I had to remove that piece of cloth from her hands and find out what she held. Ready to jump away, I stared at the blue piece of cloth, but I caught a glimpse of European shoes on her feet. Henna and sandals were the usual footwear of Arab women. I realized the woman was probably in the car against her will, and had made her shoes visible to me. The man had his left hand next to the woman. I was sure he had a weapon aimed at her, but I did not know what kind. It had to be a handgun or a knife; I hoped it was the latter which would be less lethal for her. I had to get him out of the car. I went back to his side of the Renault and casually called, "Corporal Bernard."

Being a Private, he knew something was up when I called him corporal. He came slowly, "Yes, Sir."

I moved next to the Arab; the door of the car was still wide open. All of a sudden, I grabbed the man's arm and pulled him away from the woman. Private Bernard, the strongest man on the platoon, knew why I had called him. He yanked the man out of the car and threw him onto the ground. He took away the knife the Arab had in his hand. It had blood on it. The other soldiers immobilized the driver and his buddy.

I ran to the other side. "Are you okay, Ma'am?" I removed the piece of cloth that hid her hands. They were tied. She bled from her side. I helped her out and cut the rope that was around her wrists.

"Do you have clothes underneath that Arab dress?"

"Yes," she nodded.

I removed the veil from her face and tore away the dress. I took her to my jeep. There was a combat first-aid kit on the floor. I got a piece of sterile gauze, put it on her bleeding hip, and pressed on it.

I told Sergeant Clavery, "Take over and watch these guys; I'll be back." I told the driver to rush to the base. There I helped the woman out of the jeep and into the infirmary. She kept shaking and repeating, "Thank you, thank you."

I explained the incident to the nurse on duty; she looked at the wound. "The cut is a few inches wide but it does not look too deep. She needs stitches." She took the woman into a room.

The doctor sewed up her wound and the nurse put a dressing on it to protect it. When that was done, she came out of the room, and I said, "I'm Lieutenant Alain, what is your name?"

"I'm Colette," she replied and she burst out in tears. She cried uncontrollably for a few minutes. The nurse held her in her arms. After a while she managed to say, haltingly, "I'm sorry. I'm so frightened. I thought I was on my way to a horrible death. I thank you so much."

"What happened, Colette? I need to know so I can put your kidnappers in jail. How did they get you? How did the trouble start?"

"I'm a teacher. My sister Edith picked me up at the school. We were thirsty, so we went to sit at the terrace of a café."

"How did you get in the car?"

"Three men were at a table behind ours. I was telling Edith that my son wanted to join the underground organization. I told her I thought he was too young, but that I thought of joining myself."

I was astonished. Colette had a young unwrinkled face, satin-like dark hair, a trim body, and a youthful attitude. "How old is your son? You are so young."

"You are so nice, I'm thirty-six. He's fifteen, almost sixteen. At seventeen, my sister's son is already part of the secret army. I didn't pay attention to the men behind us, but they heard me. One left the café and returned with the car. He stopped it by the curb in front of the café, and opened the back door. The two men, who had stayed behind, jumped out of their chairs; each grabbed me by an arm, lifted me, and pushed me into it. It hardly took a second. My sister could not do anything."

"Where did they take you?"

"They drove me to a house nearby. I could not tell you where it is; they had covered my head. There they put that Arab dress and the veil on me. They tied my hands and held me at knifepoint all the time. We got back into the car and drove away."

"Is that when you ran into the checkpoint?"

"Yes."

"Why didn't you tell me what was going on when we stopped the car?"

"When your men stopped us, the man next to me put a knife against my side and told me to keep my mouth shut or he would push it into my kidney."

I said, "I'm glad it worked out the way it did. I don't know what the army nurse will say, but I think you should stay here overnight. We'll go tell your sister you're safe and to take care of your son tonight."

"Thank you, Lieutenant." She gave me her address.

"I'll be back."

I went to the roadblock. The abductors were there, carefully guarded. I told Sergeant Clavery, "They took the woman because they heard her talking about joining the secret organization. They must be affiliated with the Fellaghas. Bring them to the gendarmes, tell them the story, and make sure they book them. Also send someone to tell her sister Edith that Colette is safe but will stay at the base infirmary tonight. Here's the address."

I went back to the base and stopped at the infirmary to see how Colette was doing. She was resting, but awake.

"Your abductors have been arrested, and your sister knows you're safe."

She put her head in her hands and said nothing for a minute. "I don't know how to thank you."

"Colette, tell me about yourself. What do you teach? Where do you live? Is it just your sister, yourself and your sons?"

"Lieutenant ... "

I interrupted her, "Colette. It's Alain, please."

"Alain, my son Jean Pierre and I live with my sister Edith. I teach French literature at the high school. I am a widow. The dissidents killed my husband in the first months of their insurgency four years ago. That's why I hate them. I never remarried."

"I'm sorry. Do you have other family in the area or in France?"

"None. It's just my son, my sister and her son François. She never lived with his father."

The army nurse came in and said, "Lieutenant, we are going to sedate this lady for the night. She needs to rest. She had a nasty cut and an even nastier scare. We'll discharge her tomorrow."

"That's a good idea. Colette, you need to take it easy. Tomorrow, we'll make sure it's safe and we'll take you home. Good night."

"Good night, Alain. Thank you for saving my life. I don't know what these guys were going to do to me."

"Try not to think about it."

The next day, I went to see Colette at the infirmary. She looked rested and her wound had not bothered her. With an escort of three soldiers, we went to a three-story building in a nice area of town.

I drove around and checked the nearby streets, looking for suspicious cars or persons. As a precaution, I told Colette to stay in the jeep while I made sure the apartment was safe. Her sister, a tall blond with a slim body, looked startled to see me.

"Is everything okay? Where's Colette? Why are you here?"

"Ma'am, I have your sister downstairs. I wanted to make sure there was no problem," I told her.

She frowned. "Everything is fine. Is Colette all right?"

"Yes, Ma'am," I replied. "I'll go get her."

The frown disappeared, a smile lit her face, and she said, "Thank you for sending someone last night to tell me she had been rescued."

"The nurse wanted to keep her overnight."

I went down and told Colette, "The coast is clear."

I helped her up. The reunion between the two sisters was touching. They embraced and cried. "I'm so relieved nothing bad happened to you," Edith said.

I had to leave. "Good bye, Colette, take care of that wound. I'll be in touch."

One afternoon, while I was cleaning my Thompson, Sergeant Clavery came to my office. "Lieutenant. It may be against the military rules of etiquette, but I would like you to come home with me tonight, meet my wife and taste her cooking."

I would never accept such an invitation from any of the younger men in the platoon, but I felt that getting to know the Sergeant's family would not affect the military relationship we had. I liked and trusted him. "Sergeant, as you know, I'm not big on army protocol. I would be delighted to meet her, and a home-cooked meal sounds really good."

That night, I met Madame Clavery in their modest one-story house on the edge of the European area. She was a beautiful Moroccan woman. Her light tan skin framed her almost mysterious, deep dark eyes. Little wrinkles on the sides of her mouth and eyes showed a happy person who smiled a lot. She had prepared a succulent *tagine*, with vegetables, chicken and exotic spices. Sitting on cushions, we ate it with couscous, the traditional local grain. She was intimidated at first, but I got her to relax.

"Lieutenant, my husband told me all about you. He's happy to be under your leadership."

"Madame, your husband is the one who gave me the tools to do my job. He's the one who is terrific and competent. I'm not a career officer, I'm just passing through. Believe it or not, I used to be a charming and peaceful young man, before this war."

"You are still young," she teased me.

I had to laugh. "You have to tell me how you cook the tagine and the couscous. It's fantastic."

She showed me the spices she used: turmeric, ginger, saffron and the spicy sauce, harrissa. "Come back any time. I love anybody who enjoys my cooking."

It was nice to see the gentle side of the fierce warrior I fought alongside for so many months.

Going back to the base, I thought about Colette. She was more mature than the women I had met before, but I yearned to see her again. I wanted to stroke her shiny black hair and to look into her almond-shaped eyes. I wanted to find out all about her. Having lost her husband to the war, it did not surprise me that she wanted to join the secret organization, but she had almost paid for it with her life.

One morning, I received a message from Colette. Happy to hear from her, I tore open the envelope. *Alain, I'm well now. My stitches are out. I've been thinking about you. I will be forever grateful to you for saving my life, but there is more than that. I want to see you. Please come when you can.*

Late that afternoon, I went to her place. I met her son, Jean Pierre, a good-looking kid with short black hair and a nice smile. Her sister, Edith was there too. Her son was in trouble with the law. He had been too open about having joined the secret army and soon after arrested. He was now in the hands of the government, worrisome, but better than those of the dissidents.

"Alain, I'm so glad you're here," Colette said, reaching for my hands.

"Thank you for asking me to come. Would you like to go out, take a walk, and have dinner? I'm sure you know a nice place."

"Yes, I do, Alain. Let's go."

We had a great time. We talked nonstop, about the war, France, Algeria, and its uncertain future. I liked Colette and I felt she liked me. After a few similar nights, when I took her home she said, "Alain, I've been thinking a lot about you since that fateful day. I want to know you better."

"I want to know you better too. I want to hold you in my arms and make love to you."

"That's what I want too. We must have time by ourselves."

"I have to go back to the base tonight. I'm the duty officer. I'll ask the Captain for a couple days' leave. We can go some place. Is there anywhere special you'd want to go?"

"I'd like to go to Algiers."

"That would be wonderful. I'll let you know what he says. My job here is not that demanding. I'll let you know tomorrow."

I took her home and kissed her goodnight. That long kiss felt good.

I asked the Captain the next day, "Sir. I would like to go on leave for two or three days."

"You sure deserve a break. When and where do you want to go?"

"Algiers, as soon as it is practical for you."

"You can go the day after tomorrow. I'll give you passes for the train. What's her name?"

I laughed. "How did you guess?"

"I have heard about the woman you rescued. Is she the one?"

"Yes, Sir."

Colette and I took the train to Algiers. I vaguely remembered the city from when I landed in North Africa, almost two years ago. The town seemed to be under siege. There were armed troops everywhere. I only had my hand gun and knife on me, but I did not let that bother me.

"I'm not sure it was such a good idea to come here," Colette said, getting closer to me.

"Let's get settled. We'll be fine."

We checked into a hotel and got a nice quiet room. As we walked in, we heard explosions and rifle fire. From the window I could see smoke, soldiers and civilians running. I closed the curtains.

"So much for visiting the town, but we don't have to go out," I said as I took her in my arms.

"No, we don't." She gave me a long kiss, and we did not go out of the hotel for two days, except for meals. We talked and made love.

She told me about her having never forgiven the dissidents for the death of her husband.

"I feel guilty for my hatred, but I can't help it. My son learned to hate from me. Now, because of that, I fear that he'll get in trouble like his cousin. It feels nice to be with you. You don't have the heritage that all of us have."

I told her about some of the atrocities I had witnessed without too many details and about the men I had lost. "I used to be a nice easy-going guy. I don't like what the war has done to me."

"Alain, I love who you are now. If you had not been that tough officer, I would be dead after unspeakable torments."

She was right. It was not all that bad to be a crusty old warrior.

The day before we had to return to reality, we met a friend of Edith's, a nice man in his mid-fifties who loved Algeria.

He said to us, "My hope is that the Geneva negotiations will end with a compromise which will let us stay here and cooperate with the Arabs to construct a strong, healthy country." He turned to me. "Young men like you could come and help lead construction and industry projects."

"That would be great. I hope you are right about the outcome of the Geneva talks," I replied.

Colette and I went back to Sidi Bel Abbes. My feelings for her had soared. She was a strong, intelligent woman. Her life in Algeria had not been easy and she was now apprehensive about the outcome of the peace talks. I tried to show her the downside of joining the secret organization, but she would have to do what she thought was right for her.

I went to sleep; Colette was not in my arms, but she was in my thoughts.

Chapter 19

When I woke up the next day, I felt remote from the war. For the second time in about two years, I had been away from my platoon for four days, and Colette had come into my life. I had to tell Ms. Rooth about her.

She is eleven years older than I am, but that is of no consequence to me; she is smart, strong, loving and beautiful. Some say that during wars people get into relationships hastily because the future is uncertain. It happened to us, and I am happy it did. With the stress of combat easing up, and with Colette's love and support, I'm no longer solely waging war. I now have a purpose in life.

One morning, a few days after I got back, the Captain called me to his office. The tall man stood looking out the window, his red hair brightened by the rising sun. He turned to me when I walked in. "Fellaghas have been active in the mountains west of Sidi Bel Abbes. They've attacked trucks and cars and killed or captured innocent civilians." The Captain handed me a piece of paper. "The Colonel wants to eliminate them."

The orders were for me. Puzzled, I looked at the Captain and asked, "Isn't it against the new rules of engagement?"

The Captain sat at his desk and smiled. "It seems to me it is, but he wants to re-open the road to Ain Temouchent. The Colonel told me over the phone that because the rebels will attack you when you open the road, it'll not be an offensive operation, it'll be a defensive strike."

I looked at the piece of paper I held in my hand. "Well, he's the boss; I have written orders." I shrugged. "I've done it many times."

"Lieutenant, the terrain is treacherous. It's a risky mission, and it needs to be successful; that's why he called on you. Also, the Colonel would prefer not to have any casualties on our side. There would be fewer explanations for him to have to give his line of command."

The War Inside His Mind

It was my turn to smile. "I see. I'll do my best, Sir."

Later that day, the second platoon rode to the beginning of the dangerous stretch of road. A military transport unit had stopped traffic to let me clear the difficult passage. Trucks and cars were lined up, waiting. Many cheered us when we went by.

The entrance to the canyon looked indeed unwelcoming. At the bottom of high vertical mountain walls, on the right and the left of the road, were thirty- to fifty-foot-wide strips of shrubbery separating the cliffs from the roadway; covered with an undergrowth of bushes and trees around huge rocks, they seemed to be the ideal environment for an ambush.

My men took position on both sides of the road to sweep through the whole width of the underbrush so as not to miss any insurgent. It was hard to negotiate the terrain, and risky to look under trees and shrubs, and they had to proceed slowly. The first squad and I stayed on the asphalt and had to go at their pace; that increased the danger for us. We kept the safety of our weapons, ready to fire. Our trucks followed at a distance.

After two or three miles, an Arab bounced out of the bushes on the right, less than eighty yards in front of me, his AK47 aimed in my direction. I threw myself on the ground as he squeezed the trigger. A couple of bullets went by my head. Then I heard the click of the hammer; his weapon had jammed. My soldiers and I returned fire. He crumpled. Three rebels who came out from behind the same bush were caught in our returning fire before they could use their weapons. They all fell.

I put my head down on the sand and closed my eyes for a moment, relishing the warm smell of the dry dirt. I should be dead. AK47s were not always the most accurate weapons, but they were reliable and usually did not jam. At that distance, at least one bullet would have hit me. This was a wake-up call. I was still in a war, and far from being out of danger.

I sprang up and, with the men of the first squad, rushed toward the area the rebels had come out of. There the terrain became more open. When we got closer, a group of ten or so Fellaghas took off and ran away. The troops fired. Most of the fleeing Arabs were hit and stumbled; the last two kept on running. I continued the pursuit. They disappeared into a trail going away from the road on the right. By the time we got to the beginning of the narrow path, they were no longer in sight. The tortuous canyon appeared to be twisty and full of bushes and rocks.

A Sergeant asked me, "Do you want me to go after them, Sir?"

"No. They'll be impossible to find. They could be hiding behind a rock, waiting to take you down. It'd be an easy ambush for them to set up. Let them go." I remembered that the Colonel did not want any casualties.

Three of the men lying on the road were wounded but still alive. My soldiers had disarmed them. Sergeant Clavery asked, "Are there more rebels waiting for us down the road?"

"Find out for yourself," one of them snapped back and spat.

I ignored him; I would not have believed him anyway, whether he had said yes or no.

The trucks picked up the four dead dissidents who had first fired at me and came to load the remaining rebels. The rest of the platoon had continued their search through the bushes and caught up with me. I had not reached the end of the canyon, so I had to resume the sweep.

"There are probably no more rebels ahead of us, but we've got to finish the job. Resume your positions. Let's go, and keep your eyes open."

We continued down the road until it widened and the vertical cliffs disappeared. The dangerous gorge was behind me. I stopped the platoon. The soldiers stood on the side of the road, smoking and joking with one another to relieve the tension of the past hours. I had a big scare, but neither I nor any of my soldiers had been hit.

I radioed the Captain, "Sir. Mission accomplished. No casualties. We annihilated over a dozen rebels. The road is clear. The civilians can drive through."

"Good job, Lieutenant. Let the convoy go by and come back to the base. I'll brief the Colonel."

Far from tranquil, the town of Sidi Bel Abbes experienced much violence; assassinations, abductions, and explosions from bombs left in populous places; the Arab dissidents put them near European shops and markets, and the European rebels left them in Arab bazaars. The two factions were at each others' throats.

I spent many evenings with Colette but I always went back to the base before midnight. When I left her apartment, I had to walk a few blocks to an army post where I could get a jeep to drive me back. One day, one of my Sergeants who drove me to her place offered to pick me up at her building. "Sir, the town is becoming more dangerous, especially at night. You should have an escort. You don't want to get in trouble."

"Thank you, Sergeant. I'll be all right. I have my knife and my handgun. Also, there are police and gendarmes patrols around."

One night, when I walked my usual route, I heard running footsteps behind me. I quickly turned around and saw an Arab rushing toward me, his right arm over his head, a knife in his hand, ready to plunge it into my back.

I faced him, braced myself on my left leg, and raised my two arms crossed to block his down thrust. The blow had such force that my wrists almost collapsed, and the knife came close to my face. I grabbed and twisted the hand with the knife.

I felt a sharp pain; the blade must have cut into my hand.

He struggled, breathing hard. Still anchored on my left leg, I hit him in the groin with my right knee. He froze and dropped his weapon.

I kicked him in the knee. His legs buckled; he leaned backward.

I got a glimpse of another man running at me.

With my fingers taut and extended, I aimed at his throat, exactly where I had been trained to hit. I struck him as hard as I could with the side of my right hand. He fell down on his back.

I yelled, "Police!" and turned toward the other guy.

The second dissident was getting close. My right hand hurt and bled profusely, but I was able to grab my knife, and I threw it at him.

The blade buried itself into his chest. The man stopped and screamed. He tried to pull it out. But he could not.

Unsteady, but still standing, he moved his hand toward his pocket. I drew my pistol with my bloody hand and fired a shot at his leg. He fell.

A patrol of gendarmes, with khaki fatigues and their traditional black kepis, ran toward me.

"Are you okay, Lieutenant?" One of them asked.

"He has blood all over his uniform," another one said.

I shook my head. "I'm okay. It's a couple of cuts on my hand."

Out of breath, taut, almost shaking, I pointed at the man I had just shot. "I know this guy with the scar on his cheek. I stopped him at a checkpoint and sent him to jail a few weeks ago. I guess he must have been released and wanted revenge. I don't know if he's alive, but if he is, he must be put away for a long time."

One of the men went to look at Colette's abductor and kicked his wounded leg. Although semi-conscious, he groaned.

The gendarme smiled at me. "He's got your knife in his chest, and the bullet broke his upper leg. He won't be back roaming the streets for a while."

I always hated the idea of a fight with any kind of knife. When I went through special-forces training, as we repeated the moves over and over, the Sergeant instructor told me that to struggle with a man with a blade in his hand was not for the fainthearted. "If you have to get into that kind of a fight, you will be grateful for these drills," he said. Today I thanked him as I remembered those very words. How right he was.

The head of the patrol checked the other rebel, and turned his head, his eyes riveted to me, his mouth open in disbelief. He said, "This one's dead."

I was stunned. I remembered learning from the same instructor where to hit the throat of an enemy to collapse the wind pipe and cause loss of consciousness or death, but I could not believe I just killed a man with my bare hands.

"Thanks for the help, guys," I said.

"You took care of business yourself, Lieutenant." One gendarme pulled my knife out of the Arab's chest, put a bandage on the wound, and wiped the blood off the blade on the man's shirt.

"Here's your knife and a dressing to stop the bleeding from your hand. You should have it taken care of. Do you need a ride to the base?"

"Yes. I do. Please take me to the army post. They'll take me home."

I went straight to the infirmary. The nurse on duty looked at my hand. "What did you do? You have nasty cuts on the palm and on the tips of the three middle fingers."

I told her about the attack. She stopped the bleeding and protected the wounds. She bandaged each of my fingers separately so I could squeeze the trigger of my Thompson.

She put her hand on my shoulder. "You're all fixed up. You can go back to war now, but you should stop playing with knives."

The War Inside His Mind

"I promise. They're too sharp for me. Thank you for your help. I have to go on duty now."

She shook her head, her eyes looking up at the ceiling. "Lieutenant, with all due respect, your clothes are full of blood. Before you go, how about changing into clean ones?"

"Yes, Ma'am."

The Captain's office s light was on, so I went in to see him.

From behind his desk he looked at the bandages. "What did you do to your hand?" He asked, frowning.

I told him what happened.

"You took care of two guys with knives by yourself?"

"Yes, Sir. I knew what to do, thanks to the Special Forces Sergeants."

"From now on, you will get a jeep with a couple of soldiers to drive you back late at night."

"One of my Sergeants suggested that a couple of days ago. I thought I was safe enough walking to the command post."

"You should have listened to him."

"Sir, these guys were Colette's abductors."

"How do you know?"

"I recognize the one with a scar on his face. I saved her from him. I'm sure he'd have gone after her once they killed me."

"Well, no more walking by yourself at night. It's an order."

"Yes, Sir. Hand-to-hand combat is not my favorite sport. I've learned my lesson."

"Do you want me to relieve you from duty?"

"No, Sir, it's not necessary. I'm so wired up; I would not be able to sleep anyway."

I drove around the perimeter to check on the sentries and went to my night post. As I got back to my desk, I thought about the last couple of hours. Short but intense, tonight's fight had been more extreme and more scary than any of my battles with rifles, submachine guns or grenades. I had survived, but it was sobering to realize how fierce and deadly I had become. It bothered me to have killed a man with a single chop to the throat.

Was it right to do what I did? Could I have used a little less vigor and just knocked him unconscious? Was I right to shoot the other man? Although he was still standing, I didn't know if he was reaching for a gun. Was he not incapacitated enough with my knife in his chest? I did not know. *Did I react too strongly? Have I become too violent, too ruthless?* I had no answers to any of these questions, but if the same attack had taken place a few months ago, I would have been killed.

However frightening the evening, I had conquered my fear of knives forever. The thought of having to fight with one would no longer haunt me. After tonight, nothing and no one could scare me.

I looked at my knife. It had become my most trusted friend.

The next evening, I went to see Collette. The minute she opened her door, she saw my bandages and asked, "What happened to your hand? You are hurt."

"It's not bad." I told her about the night before. She shivered at the thought of the Arab stalking her.

"I owe you my life once more," she exclaimed. She had tears in her eyes. She hugged me tight and kissed me hard.

My eyes were also teary. I told her, "You know, when I was a kid I used my knowledge and my skills to help my friends. Now, I have many tools to protect the lives of the people I love. You are number one on the list."

We went out to eat at one of our favorite places, a one-room restaurant with three tables. Kay, the cook, server and owner of the little eatery, was from Indochina. She had come here with a Sergeant from the Legion. He was stationed somewhere near Aïn Sefra in the northwestern Sahara. She cooked *nems*, deep-fried rolls of ground meat, onions, mint and cilantro, wrapped in rice paper. One ate them rolled up with fresh mint in lettuce leaves and dipped into *nuoc man,* a tangy fish sauce.

Over dinner, Colette and I talked. I shared with her my worry about my being too tough. Across the little table, she gently took my wounded hand in hers and said, "Well, it's because you are so tough that you only have these cuts in your hand, instead of a knife in your back. It's because you are so tough that we are both alive. It's a cruel war. The ones who are the most fit and the most aggressive will be the ones who survive."

As I went back to the base in the jeep the Captain ordered me to use, I thought Colette was right. We were both alive because of the man I had become. I loved her and she loved me. Nothing else much mattered.

Because of the bombs placed in crowded areas, some days we were ordered to patrol the European market. That meant moving amid shoppers who were buying food. We carried our submachine guns with the safety on and looked for suspicious people and abandoned packages. But if anything happened, we were in the middle of civilians and could not react forcefully. We may have been a deterrent to potential bombers, but we were there only to make the people feel safer. There was little we could do. We all hated that nerve-racking kind of duty. Fortunately, we never were there when a bomb went off.

One day, I received one of the infrequent letters from my mother. She said: *I am sad today. Your brother has left for the army. He'll go through basic training in France, and then he'll be sent to Germany with the French NATO contingent. I am so glad you are in Algeria. Because you are, he won't have to go there. I hope you continue to be well.*

It was good that my brother would not have to come to this crazy place. He was shy and scared of his own shadow. That would have been dangerous for him, but the letter made me angry. How could my mother be happy I was in Algeria? She had no idea how dangerous my life was, day-in and day-out. Obviously, she did not care.

I suspected for a long time that my brother was not my father's son. She treated Eric like a love child, catering to his every want and need. I felt good that she found some happiness in life, while having to withstand the nasty moods of my father. Yet I was her son too, but my brother seemed to be the only one she worried about? Her neglect and indifference were not new to me, but it still hurt.

Chapter 20

Unlike the note from my mother, the letter I received from Ms. Rooth's was upbeat.

You are right. In times of war, life goes much faster. People live for the present, not knowing what the next day will bring. It's wonderful that you have let yourself fall in love with Colette. She makes you happy, and I love her for that. But the war is not over. Don't let your guard down.

In early November, Captain Dufour called me to his office. He sat behind his worn wooden table with a single piece of paper on it.

"Please sit down, Lieutenant." With a beaming smile lighting up his rugged face, he took the letter in his hand and waved it. "I've received word that you'll be discharged from the army one hundred days from today. Congratulations."

He got up, shook my hand from beyond the desk, and sat down again, still holding the letter.

I knew the date of my discharge would be announced soon, but it hit me right in my heart. I felt like shouting *it finally happened*. I smiled. "Thanks for the good news, Sir." I thought for a few seconds. "I'll have been in uniform for just over thirty-two months."

The Captain sat up in his chair. "Now I know you'd prefer to skip the next conversation, but I've been ordered to have it with you. So you have to listen."

"Yes, Sir."

He leaned forward and read, "On behalf of the French army command, I'm urging you to re-enlist and become a career officer. You have an impeccable military record. Your promotion to the rank of captain would come within a year, and your advancement will be swift. Your chances of becoming a general before the age of forty, which is almost unheard of, are very high. What do you say?"

"Sir, I've served my country; I've done the best I could for my men, for you, and for the Colonel. I'm not sure I've done the best for me. It'll be hard to become a civilian again, but that's what I want to do. I don't want a military career."

"I understand, and I'm not surprised. I thank you for what you have done; you led your platoon brilliantly."

"I'll never be the peaceful Alain you met months ago in Mascara."

With a kind smile, the Captain shook his head. "Whatever you may think, you're still a wonderful human being. You have great leadership ability and unshakable courage. The man you are today has a bright future."

I shrugged. "I hope you're right. I guess in some ways, I grew up."

Visibly relieved that the matter of re-enlisting was now put to bed, he leaned back and relaxed. "We're done with the official business, but I want to personally thank you for your accomplishments. Your platoon has put over three-hundred-and-fifty rebels out of commission, most of them prisoners. You made the Colonel and the regiment look good, not to mention myself and the company."

I cringed. "I'm not too proud of that number." I fidgeted on my chair. "Sir, should I be worried that my record could fall into the hands of insurgents? There are many of them in France. They may want revenge."

He nodded. "I know the rebels had a price on your head in Mascara, but it's unlikely they could link you to that number, but I'll see if I can make it difficult for anyone to track you down." He paused for a moment. "It would not be within regulations, but you are done with the military. I might be able to blur your record, and you don't need to know how. I'll also minimize your exposure to what now has turned into a civil war. I want you to go home in one piece."

"Yes, Sir. Now it's my turn to thank you. I'm proud of the way I served my country, like my uncle did. But I survived because of your leadership and your guidance."

I got up. The Captain raised his hand. "One last thing before you leave; the Colonel sends his thanks and congratulations too. He can't do it personally. He's on his way to France. The brass wants to review his interpretation of the definition of non-offensive operations. They think that, although successful, your last opening of that road might not have quite fit their standard of a defensive action."

"I'm sorry that I won't get a chance to shake his hand. He's a great guy."

"He told me that he thought you were too, but he may be back."

That night, sitting in our favorite Vietnamese eatery, I told Colette about the date of my release from the army. "The nightmare is almost over. We'll be going to France. I'll get a job, and you'll teach literature wherever we are. We'll start our life away from this madness."

A smile brightened her whole face. "I can't wait." She tenderly touched my cheek. "Remember the man we talked to in Algiers? You may also consider getting a job in Algeria. He could help us find one. But, whatever happens, we'll be together some place. I'll go wherever you want to be."

"I think we would be happier in a more peaceful place where the sun shines, and we can hike mountains. The most important thing is to get you and your son Jean Pierre out of Sidi Bel Abbes."

Over two years ago, when I was about to leave France for Algeria, Madame De Sèvres had asked me to tell her the date of my release from the army as soon as I knew it. I remembered the scene vividly.

I was sitting on one of the precious blue-velvet-covered Louis XIV chairs in her elegant parlor, when she came next to me and took my hand in hers. "Alain, I am sad you have to go fight that war, but when you come back, because you will, you'll need a job, and you'll need a car."

"I'm not worried about finding work. The alumni association is quite active. Hopefully whenever I'm discharged, the job market will be wide open. As far as a car is concerned, I doubt that a lieutenant pay will let me save enough to afford one. I'll have to manage without it."

She squeezed my hand."That's where I come in. It's going to be a long time from now, but write to me as soon as you know when you'll be released. It'll give me enough time to have a car waiting for you."

Astounded, I raised my eyebrows. "You don't have to do that."

She smiled. "Do you believe your uncle Raymond would have gotten you a car?"

I thought about it for a second. "He probably would have."

"Well, Alain, I am stepping into his shoes."

I could hardly believe it. "I don't know how to thank you, Madame." I felt a surge of affection for her. I stood up. "You have become so dear to me in the past year. I wish you were my mother."

She hugged me. "I grew very fond of you and wish you were my son. Your uncle told me you were special. You are, indeed."

I could only say, "I am so grateful for your love and support."

The countess had written to me often. I always welcome news from her; it brought some normalcy into my life. Now that I knew the date I would be back in France, I wrote to her, as she requested. *I'm not sure how my reentry into a normal life will be and where I'll go next. I feel uneasy about your buying a car for me, but, if you still want to do it, I'd be eternally grateful. I must tell you I am no longer the gentle and peaceful young man you used to know. I have done and seen terrible things. I'm not sure I deserve anything.*

By return mail, the countess wrote, *It pains me to hear you talk like you did about yourself. You have done a great service to this country, however ungrateful you will find it when you are back. My promise to you stands. Your uncle Raymond would have wanted me to do that. He would have welcomed you with open arms. I will. You deserve thanks, encouragement, and love. See you soon.*

My eyes moistened. I was touched by her love for me and by her loyalty to my uncle.

The unrest increased daily. The cowardly bombing continued. One day in January, Arabs took to the streets and burned some French businesses. Toward the end of the month, the rebels planned another such demonstration. My company was sent to protect property in the European quarter. The people who lived there had been transported to the Foreign Legion compound where they would be safe. My platoon was assigned to control one of the avenues leading to the area. We were to stop the Arabs from ransacking properties.

I had my platoon lined up, two deep. I stood in front of them. "Everyone's Thompson must have the safety on. Under no circumstance will you fire on civilians, however restless and threatening they may be. The only time you will open fire will be if I give the order and then shoot above the people's heads. If anyone tries to go through your ranks, push back with the butts of your weapons, your boots and your fists. Do not kill anybody."

I knew that if we shot one Arab, it would mean mayhem, hundreds dead, including most of the second platoon. European assets were not worth that. Facing the unruly crowd of Arab men, some shaking their fists, some waving knives, all shouting in Arabic, we spent the whole day on that street. Arab women came to the front of the crowd and did their ululation. The endless, high-pitched, loud shriek they did with their tongues frayed our nerves. It was unsettling, but nothing happened. No one attempted to cross our line.

After witnessing the hatred of the Arab people, I wondered how safe Colette and Jean Pierre would be until they came to join me in France. I asked the Captain if there was any way for me to take the two of them on the ship with me.

"Lieutenant, I wish I could say yes, but it's a troop transport. There's no emergency evacuation plan or order. I'm sorry."

The answer did not surprise me, but I thought it didn't hurt to ask.

A couple of weeks later, the Captain told me the Colonel wanted to see me."

"Is he back from France?"

"I understand he is on his way to a new assignment. He might tell you what it is."

I went to the Colonel's office. "Welcome back, Sir."

"Lieutenant, I am on my way back to France. Your last opening of the road has been deemed legal, and I have been exonerated. That is mainly because you did it successfully, saved civilian lives with no infantry casualties. I have to thank you for that."

"Those were your orders if I remember."

"Yes, but it resulted from your perfect execution. My new job is to teach new cadets how to fight guerilla warfare at Saint Cyr, the French military academy. I plan to take pages from your book; you were my most effective platoon leader. But the reason for asking you to come is to thank you for your leading role in my regiment." He looked at me as if he was not sure if he wanted to say what was on his mind. Then, he nodded and smiled.

"There is one more thought I want to share with you. The last thirty-three months have been hell for you, and you have performed impeccably. I know it, Dufour knows it and your soldiers know it. Be proud of your accomplishments. Although you might find it hard to believe, your country thanks you. You will never know it when you're back in France, but your soldiers, your commanders, and the people you have saved and protected are the ones who will be forever grateful to you and the three years of your life you gave to your country."

"Sir. I will treasure your words for the rest of my life."

"Lieutenant, I wish you the best. I have no doubt you will be brilliant in whatever you do."

He got up and shook my hand.

"Thank you, Sir; and good luck to you also."

I went back to see the Captain, who thought that the Colonel's new assignment was a significant step up, and that he was on his way to becoming a general.

My last day in Algeria finally came. I saw Colette the night before I left for Oran where I would board the ship. We were heart-broken. Tears flowing, we hugged and kissed, but I had to go. "I'll write to tell you where I am. We'll be together in a few days. You better start packing," I told her with a forced smile.

The next morning, shortly after an extraordinarily bright sunrise, Sergeant Clavery assembled the platoon on the base parade grounds, next to the flying French colors. The men looked smart with their crisply pressed uniforms. As I had on my first day in Mascara, I saluted them. They presented arms in response. Almost choking, I looked every single man in the eye.

I took a deep breath. "Men, I have to say good-bye. It has been an honor to serve with you. Thank you for your sacrifice, for your courage, and for the accomplishments the platoon made. The years we spent together are etched in our minds, never to be forgotten. The war is coming to an end, and you'll soon be home. Hold your heads high. You did well. I am proud of you."

I released the troops, and against normal protocol, went to shake hands with every soldier. For so many months, the Captain and the men in my platoon had been my universe. Through many intense and dangerous moments, we trusted each other with our lives; yet I would never see any of them again.

I had to leave Sergeant Clavery. "Sergeant, I thank you for your help and support over the past years. You are a tough soldier and a great guy. I worry about what'll happen to you when this war ends."

"Sir, I'm retiring from the army in two months. I'll go to Morocco where my wife and I are from. We have family and a little farm to go back to. We'll be all right."

He saluted me. "Goodbye, Sir. Have a great life."

I saluted him back. "Best of luck to you and to your wife, Sergeant. I'll never forget you." I shook his hand warmly and went to the Captain's office.

Bidding good-bye to the man I worked for in the last two-and-a-half years turned to be an emotional moment for both of us. Neither of us could hardly talk.

"Good-bye, Sir. Thank you for everything."

He got up "Good-bye, Lieutenant."

There was much we could have said to each other, but the only words which came out were 'Best of luck till the end of the war, Sir.' He saluted me and for the last time I returned his salute, and turned away.

Incredibly enough, I was more sad to leave the army than I would have thought possible. It marked the end of a solid bond which helped us - officers, sergeants, and soldiers - bear the burden of fighting and risking our lives together every day.

A sergeant drove me in a jeep to Oran where I was going to be discharged. When I got to the armory on the port's grounds, I left all my weapons, except my knife – the symbol of my ability to survive. It saved my life as well as Colette's and would only be a defensive weapon in my hands. I swore to myself I would never hold a gun, pull a trigger, or aim any kind of firearm at any being, man or animal ever again.

I boarded the ship.

I watched the coastline disappear in the setting dusk. This was good-bye to Algeria. I had dreamt about that day for a long time. I hated the war, not only for the senseless killings, but for the destruction of lives and hopes of innocent civilians. I hated what the war did to the rebels and to us, turning all into barbarians in spite of themselves. I still hated the Fellaghas for what they did to so many defenseless victims. But I loved the country where I discovered nature in its rawest form, the unending arid ranges of the Atlas Mountains, the fascinating emptiness of the Sahara, and the boundless starry sky.

Most importantly, I had met Colette and found out how deep and wonderful love could be.

The ship rolled and pitched as soon as we got out of the harbor. I was not seasick, so I went to the first-class dining room. I met a lieutenant who had been discharged like me. Sitting in comfortable chairs anchored to the floor, the two of us had a nice dinner of veal Marsala, roasted potatoes and spinach, with an excellent red Burgundy. The Lieutenant was a doctor who spent his military service treating wounded soldiers in the Oran military hospital. He knew Chantal and worked with her at times. He talked about her. "She ran the hospital nurses with an iron hand. She also was tough on the doctors, if she thought they were not doing enough for her patients. She was the most competent and dedicated one in the hospital. She had deep compassion for the men she cared for. She personally handled the most seriously wounded."

When the ship got to Marseille, the doctor and I decided to share a taxi to go to the train station. I was going to Paris, he to Toulouse. When we got there, we got out of the cab. I was ready to pay the fare when the driver, a North African, said that each of us had to pay the amount on the meter. He would get double what he was entitled to. Local people were known to try scams of all kinds. The driver reminded me of the rebels I fought. I saw hatred for me in his eyes. I stared at him and said, "There is only one fare to be paid."

"No, this is a new rule for the people from the ships."

I grabbed my knife from my arm sheath, and pointed it at his face. "You don't make sense to me. Tell me more about the new rule."

Eyes almost out of their sockets, his mouth opened wide, he stared in horror at the knife, then at me. He shook his head and drove away hurriedly with no money at all. I stood on the curb, feeling like a fool. I had meant to pay him. I put the knife back in its holster. So much for it being solely a defensive weapon.

The doctor looked at me and shook his head. "This is not the way things work on this side of the Mediterranean."

"I know. I'm sorry."

I got on the train to Paris. I had survived the war. Here, in France, the person I was in North Africa could not exist. Despite the uniform I wore, I was no longer Lieutenant Alain, nor was I the Alain who had left Paris in nineteen-fifty-nine. I was a changed man.

I had to find out who I really was.

The War Inside His Mind

Chapter 21

France, March 1962

Many soldiers, who like me, had been discharged from the military, rode the train to Paris. Most looked happy, returning home to a loving family, a wife, a fiancée or a lover. I was not. My home would be where Colette and I would live.

Since General De Gaulle had turned his back on the war, I anticipated my dad would have contempt for my service in Algeria. In spite of that, I hoped I could stay at my parents' place for a few days until I got myself organized. My mom would probably say she was glad to see me, but she would be more concerned about my brother who was still stationed in Germany. My school buddy Thierry and his sister Nicole were the only friends I knew to be in Paris. He had seen no action during the war. I was sure the two of them had not changed much. I knew I had.

The train arrived in the *Gare De Lyon*, in the early morning; I left the station and walked around for a while. I was back in Paris, the city I knew best, the city I loved. I had been longing for that moment for almost three years, but I felt like a stranger. Looking sad and dispirited, the Parisians, their heads down, hurried toward the metro to go to work. I could barely see their white faces partially hidden by wool scarves. It was the end of winter, cold, grey, and lugubrious.

I bought the *Figaro*, the daily paper I used to read, and went to a bistro across from the train station where I ordered coffee and a croissant. The headline deplored how bad the economy was, and stated that the Algerian war was to be blamed for it. In uniform, tan, looking fit and rugged, I obviously came from there. People in the café glanced at my uniform, my black beret, and my first lieutenant rank, and looked away. A woman gaped at me with fearful eyes. Others glared, then turned away with obvious disdain. I held my head high, and I tried not to stare back.

I had left war-torn towns and deep-rooted passions. I had left a dangerous world, a world of hatred, murder and revenge. Here, I found a world of inertia, indifference, and apathy. I had left people fighting for their lives, to find people bored with theirs. I had left dear friends and despicable enemies. Here, I sat in the midst of listless and scornful strangers.

I did not know what to do. I did not want to go to my parents' this early, lest I got into a fight with my dad the minute I walked in. He was always in a bad mood before going to work; actually, he was angry most of the time.

It saddened me to see how unwelcome I was in Paris. I had risked my life and served my country well. Didn't I deserve some thanks? It looked like I would not get any. But I could not worry about it. I had a lot to do. I had to get a job and get Colette out of Algeria.

Although it was not yet eight in the morning, I decided to call Thierry. Nicole answered.

"Hi, Nicole, this is Alain."

She almost screamed. "Alain. Where are you?"

"I just got off the train, I'm back in Paris."

"I'm so happy you're safe! Can you come over? We are anxious to see you. Thierry is still sleeping. I'll wake him. Are you okay?"

"I'm physically fine, but I'm a bit confused. I'll see you in a few minutes."

I took the metro. Again, people gave me strange looks. I felt uncomfortable, but I stared down the ones who gave me contemptuous sneers. In Algeria, people looked at me with respect because of my uniform. I protected them. Here, people looked at me as if I were a convict.

I went up the stairs to the third floor of the old grey six-story building on the rue de Rennes. Nicole opened the door. She gave me a big hug, stepped back and looked at me. "It's so good to have you back in one piece. We worried so much about you."

We went to the familiar tiny living room with its old faded pink armchairs.

"The war is over for me." I added, "It has been difficult."

She did not say anything for a few seconds. "I see that."

She took my hands and said, "You look terrific, but you have changed. I can see that you are stronger, more confident. Your hands are rough. Your face is different. Is it leaner? It is definitely sadder."

I tried to make light of it. "Well, army fare and combat don't fatten anyone up."

She shook her head. "If I did not know you, I'd be intimidated, maybe scared. There is something changed in the way you look at me. It's like you had seen darkness and it went into your eyes."

She gave me a peck on the cheek. "Anyway, I'm so glad you are here, alive and well. Thierry is coming in a minute. Would you like some coffee?"

"Yes, please. It's so nice to see you. I must thank you for being the mail relay between Ms. Rooth and me. Her letters were a source of strength when I was struggling with the war."

"I was glad to do it, and I'm happy it helped you."

I smiled at her. "Nicole, I'm a different person. I've become a tough guy. I can turn violent in an instant. I have learned to be fierce and ruthless. I need to turn it off, but I'm not sure I know how. It's scary."

"We could help if you would let us."

"I might need it. What about you? What's happening in your life?"

"I'll be finished with dentistry school in a month, and I'm getting married in June. His name is Michael and he's a professor of mathematics."

"Congratulations. I'm happy for you."

"I'll work in my uncle's practice. Michael and I will live in Paris. We're looking for an apartment." She added, "Your old flame, Josette, is a doctor, now. And, I hope you'll be okay with this. She and Gerard just got married. She now lives in Nantes. I went to the wedding. She looked radiant."

"That's terrific. She's a great woman and deserves to have a good life. We shared wonderful times together. I remember her fondly. I have met someone, too."

"You have? Who is she?"

"Her name is Colette."

"I want to meet her."

"You will. She's still in Algeria. I'll bring her here as soon as I can."

Thierry came in. Same bushy hair, hairless baby cheeks and the warmest smile; he had not changed one bit. I greeted him. "Hi buddy, how's the atomic bomb?"

"I wish I had never gone near that project. What a waste of money. Anyway, I'm out of it now. It's so good to see you, Alain. You look like a real warrior. How are you?"

"I'm different from the guy who left Paris over two and a half years ago."

"How is it to be back in the city?" Thierry asked.

I looked at him, not sure of what to say. "I feel like I am in a strange world here. I don't know how to fit in."

Thierry nodded and smiled. "You just got in; it'll take you a while."

The three of us did not say anything for a while, then I said, "I wanted to stop by and say hello."

"I'm glad you did," Thierry said. "What are your plans?"

"I have to get a job. I told Nicole there's a special woman in my life. She's waiting for me in Sidi Bel Abbes. I have to get her to France wherever I will be."

"That's great. How was it being in the infantry?"

I took a deep breath. "I saw many atrocities and much killing. It was an unreal world. I survived, but some of my men did not."

"Did you fight a lot?"

"Yes, and I hated the war. I'd rather not talk about it."

"Were you in the desert, in the mountains?"

"Both. I spent most of my time outdoors. I loved the splendid scenery. I despised the insurgents, but I loved the people I protected." I stopped for a few seconds. "I think I'm not making any sense, I'm sorry."

"Don't be. You were in combat. It must be hard to re-enter a normal world."

"I don't know what normal is any more."

"Do you know where you'll work?"

"Not yet. I have a job offer in Bethune in the north. I'll go see what the job is. I think I would prefer to live in a sunny place or near mountains. I can go to the alumni association. I'm sure they'll help me." I did not know what else to say. I stood up and shook his hand.

"Listen, I'll be in touch."

I almost ran out. I was uncomfortable, even with my best friends.

I knew my dad would not be home at that time, so I went to my mother's. She gave me a peck on the cheek, but no big hug. She did not look particularly thrilled to see me, although I had been gone almost three years.

"Welcome back. You have changed. I'm not sure how."

She had not changed much, a few more wrinkles, a few more pounds, and the same distant attitude.

"I need to get into civilian clothes. I'd like to stay here for a few days if it's okay with you."

"Sure. You can use your brother's room."

I took my uniform off for the last time. There was no more Lieutenant Alain. The ferocity of combat was behind me, but the memories of it were still in me. I had to forget all of it.

My dad came home for lunch, with the same old suit I had known for years, less hair and a few more frowns on his forehead; he looked as irascible as ever.

"So you are out of the army. What are you going to do next?"

"I'm going to get a job and get on with my life."

He shrugged. "Your life up to now has been kind of useless, don't you think?"

"Why do you say that?"

"The war you were in was for nothing. Thanks to De Gaulle, it'll end soon. The stupid Pieds Noirs will have learned their lesson for rising against him."

He sat at the dining room table. I did not remember the rooms being so small. The apartment smelled musty. I looked at him. *Already on the attack*, I thought, but I was determined to try not to get into a fight with him.

"Don't you remember? It was your De Gaulle who escalated the bloody war and made promises to the people of Algeria that he did not keep. You don't know anything about that country or about its people. You have no idea what I have done for France, for almost three years. You don't know how hard it was and how well I did. You have no idea how many of us died, but you still insult me and people you know nothing about. Why?"

"Well, it's pretty obvious. The General knows what is best; you don't."

That did it. I exploded, "You have not changed. You just have stupid opinions. They're not even your own."

I stood up and towered over him. I looked down at him. "Now, you listen to me. You can't imagine how powerful I have become and how dangerous and violent I can be." I showed him my hands. "I've killed men, even with my bare hands. You can thank your friend De Gaulle for that. He's the one who made me that way. I'm here because I can use a place to stay for a couple of days. You're a pathetic old man. I don't want to harm you, but if you continue to provoke me, I'm not sure I can trust myself not to."

He stared at me. I had scared him.

"I mean everything I said." I told him.

He looked away. My mother turned white.

"We have a television. Let's look at the news," my dad said after a while.

He rolled the set with a little screen into the dining room. Flickering black and white lines showed a blurry picture. It did not impress me, and I was not interested. What my father had said did not surprise me, but it made me angry that he had. I had fought for our country for almost three years and on my first meal back, he did not even try to understand what my life had been? We had to watch television? It had a single channel run by the government. The news praised De Gaulle and dumped on Algeria and its residents. I almost threw up.

I got up. "I can't stand that propaganda. It's revolting." I turned to my mother. "I'll be in touch."

I went out and called the firm which had offered me a job. They had posted an ad in the Oran newspaper, so I responded, thinking they had a soft spot for the veterans. They agreed to pick me up at the railroad station that afternoon.

I took the train to Bethune, a little town of twenty-five thousand people in northern France, about one-hundred-thirty miles north of Paris. A company executive greeted me at the station, and took me on a tour of the city. Every house and building was grey like the sky above us. It was damp, cold, and there was no sun. There was hardly anyone out in the uninteresting town. There were a few shops, seemingly as colorless as the streets.

He then took me to the factory which did not look more promising than the town. It was a tire manufacturing business, dark, full of black dust, and it smelled of burnt rubber.

He said, "You and I will sit and talk about your job, but we have to go see the director, first. He likes to welcome every new employee."

The director of the firm did not get up but greeted me from behind his enormous, gaudy desk. Bald, short and overweight, he had a reddish, fat face, and sported thick eyeglasses. He was overly dressed with shiny gold cufflinks, a three-piece suit and a nauseating red tie.

I went to shake his hand; he gave me a limp wrist, and the handshake had no energy. He looked at me and spoke with what he thought was an intimidating and authoritarian tone of voice. "Welcome. You'll work in the plant. We don't tolerate lateness and we expect you to comply with all the rules. If you do and if you work hard at your job, all will be well."

Was this his welcome?

I smiled at him and said, "Sir, I only obey rules if they make sense to me."

He stared at me, speechless for a second. "Are you for real? You were in the army. Didn't they teach you to respect authority? Don't you follow orders? Is that what you learned in Algeria?"

"Sir, I only respect earned authority. I don't know you. As far as I'm concerned, you have not earned it. You know nothing about my service in Algeria. I expect you to respect what I did for my country. Your insinuations are offensive."

"You have some nerve, young man."

"Yes, I do. I am proud of who I am and of what I have done. For almost three years, I ran an elite infantry platoon of forty-five skilled soldiers. I'm not intimidated by your airs and petty admonitions. If you want me to do a job, tell me what it is. It will get done. If you want me to kiss your butt, get yourself someone else. I won't be pushed around and treated like a slave."

His face turned crimson. He said, "But you have to fit in."

"No, I don't. Actually, there's no way I would work in this place. It's dirty, probably unhealthy, and I could not work for someone like you. I want to go back to Paris."

His mouth open, he stared at me. He could hardly talk.

"You have to learn to be civil, young man. Whatever you did in the army, you have to face the fact that you can't push people around with your guns anymore "

He turned to the manager, and said, "Go ahead. Take him back to the train station."

On the train, I thought about what just happened. Since I had gotten off the ship last evening, less than twenty-four hours ago, I had lost my temper three times. Sadly, France did not welcome me. I was confused. I missed Colette. I had hoped that my parents would at least be neutral and accept me for who I was. None of that had happened. Both the Colonel and the Countess had warned me about the cold reception from the French people, but it was still a letdown for me.

Restless, I did not know where to turn; I was on edge. I thought that the agreements in Geneva might leave some room for Europeans to participate in the rebirth of Algeria. There, people would understand who I was and would respect what I had done for them. I did not really like the idea of going back to Algiers, but a talk to Edith's friend about a job there seemed to me to be the best thing for me to do. I would also be back with Colette faster. I really missed her.

I went back to my mother's place and said, "I need to stay here a couple of nights. I'll be out at meal times. Just give me a key. Dad will never see me."

"Fine, but you scared him, and you scared me too."

"He earned it. Don't worry. I'll be out soon."

I thought about the Countess. Should I go to her and share my confusion? I did not know how to explain what I grappled with, so I wrote her a note *I'm sorry. I'm still trying to figure out where I am and what I'll do. I'll come to see you as soon as I settle down.*

I wrote to Colette, *I'm coming back to Algiers. I want to meet with Edith's friend. I'll meet you in two days at the hotel we were in. Wait for me if I'm not there. I love you.* Even in Algeria, the post office delivered the mail within twenty-four hours like in France.

I went to Air France to get a plane ticket to Algiers and found out that I had to have a permit from the French authorities to fly there. In the dirty room of the police station, the policeman on duty sat behind a desk covered with stacks of papers.

When I asked him for the permit, he frowned. "Why do you want to go there? It's dangerous, and there is nothing there for Europeans anymore."

Anger would certainly not work here. I curbed my instinctive

The War Inside His Mind

reaction and said, "That may be true, but it's not the case for me." I smiled at him. "Her name is Colette. She's beautiful, we're in love, and she's waiting for me."

He smiled and shrugged. "Ah, young men, always looking for gorgeous women. We are not supposed to give out these permits anymore. I fought in Algeria myself. I liked the people there and I like you. I'll give you one. I'll predate it."

I went back to Air France and booked a flight to Algiers for the next day.

After all the months I spent waiting to get out of the country, I was going back to Algeria. I looked forward to being with Colette, and ready to enjoy the warm sun and the light blue sky I loved.

I landed at the Maison Blanche Algiers airport, early afternoon, and went to the hotel. Colette was not there yet. I decided to go to the railroad station and meet the train from Oran.

The train pulled in late. People got off on a crowded platform, and I saw her. I fought my way to her and called her name. She heard me. She saw me and ran into my arms. We held each other for the longest time. I had left her in Sidi Bel Abbes less than a week ago. It felt like an eternity.

I took her hand and we walked slowly to the hotel, savoring being together again. We went to the hotel and made love until dinner. She had called Edith's friend. We had an appointment for early the next day. We went to dinner. There were still romantic little places, although they were busy. I could not stop looking at her throughout the dinner.

"How was Paris?" she asked.

"A big disappointment. I did not know what to do. I wanted to be with you more than anything else. So here I am."

She looked so beautiful. I loved her flowing dark hair and her mysterious eyes. I took her hands. "I missed you. I love you so much."

Her eyes were riveted to mine. "I love you too. Soon the nightmare will be over. We'll be together forever."

The next day, the meeting did not go as I had hoped it would. Edith's friend said to us, "The word is that the provisions of the agreement which will come out of Geneva will not protect European businesses or people. I'm afraid the French companies will have to leave and forego their assets. There is talk of civil trouble. I'm not sure if there's any fact to support that, or whether panic is starting to set in. My recommendation to you, Alain, is to go back to France. Take her with you and start your life there."

Colette and I were not completely surprised, but we were disappointed.

We went back to the hotel. "Colette, fly to France with me today or tomorrow," I said to her. "We'll have Edith join us and bring Jean Pierre as soon as she can leave."

"I could not do that. I can't leave my son here. I have to go back and take him with me."

We were both standing."All right," I held her tightly in my arms. "I'll go with you to Sidi Bel Abbes this afternoon. The three of us will leave for France tomorrow or the next day."

She put her head on my chest. "It takes a week or two to book a passage on a ship from Oran, and it's difficult to get plane tickets. The best thing to do is for you to go back to France from here. Get a job and I'll join you as fast as I can. Hopefully, it'll be in less than two weeks."

"Get a passage in the class which offers the earliest sail. Money is not important; your safety is."

"I'll try everything. I promise. I'll be there soon, and then we'll never leave each other."

"Fine, I'll find work somewhere. I'll write to you to tell you where to go. In case the letter does not reach you, go to the main post office in Marseille. There will be a letter from me in the to-be-collected mail. I think that's the best we can do."

Early afternoon, I put her on the train back to Oran. I kissed her warm, voluptuous lips and held her until it was time to board. She leaned out of a window, waved and blew kisses at me. I waved back, but I could not see her; my eyes were full of tears.

The War Inside His Mind

Chapter 22

At the Algiers airport, the Air France counter employees were dealing with more people than they had seats for. I had a ticket to Paris, but no confirmed reservation. I saw near the head of the line two people I knew well, Tom and Francine, the farmers I had helped when rebels attacked their ranch near Mascara. I elbowed my way to them. "Tom, what are you doing here? You have not left yet?"

"I guess we should have; we kept hoping we would never have to go, but now, it's time. What about you, Lieutenant? It's nice to see you, but what the hell are you doing here? And in civilian clothes?"

"I'm trying to get out. It's a long story."

"Stay with us. We're going to Paris. We found a farm with vineyards in Provence. Francine's brother left two weeks ago by ship with most of what we can bring out of the country. I still have his plane ticket. You can use it."

We were three of the last people on the plane. I had saved their lives a-year-and-a-half ago; Francine's brother's plane ticket would spare me a lot of waiting, and maybe save me from dire trouble. Algiers was a dangerous city.

Back in Paris again, I had a great sense of urgency. I went directly from the airport to the Ecole Centrale Alumni Association. The receptionist directed me to the job-offer department. In the elegant but severe room, with light grey walls and pictures of stern old men, former directors of the school, I walked to the desk. Smiling, the woman who worked there shook my hand.

"Welcome, I suppose you're looking for a job."

"I am. I just got out of the army." I gave her my name and the year I graduated from the school.

"We actually have a long list of job offers. Just wait a few minutes while I'll go get your file." She went to another room and retrieved my records.

"We have quite a few jobs available in automobile design and manufacturing."

"I'd prefer something other than the car industry."

"There's a new secret project for the army at Sud-Aviation."

"I just got out of the army; I'm not ready to go back in."

"Sud-Aviation is not a military firm. They build airplanes. They're working now on the supersonic Concorde. But they're anxious to staff a new contract they agreed to do for the army. They're having a hard time doing it because the project is not in Paris; it's in Cannes."

My mouth opened wide. I almost cheered. "On the Riviera? That's fantastic. Can I go interview?"

"Let me make a call."

She did and said, "You can go to their Paris headquarters for an interview today at three. Ask for Mr. Benoit. Here is the address." She gave me a copy of my grades and evaluations.

I thanked her profusely and went to have lunch.

At three, I was ushered into the immense office of Sud-Aviation's personnel senior vice-president.

He reviewed the file I gave him and said. "Great. You did well in all subjects, except for metallurgy. We don't work in that industry at all, so it's not a problem. Are you single?"

"Yes, Sir."

"Are you amenable to moving to the south of France?"

"I'm free as the wind. Actually, I'd love to go to Cannes."

His smile told me that my response pleased him. "Most graduates prefer to stay in the Paris area, so it's great you're willing to go. What did you do during your military service?"

"I was an infantry lieutenant in Algeria."

"Infantry? I don't see many guys like you. Did you see combat?"

"Yes, Sir. Quite a bit. My platoon had Special Forces rating."

"They'll love that in Cannes. They're looking for leaders." He outlined the position and the salary attached to it. "I have the authority to hire you. The job is yours if you want it."

"I'll take it, Sir. Where do I go?"

"First, you have to have a security clearance. It takes a few days."

"Can I work here, in Paris, while they process the paperwork?"

The War Inside His Mind

"I can arrange that. Sud-Aviation is working on the design and development of the Concorde supersonic aircraft in their lab in Paris. Be there tomorrow at eight. You'll get the same salary. Ask for Mr. Boulot; he runs the design of the wings. I'll let him know. Here's the address."

"Thank you so much."

I finally got a break. I had a job, and Colette and I would live in a sunny place, near mountains. I did not know the Southern Alps, but I heard they were pristine.

It was not too late to call on Madame De Sèvres. The same old butler opened the door. The usually reserved man gave me a hug. "I'll go tell Madame. I know she's anxious to see you." He took me to the parlor and went to get her.

She almost ran to me. We embraced warmly. "You are back and you are safe." She stepped back, put her two hands on my cheeks and said, "You look strong and healthy. I'm so glad to see you."

The Countess looked just as she did three years ago, elegant, trim, her hair and face perfectly groomed.

"I'm so grateful for your letters and your support over the past years, Madame. You'll never know how much they meant to me."

"I'm proud of you; your uncle would have been too. I knew your life there was hard. I thought of you every day, and now here you are." She hugged me again. "I have your car in the garage. Shall we go look at it?"

"Yes, I'm anxious to see it. Thank you."

She showed me a shiny brand new blue Peugeot. I was speechless. "Madame, I don't know how to thank you. It's magnificent." I gave her a big hug and a kiss on the cheek.

"Your uncle would have loved to be the one giving it to you. Enjoy it, Alain."

"I will, and I'll think of you every time I drive it."

"I'm glad. Do you know where you'll work?"

"Yes, I have a job with Sud-Aviation in Cannes. I'll be going there soon."

"I'm sure you'll do well. Please keep in touch and drop in to see me when you are in Paris. Here are your keys and the car documentation."

I drove away. I went to a café and called my mother. "I'm in Paris."

"You're back from Algeria? Again? Already?"

"Yes, I am. Things did not work out but I have a job in the south of France. I'll be going there in a few days. Can I stay at your place with the same arrangement as before?"

"Yes, you can."

When she opened the door to let me in the apartment, although the entrance hall was dark, I could see she had a frown on her forehead and the corners of her lips were down.

"What's wrong? You look worried."

"Your brother's having a hard time."

"You've got to be kidding me. A hard time? Why? He's in no danger. He does not like the food?"

"They go on maneuvers, sometimes even at night. It's scary and it's tough on him."

How could she say that? She never showed any concern for me, when for almost three years, I lived in constant danger.

I said, "Poor baby. He must still be afraid of the dark."

I went to my brother's room, sat at the tiny mahogany desk and wrote to Colette to tell her about the job in Cannes. *It's perfect for us. Write to me, so I know when you are scheduled to sail. Send the letter to the to-be-collected mail at the Rue Turgot post office in Paris.*

At Sud-Aviation, the design of the supersonic transport was going strong. The manager assigned me to the wing section. In a huge room, full of desks, each one with an engineer working silently with pencils, slide rules, and paper, I integrated differential equations all day to define the profile of a section of the delta wing. Amazingly enough, I remembered how to do that.

After a few days, I grew impatient. I called the personnel man and asked him, "What's happening with my clearance, Sir?"

"The army does not move fast. It takes time."

"For almost thirty-three months, I could handle all their weapons and do their dirty work. I was good enough then. What has changed?"

"I understand. I'll see what I can do."

A letter from Colette waited for me at the post office. She said that she was booked on the ship leaving in seven days. I would be in Cannes then.

Two days later, Mr. Benoit called me to his office. "You have your clearance; you can go south."

"Thank you, Sir. I'll be there the day after tomorrow."

I went to get my stuff and tell my mom I was leaving. When I was ready to go, she asked me, "Who is Colette?"

She stood in the tiny, dark entrance hall in front of the door. I had my bag in my hand and I stared at her. "Am I to believe that you read the letter I left in my personal things?"

"Well, you don't talk about yourself. I was curious."

"You should be ashamed of yourself. You had no right to do that. You violated my privacy. "

"I don't know much about you, and I'm your mother."

I put the bag on the floor and my hands on my hips. "What do you mean you don't know much about me? When did you ever try to find out? You don't even know what I did in Algeria and never asked. You never wrote to me. You didn't care if I got killed. You ignored me like you have all my life. And now you're interested in me?"

"I was always concerned about you."

"That must be the best kept secret in the world. "

I opened the front door. "If you want to know, Colette is the woman I'll spend my life with."

I glared at her, slammed the door, and left.

I drove all night, so I could get a place to live and report to work the following day. I arrived in Cannes early morning and found the Sud-Aviation building. I rented a furnished apartment that would accommodate Jean Pierre and Colette. I wrote to give her the address. That afternoon, I wrote to Ms. Rooth to bring her up-to-date as to my whereabouts. "Colette is joining me in a few days. We will come to see you this summer. You'll meet her then."

After the first days at work, I received a letter from Colette saying that her principal knew one of the top people in one of the high schools in Cannes. She had a letter of recommendation for the next school year. Things were falling into place.

At the end of the week, when I got home, there was a letter from Sidi Bel Abbes. It was from her sister. *Colette was one of four people killed yesterday by an Arab bomb in the European market. I am leaving Algeria for Alicante in Spain where I have friends. I will take my son and Jean Pierre with me. I am sorry.*

Y.M. Masson   195

Chapter 23

Cannes, France, Spring 1962

I read and re-read the cursed sixteen words that turned my life upside down; *Colette was one of four people killed yesterday by an Arab bomb in the European market.* I did not want to believe it; yet I knew it was true. I tore the letter into little pieces and threw it in the trash. I left the apartment and walked to the beach across the street. Although it was early evening, it was August so the sun was still high, but I ignored the bright sky. Many people played in the gentle waves; I did not see them either. I just stared into space.

I put my head between my knees so people could not see my tears. My mind was racing; I should have gone with her to Sidi Bel Abbes. I probably would have been killed by the bomb that ended her life. We would have died together. That would have been so much better.

In my young adult life, Josette stood by me when I struggled during my uncle's terminal illness and helped me get over his death. Later, our lives went different ways. We had to let each other go. I was sad, but not devastated. Colette came into my life and gave me the strength to regain my sanity at a time when the Algerian conflict was taking a toll on me. She loved me the way I was. She promised me we would never leave each other. We did not. The Arabs took her away from me.

My stomach hurt and my head throbbed. I got up, left the beach, and started to walk, following the shore line. Throughout the weekend, I could not eat and I could not sleep. I walked aimlessly for miles, talking to myself. At times, I wanted to go back to North Africa to punish the ones who were responsible for her death, but I knew I would never find them. I thought about going there, just to kill dissidents, but I promised myself I would not kill anymore. At other times, I just wanted to cry. I did. Without Colette I was nothing. I had no purpose left in my life.

I did not even have a picture of her. I wanted to close my eyes and never open them again.

Back in the apartment on Sunday night, my hatred for the insurgents knew no bounds. I despised the dissidents for their ferocity and madness, but I also hated all other Algerians. They were their brothers and did nothing to stop them. They were all responsible for the deadly act. I would never forgive them for that bomb.

Looking out of the window at the moonless sky and the dark sea, I thought about the damned rebels. For three years they had tried, but were not able to kill me. Although devastated by my loss, I did not want to do the job they could not finish. I resolved not to take my own life. I had to face my distress and confront the emptiness in my heart.

I had to think up some principles to live by: I would work hard and be successful at my job; I would seek to make friends so as not to be alone; I would consider a relationship with another woman, but that had to be a long way in the future. That was hardly a plan, but it was the best I could come up with, and my heart was not in it.

That night, I wrote a long letter to Ms. Rooth. I told her what had happened and all the states of mind I had gone through since I had learned of Colette's murder. I told her of my new resolve and said *I'm not sure I will have the strength to uphold my decision every day. You are the only person in the world I love and trust to help me overcome this. I need you. I cannot go to England now; I'll come to see you in July when the plant closes. In the meantime, I will keep writing to you. This struggle is too tough for me to take on alone.*

Monday morning, I went back to work. My boss, Mr. Abadie, called me. "Management has decided to build a simulator for the flight of the rocket we are commissioned to design and manufacture for the French military. It'll require a computer, a digital converter and a flight model. You were selected to head the design team for the new system. It'll involve procuring a powerful digital computer and specifying the converter."

"Do I have to do it by myself?"

"No. It's too big a job, and there's some urgency to getting it done. You have to do the overall design and estimate the cost of the project. I'll give you three or four engineers to help you. Tell me if you need more manpower."

"I'll get started right away, Sir."

I welcomed the news. I would have something to occupy my mind. I spent the day researching companies which had the capability to build the converter; most of them were American. I worked with IBM to identify local technical people who could understand my needs and help me with the choice of the computer. It was way past clock-out time when I finished what I wanted to accomplish. I had spent the day absorbed in my new assignment. I did not have time to feel sad.

The evening was another story. At home, I struggled with my anger. All the sacrifices I had made were for nothing. Why did I survive? I stared at the walls. I had no one to talk to. I slammed my fists on the table and on the kitchen counter. When I closed my eyes, I saw Colette's face and her beautiful smile. I cried helplessly. I went to bed late; then grenades exploded in my sleep. The clamor of the battles woke me up, sweaty, anxious and depressed.

I got up early, and went to work before clock-in time. The company had a strict schedule for everyone's work day. All employees punched in when they came in at eight in the morning and punched out at five thirty-six, the end of the work day; this made the work week exactly forty-eight hours in five days. I hated that rigid schedule. I went to see my boss, "I'm getting started with design of the simulator. I would like not to have to stick to the regular hours. My project requires intense concentration; there's a lot of work to be done. I would like to come in early and leave late."

"The personnel folks hate that," he replied, "It makes work for them to calculate the overtime. May I ask why you have such a request?"

"For years in the military, I ran a platoon. My captain gave me missions. Nobody told me how to run them. That's what I'm good at. More importantly, a recent personal tragedy has affected me deeply. I need to immerse myself in work. It'll help me."

"I understand. Go ahead. I'll let you know if the personnel people balk."

That was good enough for me. I was my own master. My boss gave me three engineers, and the promise of one more to help me. I had a project to concentrate on and to keep my mind busy all day. I buried myself in work all week. I worked at home on weekends.

I worked hard, but I was adrift. After years of hiking day and night, I could not get used to the lack of physical activity. The company had an employee association which owned three twenty-seven-foot sailboats. I had learned to sail in England and love the closeness to the sea, so I talked to Robert, the guy in charge of them. "My name is Alain. I'm a good sailor and I'd like to use the boats on weekends. What do I need to do? Just schedule a boat when I want to go out?"

"Where did you learn how to sail?"

"In southwest England, on the English Channel."

"I have to take you out for a test sail."

We sailed around for an hour. The wind was brisk. I enjoyed the sound of the water lapping on the hull. I loved the feeling of the wind on my face. Easy to handle, the little boat proved to be reasonably stable. Steering the small vessel and using the waves to smooth out the ride was fun.

"You're right," Robert said when we got back to shore, "You are a good sailor, you can take the boats out."

So I sailed a couple of times, but my heart was not in it.

Deep inside, I was miserable. Lonely evenings were difficult, the nights fitful at best. Sitting inside most of the day, I ached for more physical outside activities. One Friday at lunch in the company cafeteria, I overheard a woman, Catherine, a programmer at the plant, talking to her friend about hiking in the Alps.

I went to sit next to her. "I didn't mean to eavesdrop on your conversation, but I heard you talk about hikes in the mountains. Are they far from here?"

"Not at all. You can get to a trailhead in a little over an hour. My husband and I go quite often."

"I love mountains. I bet the Alps are beautiful."

"They sure are. I know you were in the war. I can see you are still in great shape. You'd love hiking the local Front Range."

"I'm sure I would, but I don't know how to get there."

"My husband and I can take you next time we go, if you'd like."

"That'd be wonderful. I miss being outdoors, and I'd love to know the area."

A week later, Catherine called me. "Alain, we are going hiking this Saturday. Would you like to come with us?"

"Yes, definitely, where shall I meet you?"

"We'll pick you up."

Her husband, Albert, was a nice guy. We rode in their car for less than two hours northeast of Cannes. We stopped at a trail head. Albert spread out a detailed map on the ground.

"Here's where we are. As you can see, there are several trails leaving from this spot."

Indeed, I saw many paths going up to the east and to the north. One went around grey granite rocks. Most trails started through a forest of tall green trees. There I saw grass on the ground; birds sang, and the wind whispered through the forest. The sky was light blue and the temperature moderate. It was different from the hot and arid Atlas range I knew.

Catherine said, "From here, we can go anywhere. Some trails are more rugged than others. What would you prefer?"

"You lead the way. I'm game for anything."

She selected one which meandered through the forest. As it went up, it steepened; the trees became sparser and the trail ended up on a crest. Down from it to the east I could see a small lake; its clear water reflected the periwinkle hue of the sky. It took almost five hours to go up; then we had to turn back. As the sunset got closer, the colors changed. The tree trunks became redder. Even the green of the trees and the grass of the prairies turned darker and warmer.

Riding back in the car with my friends, I felt good about the day. "Catherine and Albert, I thank you so much. I loved the trails, the views and the peacefulness of the mountains. Do you know if there are any restrictions on sleeping out, anywhere in the hills?"

"None that I know of," Albert replied.

"I'll get myself a map and come back another day to spend one or two nights up there. I can explore further and learn more about the peaks and the lakes. I miss looking at the stars. You may want to join me, you'd love it."

Albert said, "No, we don't camp. We like to sleep in our bed, but I'm not sure you'd be safe alone in the wilderness? One never knows who might come in the middle of the night, people, or animals. There are smugglers around, you know. They can get nasty."

"I can take care of myself. I'm a light sleeper. I learned that the hard way. No one can surprise me during the night. I'll carry my knife. I'll be perfectly safe."

The War Inside His Mind

"Really? A knife?"

"Yes. In my hands, it's a weapon. To tell you the truth, there are not too many people who scare me."

In the office, I concentrated on my objectives, guiding the three engineers assigned to me. No one, including my helpers, had any clue about my internal struggles. The deadlines and the complexity of the project made the work challenging, but to me it was no stress. I kept to myself. I had no friends.

One day, at lunch, in the cafeteria, Vanessa, a petite vivacious blonde woman who worked in the programming department came to sit next to me. "You work all the time. Do you ever have fun? Do you have a girlfriend? You seem so serious all the time."

"Well, I go hiking in the mountains on weekends."

"Some people say you were in the infantry in Algeria, and that you're sorry we lost the war. They think you have a chip on your shoulder."

"If that's what people think, let them. The truth is far from that."

"What do you mean?"

"The soldiers didn't lose the war; the politicians sold us out. You're right; I like being alone. The insurgents killed some of my dear friends. I'm still grieving."

"I didn't know. I'm sorry." She tilted her head and gave me a warm smile. "Would you like to take me out? We could do fun things."

"Vanessa, you're so sweet, but the truth is I don't think I'd be a fun date."

"Well, when you're ready, I'll be here. If I can help, talk to me. I'm a good listener."

That night lying in bed and dreading another night of bad dreams, I asked myself why I did not go out with her. But what if Vanessa and I liked each other and then drifted apart? What if I got hurt again? I had no answer to any of these questions.

Would I ever?

Chapter 24

In late May, I received an invitation to attend Nicole's wedding in Paris. I started to write to her, *I told you about Colette the day I got back from Algeria. She was killed before she could make it here. It is a difficult time for me. I won't come for your big day, but I wish you the best.*

But I did not send that letter. Nicole was more than a good friend. She was like a sister to me. I should show her my love and my support. There would be many people I knew at the wedding. It might do me some good. So I wrote another note saying I would be there.

After the ceremony, standing outside the church, I congratulated Nicole and met her new husband, Michael, for the first time. Tall, dark hair, and handsome, I could see from the way he looked at her that he adored her. Beaming with happiness, Nicole said to me, "You didn't bring Colette? I was looking forward to meeting her."

My heart sank. I should have anticipated the question. It hurt me to say the words. "Nicole, a bomb killed Colette in Sidi Bel Abbes before she could come to France."

Nicole hugged me. "Oh, no! I'm so sorry. Why didn't you tell me? Are you okay?"

"Please, I'd rather not talk about it."

She gave me a long, warm hug. "Of course."

Everyone gathered in a private room in a nearby restaurant. I enjoyed seeing old buddies; Thierry had a new woman friend, Claudine, a very pretty petite brunette, who seemed very shy. Josette and her husband also made the trip to the wedding. I had not seen her for over four years. Trim and fit, her gorgeous blond hair flowing in the wind, her energy showing through her irresistible smile, she radiated a picture of happiness.

"Congratulations on your wedding, Josette."

"Thank you, Alain. This is my husband, Gerard."

I shook his hand. "I'm so glad to meet you, Gerard, my congratulations to you too."

Josette beamed. "It's so nice to see you. Nicole told me you had a tough time in North Africa. I can see that. Your face is more chiseled ... but you look sad. Are you okay?"

"I'm fine, Josette. It's hard to re-enter the normal world, but I'm doing my best."

We all sat down for lunch; the day went on. I got tired of smiling. Here, everybody was happy.

On the train back to Cannes, I admitted to myself I was not too sociable these days. I shied away from any kind of relationship which might stir emotions in me. My inner struggle consumed me.

One day, I sat on the beach and watched young men and women enjoying the French Riviera. Most of the women were bare-breasted. The sight stirred some yearning in me, but I was not ready to go talk to them. What if they agreed to go out with me? What if I liked them? What if they would not measure up to Colette? So I just watched.

A young pregnant mother with her two sons, one about five, the other younger, came to sit on the beach not far in front of me. She sat down on a large pink towel and watched her children play in the sand. An Arab man who sold straw hats walked toward her. The smile, or I should say the grimace, on his face revealed a gold tooth. His eyes darted right and left. He put his right hand in his pocket and took out a long, thin, shiny object. *A knife!* I sprang up, ready to jump on him. With his thumb he opened a glittery fan. *It's not a knife!* He did not intend to slaughter her and her kids. I sat down, broke into a sweat, and started shaking; I put my hands over my face so nobody would see my pain. This was the summer in France, not North Africa. I had to stop fighting the war. *I can't turn off the damned memories. I don't know how.*

Back at work, I found out that because I had not worked the previous year, I would not be paid for the four weeks the plant would close. I did not expect that. What a blow! The most important thing I had to do was to spend time with Ms. Rooth. We had been writing to each other, but I needed to be with her. I could not swing the cost of going to England and have enough money to survive until the next paycheck.

I wrote to her to tell her I was trying to figure out how to finance my trip and not starve for the rest of the summer. She wrote back and told me she could not help financially, but suggested I write to Madame De Sèvres. *It is important for you to come and be with me for some time. Tell her about Colette. She lost the man she loved five years ago. She will understand how hurt you are. She will help you.*

I was reluctant to ask the Countess for money after she had given me the car; on the other hand, I was afraid of spending the whole four weeks by myself. I was depressed enough as it was. It would not be good to add more anxiety to my current state of mind. I was unstable and I might do something crazy. So I wrote to the Countess and told her about Colette, and not being able to pay for going to see Ms. Rooth. I told her I needed to borrow some money from her and would pay her back before the end of the year.

I received a letter and a check by return mail. *Don't even think about paying me back. I remember being hurt and alone when I lost your uncle. Let your English mother heal you. Next time you are in Paris, stop in and give me a hug. That will be your way to repay me. Love to you.*

I wrote back and thanked her for her generosity. I added, *Is not destiny cruel? I can't help but dream what our lives would be today if Uncle Raymond had not died and the three of us were together in a warless world.*

The following weekend, I went back to the place where I had been with Catherine and Albert and hiked a long way beyond the crest where we turned around. Any time I came to a fork in the road, I took the path which went up. I crossed a gorgeous little stream, jumping from rock to rock. There were yellow wildflowers everywhere. I reached an area where I could get a glimpse of the Mediterranean Sea. It was not close, but the glow of the sea lit up the horizon and the faraway sky. It was quiet, cold and beautiful. I had a poncho so I could sleep on the ground without getting wet. I settled in for the night. It rained. I rolled myself in the poncho. I loved the feel of the droplets on my face and the smell in the air after the gentle shower.

That night, alone in the mountains, I was at peace.

The plant closed. I braced myself for the long trip to the hamlet of Bishopsteignton in Devonshire. After an overnight train to Paris and the train-boat-train trip from there to my destination, I got to my final stop almost twenty-four hours after I left Cannes.

Ms. Rooth waited at the station, in her usual spot on the platform. Her hair was a little grayer than I remembered. Our reunion was tearful. I buried my face on her shoulder. She held me tightly in her arms. I let my emotions take over. For a moment all my hurts and worries were gone. It had been a long time since I needed to feel the love of my mother. I told her, "It's so good to be here. I'm sorry for the tears."

Her eyes were not dry either. She let go of me and said, "Tears of happiness are nothing to apologize for."

"Today, I'm happy, but I often cry by myself for no apparent reason."

She wiped my eyes with her gentle fingers. "Let me look at you. You're very fit, and your tan makes you handsome. You're still the Alain I love."

I touched the sides of her eyes where there were a few more wrinkles than the last time I saw her. "Your face is even more lovely with these," I said as I kissed the new little furrows.

We got in the car and drove home. Mr. Rooth had aged a little, but he still looked good. He must have been just over sixty-five. It was time for tea. Ms. Rooth had prepared my favorite cucumber sandwiches. There were, as usual, a few foreign kids staying at the house to learn or to perfect their English. They were in their late teens, and looked so young. I remembered that I had been one of them a long time ago. Ms. Rooth said, "We'll talk tomorrow. You need some sleep."

"I'm fine. I can stay up."

"You are not in the military anymore. You don't have to."

I smiled. "Okay, Mom, I'll see you in the morning."

The army had taught me to go to sleep instantly, anywhere, at anytime. I went to bed and had a long and dreamless night.

The next day after a hearty breakfast of bacon and eggs, Ms. Rooth and I went to the garden. We sat in the shade of a tree, surrounded by bunches of flowery bushes. The rattan armchairs with their colorful cushions were comfortable. I relaxed; she smiled at me. "Now, you have to tell me everything that happened since I last saw you."

"What happened in North Africa is the past. What's happening to me now is what I can't understand and what I'm struggling with."

"I know, but what you're going through is a result of the years of war. I need to know what they left in your mind. So I can help you."

For the next day or so, Ms. Rooth and I talked a lot. Actually, I talked and she listened. I told her everything I could about Algeria; I knew not to try to explain combat. There are no ways to explain what happens in a soldier's mind when he is involved in the height of deadly actions. So I shared the fear I had to ignore, the boredom between battles, and the loneliness of being in charge. A few times, when I choked up, she got up and came to put her hand on my shoulder to show she knew the pain of remembering.

"Let's take a walk," she would say, and we would amble through the quaint narrow lanes of the little village.

I got angry when I described the ruthlessness of the insurgents and the atrocities they committed. I tried to explain my feeling of responsibility and guilt from our killing rebels, and the price my platoon paid for it with our own casualties. I tried not go into a rant about the insurgents.

Although Ms. Rooth knew much about her from my letters, I entrusted to her some of my special moments with Colette, and I cried. At that moment a yellow butterfly came to rest on my hand.

Ms. Rooth smiled. "That's Colette coming to console you." The thought generated more tears.

I also described the beauty of the country, the Atlas Mountains, the desert, the sun and the endless skies, the exotic fruit.

When I was talked out, I added, "I said to you, all of that is the past, but it really is not; the past is still with me. I told you all the events and the feelings I experienced, but I'm not sure how I developed the strength to deal with these challenges and the intense emotions I went through."

"You did what you had to do to lead your men."

"I did and I am proud of that. My platoon fought well. But I did not realize at the time I would have to pay such a big price later. I did not know then that the relentless and ever-increasing stress would have such a considerable impact and change me."

She bent toward me and looked into my eyes. *Was she reading into my soul?*

"What changes are you aware of?"

"Most nights I have nightmares about combat, noise, explosions, screams, and during the day, flashes of horrible images. I can't stand crowds. Noise hurts my ears. I'm suspicious of any man who comes too close. My fighting days might be over, but not in my mind. It wears me down."

She tilted her head, and said tenderly, "Do you remember, when you were a child, you were strafed and hurt when you ran away from the German planes? You were scared of being buried alive in the dark cellar during the bombing raids. Those memories are still there, aren't they?"

I chuckled. "Yes, they are. I still don't like low-flying airplanes, and you'd never get me to go into a cave."

"That's because of what happened to you in your first war."

"I know, but I was a child then. I may have been a strong kid, but I was impressionable."

"Alain, it doesn't matter how old you are when something terrible happens. You never forget these moments. They become scars in your mind. The horrible war you just went through will have many such lasting impacts."

"I'm sure you're right, but you said these memories become scars. If they were, they would not be painful, but they are."

"It's too early for scars. Your mind is deeply wounded; the injuries are still raw. They hurt, like a scraped elbow that's oozing blood. The pain in your mind makes you depressed and angry."

I reached for the cup of tea she had poured for me. Clumsily, I dropped it and it shattered on the patio tiled floor. I stood up and hit the ground angrily with my right foot.

"What an idiot, I'm so sorry," I almost shouted.

"It's okay, Alain. Don't be upset. Things happen."

"I'm jittery, my nerves are frayed, and I overreact. I lose my temper easily, sometimes on trivial matters. I don't know why, but I can't help it."

"That's to be expected. You've spent almost three years at war, and you came back less than six months ago. For a while, you'll get mad when you think someone is attacking you or your friends, whether the threat is real or not. Instant reactions to threats and danger have been the way you survived. You can't forget that overnight."

"I also blow up sometimes when I read the paper or listen to the news. They print a one-sided bunch of lies. The French government betrayed me, and the news continues to do so. Nobody ever thanked me for what I did in Algeria for my country."

"Nobody will. The French people know nothing of what you went through in North Africa, and they never will. The French leadership will erase and suppress all the information they can, to make sure their change of direction, or their betrayal, as you'd call it, is forgotten. They'll rewrite history."

I nodded. "The French have no idea of the sacrifices my soldiers made, the ones who came back and the ones who did not. The government never disclosed the number of French soldiers' casualties."

Ms. Rooth shrugged. "Governments can do and say anything they want. That's power."

It was close to tea time. I went to the kitchen with her to help with the slicing of cucumbers and tomatoes, but Ms. Rooth did not want to stop our conversation. "On top of the trauma from the war, you're also dealing with the death of Colette."

"Yes. It's a double blow. I loved her more than Josette or anyone else. Yet I failed to protect her one last time."

"You did not. Colette felt rightly responsible to get her son out of Algeria. You could not have prevented the explosion of the bomb. Had you been there, you'd have been killed too."

I handed the sliced tomatoes to her. I sighed. "Sometimes I think it would have been better. There are days when life does not seem worth living anymore."

"Don't say that, Alain. Remember that you wrote to me about your resolve to be open to a relationship sometime in the future. You have a lot to offer a woman. Be patient. You won't forget Colette, but your wound will heal. Thanks to her, you know what love can be."

"That may be, but it'd be difficult for me to get in any kind of relationship. I don't want to be hurt again."

"You have to give it some more time."

"You know, during my first war, as you call it, I feared the Germans, but I never let them see it. When they left, I didn't have any desire for revenge. I still don't. This is not going to be the case with the Algerians. I fought them. They committed crimes. They killed Colette. I hate them with passion, and I'll never forget what they did."

"That's understandable. It may take a long time to go away, but you'll have to watch out for that. You don't want hatred to eat into you. You were a courageous infantry officer, respected by your men and by your superiors, but it was not your career. As hurtful as it may be, you have to face the fact that, like most, this war was useless. If you don't talk or think about it, the memories will fade."

I helped her bring the dishes to the table. "Talking to you about it has helped me, but there's no one else I can be so open with. I never talk to anyone about my pain, except to myself."

"You're a changed man; you have to let the new Alain be the strong and fearless human being you've become."

"You're right about that, there's not much that scares me." I paused for a few seconds. "Except what's inside my head."

I got updated on the family. Her youngest son, Kipper, a Royal Marine, attended officers' school. Alistair was going to be a father, Ms. Rooth a grandmother. After two weeks, I felt better.

When it was time to leave, she said, "Alain, go to the mountains, sail, do the things you love to do. Finding new friends was your forte. You can still do it. Meet people, young women. It's not good for you to be alone at this time."

"I'll try. You're right, I do love the mountains. I have to thank Algeria for that."

"Enjoy hiking in the Alps. Don't think about the war; focus on the future. I hate to see you go. I love you. Keep writing to me."

She looked at me tenderly and added, "I think it's important."

Chapter 25

I arrived in Paris in the early afternoon. I had time to go visit Madame De Sèvres before catching the night train south. As usual, the butler escorted me to her parlor.

"Alain, you're back from England."

"I came to give you the hug I owe you," I teased her.

"I accept payment," she joked back. "How is Ms. Rooth? Was she helpful to you?"

"She certainly was. She helped me see some positives out of the past three years, even out of Colette's death. She said that now I know what love can be, and even if I'm not ready, I should be open to meeting new women. But I'm afraid there might not be another Colette out there."

"Yes, there is. She's somewhere, but don't look for her. She'll appear when you least expect it; you're still young, unlike me. I'm an old woman. It has been five years since your uncle died, and I still miss him."

"You're not old. You're beautiful and vibrant."

"You're so sweet. You know, when you wrote to me about your uncle, you and I being a family, it brought tears to my eyes."

"I didn't mean to make you cry."

"I know, it just sounded so good, but now I worry about you. Are you going to be okay?"

"I think so. Ms. Rooth helped me begin to accept my life as it is. I'll go hiking in the mountains, and I'll try to force myself to meet people. I'll write to you and tell you how I do. Ms. Rooth and you are the only people in the world who care for me. I treasure both of you."

She gave me a big hug and a kiss. "Please, come anytime you want. I'll always be happy to see you." I went out and ran to catch my train.

The War Inside His Mind

On the night train to Cannes, I went to the dining car. I had bought a ticket for the last dinner service. Two young American women seemed to have trouble communicating with the waiter.

I asked them if I could help.

"Thank God! Someone who can speak English," the brunette exclaimed.

"Please, all we want is to have dinner," the blonde one said, "There seems to be some problem, but we can't figure out what it is."

I asked the waiter what was going on. "They don't have a dinner ticket," he told me, "I try to explain to them they could buy one, but they don't understand me."

"Do you have space for this service?"

"I sure do."

I turned to the American women. "You're supposed to purchase a dinner ticket before the train leaves, but he has room. You can buy it now."

Grateful, they paid for their meal and asked me, "May we sit with you?"

"Please do. My name is Alain, what are yours?"

"I'm Sarah," the blond one said, "and this is Esther."

"Nice to meet you both."

"Nice to meet you too. It's our first time in France. We spent three days in Paris. We loved it. Now we're on our way to visit the Riviera. We are going to Nice. Is it as beautiful as everyone says?"

"I don't know what people say about it, but it's a typical Mediterranean setting, palm trees, blue sea, blue sky and sun."

"That sounds good. How's the beach?"

"There are plenty of beautiful beaches along the coast, but the one in Nice is different. There's no sand. It's made of blue and grey round pebbles. It's really cozy; the water is warm, and the waves gentle."

"Wow. That's not what a beach is. Where are you heading, Alain?"

"I'm getting off in Cannes, a couple of stops before Nice. Where are you from in the States?"

"We're from Scarsdale in New York, twenty miles north of New York City."

"I always wanted to go to New York since the GIs liberated me from the Germans. What do you do there?"

"We graduated from college this last May. This trip is our graduation present. We went to England, and Paris. Nice is next. Then we go to Italy. What about you? What do you do?"

"I'm an engineer, I work in Cannes, but I'm on vacation."

"Could you come meet us in Nice and show us around?"

"I guess I could do that. Where are you staying?"

They gave me the name of their hotel and I agreed to pick them up the next day, after lunch.

When I got home, I thought I should go meet the two American women the next day. I had to force myself not to stay isolated from the rest of the world. Besides, there was no danger of getting involved with Sarah or Esther. They'd leave in a couple of days.

The next day, I met the two women at their hotel. They got into the car, and both sat in the front seat, Sarah next to me, Esther on her right. Sarah put her arm around my shoulders. I drove to Monaco and took them to the palace. They loved the sumptuous building with the guards in their splendid, colorful uniforms. I told them that Prince Rainier and his American wife, Grace Kelly, lived there. They must have taken a million pictures.

Next, I drove them to the famous Monte Carlo casino. Inside, the stilted, gaudy baccarat and roulette rooms were crowded with well-dressed gamblers. Sarah said, "This is for rich people. We have no money to give away to the casino. Let's go someplace else."

I took one of the roads which climb on the hill overlooking the Mediterranean. We stopped in Eze, the little village high above the coast line. I stopped the car and bought them a glass of wine so they could admire the splendid view of the blue waters.

"How beautiful. We have nothing as spectacular in the United States. This hill is so steep."

"You have the National Parks in the West of the country. I read about them. They seem to be fascinating."

"We have not been there; we only know the east coast, and it's pretty flat."

I told them, "The mountains are special here, because they're so close to the sea. What would you like to do next?"

Esther turned to Sarah, "I wouldn't mind going swimming, what about you?"

She turned to me. "Can we?"

The War Inside His Mind

"Sure, I'll drive you back to Nice, and drop you at the hotel. From there it's an easy walk to the beach."

As I was preparing to say good-bye, Sarah said, "Alain, do you have a male friend you could call? The four of us could go dancing tonight."

"To tell you the truth, I'm new to the area and I haven't made many friends yet."

"Would you come by yourself, then? It'd be just the three of us."

I did not feel like holding a woman in my arms. I managed to say gently, "I'm afraid this is not what I'm good at. I hike in the Alps, and I sleep outside in the mountains. I enjoy being close to nature. I'm not comfortable on crowded dance floors, actually in any venue with lots of people."

She looked at me a bit puzzled. "Sleep outside? On the ground?"

"Yes. It's marvelous. It's peaceful, and it smells good. The stars are dazzling."

That was definitely not her thing. "Well that's not for us. Thanks for a lovely day. You have been so nice."

"You're welcome. I enjoyed your company. Have a good trip. Enjoy old Europe."

I left them and went home.

That had been a timid attempt at being sociable, but I had to admit to myself I had not made great strides toward my recovery. I had talked to two women and had a reasonably good time, but I ran away when Sarah tried to get too close.

I still had over two weeks to wait for the plant to reopen. The French Riviera in the summer attracted thousands of tourists. When I shopped for food, the markets were crowded. I dreaded being in the midst of too many people. It reminded me of the patrols in the Sidi Bel Abbes market. It also made me think of Colette and the way she died.

But I had to go do my shopping almost every day to get the food I needed for the next day. I had no way to refrigerate anything. The store was crowded. People with their grocery bags were going through the aisles, picking up fruit and vegetables. I looked behind me to know exactly where to find the exit in case I had to get out in a hurry. Choosing fresh figs, out of the corner of my eye I saw a little red bag abandoned on the ground, no one near it. In a flash, I dropped the figs, turned around and bolted out of the store, almost knocking down an old man on the way. "Sorry," I mumbled.

Once outside I stopped, panting. After a while, I stopped shaking. I had to face the crowds and go back in to get food. Then I saw a little old lady come out of the store, carrying the red bag. I shook my head in disbelief.

The War Inside His Mind

Chapter 26

Ispent quite a bit of time alone in the mountains. I had fewer nightmares when I slept up there. The Alps were healing me. I had bought a backpack to carry food and water. Sometimes I went for two or three days without seeing anyone. I did not have a tent; I didn't need one. It seemed to me that up there, time slowed down, and the serene scenery and the rhythm of life calmed me. I immersed myself into nature. Animals were friendly, even if skittish. Rabbits, wild goats, and marmots went about their business accepting my presence. I felt safe, day and night.

One evening, resting on top of a hill, I started to have chills. My body shook. I did not know what was happening. I was sweating one minute and freezing the next. In the morning, after a difficult night, I felt better, but I was weak. Something was wrong. I had to rest several times on the way down, so it took me a while to walk back to the car. In Cannes, I hardly knew anybody and certainly no doctor, so I decided to go to the hospital.

The brightly lit reception area had white walls, and smelled of antiseptic. A receptionist asked me if I were here to visit a patient.

"No, Ma'am, I need to see a doctor." She wrote down my name and took me to a little room near the entrance. After a short while, a nurse came in and asked me for my name and what brought me there.

I told her what had happened the night before. She wrote a few words on a board, and said, "I'll get a doctor. Just wait here."

Within a few minutes, a woman in a white coat, a stethoscope hanging from her neck, came into the room.

She read what the nurse had written and sat down at the little desk in a corner of the room. She frowned, then looked at me and smiled. "Alain, I'm Doctor Merle. Tell me what happened last night."

I described to her what I went through, the alternate chills and sweating episodes, and sometimes the uncontrollable shaking.

She nodded her head. She looked at my throat, listened to my lungs, took my temperature, and asked me, "Did you do your military service in Algeria?"

"Yes, Ma'am. I was an infantry lieutenant for over thirty months, and I've been back since March."

"Did you take pills against malaria when you were there?"

"Yes, we all did, every day."

"Didn't they tell you to keep taking them for three months after you returned?"

"Yes, they did, but I had too much on my mind. I forgot about it."

"Well, you should have. You just had an attack of malaria. Fortunately, it was a mild one. I'll give you something that will fix you up. Do you have family in Cannes?"

"No, I live by myself."

"Okay then. We'll keep you here until tomorrow to make sure there's no relapse."

I thanked her. The same nurse came back and took me to a room. She wrapped me up in a blanket and gave me some pills. I had nothing to do, nothing to read, so I took a nap. They woke me up for dinner and gave me more pills. I went back to sleep. I spent the night without nightmares. I suspect that the pills they gave me contained some sort of sedative.

The next morning, Doctor Merle came by, took my vital signs, and said, "You have no fever. You're fit to go. I'll give you a prescription for Quinine. If you have another attack, take it for four days. That'll take care of it. Your malaria attack went away by itself in a few hours. It may not happen again, yet it might."

"What would cause that?"

"Probably change in temperature. The disease is in you. You shouldn't ever go to a malaria-infested area. That could be catastrophic for you if you were bitten by carrier-mosquitoes."

I thanked her. Nightmares, grief, and now malaria? Great! What next?

I went home and rested. The day went by slowly. I languished.

Tired of struggling alone, I curled up under the covers and withdrew into myself. I was only conscious of my body and of my slow

The War Inside His Mind

breathing. I had no desire to be part of the world. I did not want to do anything: work, play, read, write, eat or drink. I hoped I would not wake up. I almost wished Doctor Merle had kept me in the hospital. At least, there would be people there.

I woke up and I tried to think of anything that could help me regain the energy I needed to do things and be happy. I thought of Mr. Boucheron who shook me up after my uncle's death, and of Sergeant Clavery who told me to just do my job. Today I was not only feeling sorry for myself. I was not in complete control of my being.

I did not know how to help myself, but I did not want to give up. Ms. Rooth told me not to think about the war, but I could not do it. I could not forget the ferocity, the fury, and the energy of the battles. I remembered the bond and the sense of belonging with my soldiers. We helped and protected one another. It was not that I missed combat, but now my life was so utterly different, so tame, subdued, and lonely. I faced a difficult battle, but this time I had to fight alone. She told me to meet people. I had not been able to do it, but I had to try again. I had to get out of the apartment. I had to feel the sun, look at the sea and breathe the mountain winds. It was not good for me to be alone for too long.

I went out. Sitting on the beach, I remembered the hot sand of the Sahara. Images of the raima we protected went through my mind. I looked at young men and women playing on the beach, throwing water at each other and having a good time. The young men in the desert had no time to play; I felt close to them. Part of my soul was still in the desert with the Berbers.

I used to meet people easily before the war; now I could not do it. I was afraid of meeting and talking to anyone. I did not know how to behave in a friendly social environment anymore.

So I kept going to the mountains by myself. One evening, I camped by a lake. Although it was August, it was chilly. I had matches with me. I gathered some dead wood and built a fire. It provided heat and the special smell of burning dry wood. There was little smoke. I stared at the dancing flames; I dreamt of other mountains, other peaceful venues, away from other human beings. I knew I had to stop this isolation trend, but work would resume soon, and I would be with my coworkers.

The small fire soon went out. When it did, I made sure all the wood burnt out and I buried the ashes under dirt. As I was doing that, a couple of rabbits came by. They were leery of me, but they must have been curious about the fire. They probably wondered what had happened to it. I spent a cool, but restful night.

The next day, the third one of my hike, I followed a long and narrow path which brought me to a beautiful lake; deep blue, lined with evergreens, huge, grey round rocks graced its edges. I saw a steep trail going up on the side of a moraine. A herd of goats jumped from rock to rock high up toward the top. They could have been ibexes; it was too low for chamois. Although I was out of food and low on water, I decided to go up. The animals would most probably be afraid of me, but I could get a better look at them, and I would see what was at the end of the trail.

Chapter 27

Wednesday, August 15, 1962

It took me longer than I expected, but three hours later I reached the top of the ridge. There, a narrow path snaked up to the crest of the no-name mountain. I sat on a rock. Below my feet a vertiginous slope went down into dark nothingness.

Here you are again, I told myself, *alone and depressed, full of guilt and anger.*

The sky lit up in intense reds and oranges; the mountains turned purple, and the hazy, almost violet, distant Mediterranean Sea disappeared. The fragrance of the evergreens intensified, and the temperature dropped. Slowly, the world went dark.

I closed my eyes and my thoughts drifted to the faraway Atlas range of northern Africa and to the flaxen gold of the sands of the Sahara. An eerie parade of the sergeants and privates who were killed under my command, came out of the night sky. They had visited me several times before, but never in the mountains. I felt betrayed because the high wilderness was my refuge, where I could be alone, but they found me here. Once again, I watched hopelessly the victims of the brutal conflict walk before my eyes, and once more, I tried to tell them I was sorry, but they were no longer alive; they were at peace while I fought every day to forget the war.

More visions of the maimed bodies of innocent victims of that useless conflict flowed in front of my eyes. Oh no. A flashback of George's body lying on the ground, next to the dining room table, covered with his own blood was a prelude to ... I screamed, *I don't want to see Thérèse.* To no avail. Once again I had to look at her mangled body and those of her sons.

I tried to stop the horrible series of pictures of the worst time in my life. My brain went mercifully dark for a few seconds, but it brightened again. This time, I saw my uncle and his unforgettable smile. I watched him again close his eyes for the last time.

I felt the soft caresses of Colette on my face. I looked at her tender smile.

I thought about all those dead people, the ones I loved, the ones I respected and admired, and even the ones I hated. They were all resting, away from fights and struggles. Why couldn't I be like them? I looked down at the chasm below me.

I could exit this savage and unforgiving world right here, tonight, just one step from the edge and an endless flight down to eternity.

In a daze, I opened my eyes, or did I? I could not see anything. But I sensed the moonless night. The breeze gently stroked my body, and the mountain air filled my lungs. I embraced the idea of taking my own life. All I had to do was to stand up. It would be over in an instant. No more pain, no more anger, no more guilt, no more sadness, no more struggle, and no more broken heart.

I was ready. I got up. I looked down at the abyss. I hesitated.

Was I afraid to die?

I froze and kept staring at the darkness of the abyss. Then, all of a sudden, a brightly-lit white cloud illuminated the sky. Blinded for an instant, Ms. Rooth appeared in the center of the white mass, dressed like she had been when we said good-bye. She looked at me lovingly. *I love you. Keep writing to me. I think it's important. I love you. Keep writing to me. I think it's important,* she said, and within a split-second, vanished.

Was this real? Did I really see her?

A cold gust of wind wiped out the cloud and froze me to the bone; then I heard a voice, a woman's voice. *Wake up, Alain. You loved the Atlas Mountains. You love the Alps. I am the Goddess of the Mountains, and I love you. Don't jump.*

I had never heard of the Goddess of the Mountains, and I was astounded that both she and Ms. Rooth came to find me all the way to this remote promontory to tell me not to give up. In the twenty-six years of my life, more than half of it spent in war or preparation for one, I never gave up hope. The rebels tried to kill me for almost three years and never succeeded. Why do the job they failed at? Why take my life now? Today? Ever?

I sat down.

The War Inside His Mind

I opened my eyes. This time I could stare into the night. I did not feel the cold. I had no idea of the time. I did not remember where I had been, but I sensed that it was a dark and dangerous place, a faraway corner of my mind, an eerie kingdom, a realm of doom and nothingness that I did not want to go back to ever again.

I shook myself awake.

Where was I? What happened?

Then I knew.

Why did I go there? Was it hunger? Was it loneliness? Was it despair?

And what scared me the most: could it happen again?

Chapter 28

Now fully awake, freezing, starving, and dying of thirst, I welcomed the discomfort because it reassured me I was alive. I inhaled the cold air of the night, relished the scent of the trees and that of the wet ground. I touched the stone I had almost jumped from; I looked up at the sky and its multitude of bright, friendly stars. There I detected a faint glow to the east. Morning would come soon. I would wait and watch the sun rise. I was not about to close my eyes again.

Soaking up nature through all my senses, I thought about the last few minutes and believed that the aberration of the night might have pulled me out of the depth of my sorrow. In spite of the debilitating events of the last three years, I was as resilient as when I was a child struggling to survive in Paris, at the end of the German occupation. I battled the liver disease I had contracted after years of food deprivation. My mom thought Doctor Marteret saved me when he diagnosed the disease, but he told her my will to survive was what made the difference. I still had that determination in me.

I looked at Mother Nature's paradise around me, and I was sure that again today, I wanted to live.

The mysterious voice I heard intrigued me. I loved nature, especially the mountains. I trusted them, I was at home on their slopes, and they loved me in return? *Was there a Goddess of the Mountains? And she cared about me?*

The trails I hiked were gentle and rugged, narrow but boundless, and generous to me, sharing flora and fauna. Each one had a distinctive aura. Tonight, I saw clearly that every trail, hill, and peak was under the eye of spirits who were inspired by a single supreme being. I had no religion, but I had to believe there was a Goddess of the Mountains who oversaw all the high ranges around the world.

The War Inside His Mind

She knew everything that happened in her domain. And I became convinced she must have been the one who spoke to me. She knew I had a long way to go to be well again but she would never abandon me. I loved her and I felt comforted to have such a powerful friend.

I smiled.

The wind came up; it got colder than I anticipated, but the wise thing for me to do was to wait until sunrise to go down from the mountain. It would be risky to hike the down-trail in the dark. I was no longer inclined to topple down a steep slope. Biding my time, I thought about what was next. I had to regain control of my life. My English mother had told me how, but I failed to do it. Now, I was determined to find a way.

I was not ready for a new love; Colette's death was only a little over four months old, but at least I had to be open to new friendships, even if I was afraid of being hurt again. The mountains would always be ready to welcome and shelter me from the troubles of day-to-day life, anywhere in the world.

The eventful night had made a significant change in me. I wanted to get better.

Early in the morning, the sky exploded into a symphony of fiery colors. Filled with energy, I started down the trail I had hiked up for three days; it took me the better part of the day to walk back down to my car. As I drove down the twisty mountain road, I saw a food stand. An old man was stoking his wood stove. I stopped.

"Good afternoon, Sir. Do you have any food? I'm starving."

The old man said, "Actually, I'm closed. I'm cooking my dinner. I could roast a few red peppers for you. It'd take me only a couple of minutes."

"Could you? That'd be wonderful."

He put the peppers on his wood fire. They were the best I ever tasted.

Tired, I finally got home, but I did not want to go to sleep. The peppers had helped, but I was still hungry and needed to have a meal. I was also leery of being alone. I needed to be with people. Last night was still vivid in my mind, and I did not want to risk a relapse.

I went to my favorite restaurant, located in one of the back streets of Cannes, away from the tourist places. The small eatery had only five tables; the kitchen was in one corner of the room. The cook and owner, Madame Filla, was old but full of energy. Born in the area, she spoke with a delightful local accent. She sang the end of every word. Her laugh carried all the way to the end of the street. She prepared local dishes and was a fabulous cook.

"I'm glad to see you, Alain. Are you hungry?"

"Madame Filla, I'm starving."

"I can fix that; I'll make you my chicken Provençal, with tomatoes, olives, onions, lemon, capers and lots of garlic. While I cook your meal, have a piece of bread and munch on this piece of gruyere. Wash it down with a glass of wine."

"That's sounds wonderful. Thank you."

She finished cooking my meal. I enjoyed every bit of it. I sopped up the sauce with my bread.

"It was delicious. How did you cook the chicken?" I asked.

"It's easy. The secret is good olive oil and good wine; don't burn the garlic and don't overcook the chicken." I was sated.

"Thanks, Madame Filla. I'll see you soon."

The meal, the wine and the weariness of the last few days caught up with me. I was ready to go to sleep. I went home, got into bed, and was gone in seconds. I slept for ten hours. I woke up rested. *No more sadness* had to be my new resolve. I had to face the world. The trouble was that, while I might have enough strength to put up a good façade and let people believe I was fine, it would still be difficult for me to feel good, deep inside. Actually, I had to figure out how to control the demons hiding in my mind.

I had promised myself I would never tell anybody about the night that had almost been my downfall, but I changed my mind. I had to put it out of my mind and I thought that sharing my story with someone would help me bring it to closure. I wrote to Ms. Rooth who was obviously the only one I could tell. After all, she had a part in saving my life and would want to know that she had.

A few days remained before I would go back to work. I returned to the mountains, but to a different place. I felt at peace in the midst of the hills covered with the blue columbine and larkspurs, and other wildflowers, the names of which I did not know. I felt different now that I knew the Goddess would keep an eye on me. I was relaxed and happy, yet I believed it would be wise not to spend the night up there.

The next day, I received a response from Ms. Rooth. *I'm so re-lieved the dark night did not end as your last night. I was horrified to read your story, but I must tell you that I was not really surprised. I feared something like that might happen. That may be why I told you it was important to keep writing to me. If you think those words saved your life, I'm glad for that plea. Now that you survived that frightening night, I feel I don't have to worry as much about you. Keep on fighting. I am with you. I love you.*

She did, and so did the Comtesse de Sèvres; I loved them to. Mother Nature had touched me through her star-studded skies, through her gentle animals, and through the colors of the desert, the mountains and the endless blue horizons. I shivered at the thought that I had almost given all that up because, once more, I had felt sorry for myself. But, not unlike the dean of my school and my Senior Sergeant, the Goddess of the Mountains had protected me and saved my life.

The war was still in my mind, but the difficult summer was be-hind me. Full of energy and faith in my survival, I went back to work, eager and ready to face my future.

About the Author

As a young boy Y. M. Masson (Yves) struggled through four years of hardship under German occupation of Paris until he was liberated by the American Third Army. Twenty years later, after having served in the French army in North Africa during the French-Algerian war, he left France for New York City and became a United States citizen in the early seventies. After working as a marketing executive in corporate America, and then running his own consulting business, Yves turned to the arts. He is an accomplished portrait artist, but loves to share his life experiences with his readers. He knows what war does to people and especially to children. His ability to describe their daily fears, their devastating hunger, and the despair of deprivation draws his audience into their conflict.

The War Inside His Mind won second place in the Royal Palm Literary Awards from The Florida Writers Association 2018 competition.

2018 Royal Palm
Literary Award
Competition

2nd Place
Florida Writers Association

Another title by Y.M. Masson:

When Paris Was Dark, ISBN 978-1-946886-09-5. Visit his website https://www.ymmassonauthor.com